THE ROOMMATE

GEMMA ROGERS

B
Boldwood

First published in Great Britain in 2023 by Boldwood Books Ltd.

A CIP catalogue record for this book is available from the British Library.

Paperback ISBN 978-1-78513-802-7

Large Print ISBN 978-1-80048-707-9

Hardback ISBN 978-1-78513-800-3

Ebook ISBN 978-1-80048-710-9

Kindle ISBN 978-1-80048-709-3

Audio CD ISBN 978-1-80048-702-4

MP3 CD ISBN 978-1-80048-703-1

Digital audio download ISBN 978-1-80048-705-5

Boldwood Books Ltd
23 Bowerdean Street
London SW6 3TN
www.boldwoodbooks.com

For Lucy

PROLOGUE
LIVVY

The club is loud and sweltering. Condensation drips from the ceiling, mixed with spilt alcohol, leaving an oily film on the dance floor. Bass from the speakers reverberates through my entire body, making my organs throb in rhythm to the beat. My fingers and toes pulse, tiny little shocks quivering as I sway in time with the music. Lifting my arms in the air, I close my eyes, music flooding my system, enjoying the sensation of my hair stroking my shoulders as I move.

Sweat pools in my cleavage, the top I've worn is too tight and I long to be free of it. In the distance, across the dance floor, I see my friend and work colleague. Ria has her tongue down Jayden's throat, but no matter. It's all good. Lights blind my eyes, as the strobes and lasers bounce off the packed dance floor. There's a hand at my waist and then it's gone. Sticky bodies collide together in the small space.

I've forgotten about my aching feet, how tired I was before, longing for my bed. It's already past midnight, yet the party is just getting started. The night is still young and the DJ drops another tune, making the crowd whoop. Their gyrating becomes more energetic, more exaggerated. I love them all. Every, single, one. We are in this together. The people I know and the ones I've yet to meet. All part of the euphoria.

My heart is racing, beads of perspiration cling to my forehead, hair matted. Mouth dry, I crave water, but I can't stop. I have to keep moving, absorbing the atmosphere despite the strange tingling and warmth spreading through my body. Every track the DJ plays glues me to the dance floor until finally I give in, breathless and dazed, leaning against a smooth pillar for support. Its surface sleek against my palms. Every sensation is amplified and I've never been so at one with my body.

A dark-haired stranger tries to talk to me, but I can't understand a word he is saying, despite him leaning in, his hot breath on my neck. The music is too loud and my head fills with a throbbing beat that will not stop despite moving off the dance floor, longing for fresh air.

Struggling to swallow, my mouth full of sand, I begin to shiver. Something isn't right. My balance is off and white streaks of light invade my vision. Stumbling in the direction of the toilets, I look around for my friends, but they are nowhere to be seen amongst the throng of clubbers. They are too busy celebrating the yearly internal awards after-party.

Typically, there is a queue and a girl grumbles when I knock her arm as she waits, my spatial awareness off.

'Watch it,' she snipes, as her friend giggles.

'She's off her face!'

I sway, knees weakening with every minute that passes. I long to feel the cool tiles against my skin. The sensation of my insides burning makes me hunch over.

'Is she gonna be sick?'

'Let her go first, otherwise she's going to spew everywhere.'

We reach the front of the queue and the girl shoves me ahead. I skid to my knees amongst high-pitched cackles. Crawling into the empty cubicle and pushing the door shut behind me, not even bothering to lock it. The laughing outside taunting me.

I heave but nothing comes up and I rest my forehead on the bowl, the temperature of the porcelain a relief. I have no idea what is happening, but I know it is bad. I didn't drink that much, but I need help. I open my mouth to speak, to call out to the girls at the sinks, but my tongue is too large and I can't form the words.

My eyes roll, breathing shallow. Time is slowing down. Chest in a vice, shooting pains fire up my arm, but I can't make my legs move at first, despite trying to draw them in. With enormous effort, gripping the seat, I heave myself upright, leaning against the wall for support. My legs are made of sand and I'm dripping with sweat from the exertion. I close my eyes for a second. I have to get help, but I'm not sure I can walk.

Forcing my weight away from the wall, I wobble, knees giving way beneath me. The fall seems to happen in slow motion, yet there isn't time to engage my brain and get my arms to brace. My knee hits the bowl first in the cramped space and my body crumples forwards, forehead connecting with the porcelain cistern with a thump. Slumped on the floor amongst the discarded cigarette butts and toilet paper, my vision fades and everything goes black.

1

As soon as the wheels touched the tarmac, my lungs constricted. An iron-clad grip squeezed until all I could focus on was my breathing. I was back on English soil, autumn in full swing, but there was no comfort. Everything I'd been running from the past five months – the pain, guilt and grief – came flooding back and in a split second it was like I'd never left. I'd exited one nightmare into another.

'Come on, Ria, you can do this,' I muttered as I patiently waited for the seat belt light to go off, my palms beginning to sweat, anxiety rocketing.

'I'm sorry?' the woman next to me said, believing I was talking to her, despite neither of us uttering a word since we'd taken off from Nice.

'Oh, nothing,' I replied, smiling tightly as passengers around me jumped up, spilling into the aisles like someone had fired a starter gun for a race I didn't know I'd entered.

'I don't know why people have to rush,' the woman tutted, taking off her glasses to clean the lenses on her jumper.

I gave a noncommittal shrug, staying in my seat and ignoring the urge to join the throng. If I was getting back to my life, facing my demons head-on, I might as well get on with it.

Five months ago, I'd boarded a plane to Seville with the intention of travelling around Europe, although I didn't get further than across the border to France. I winced as I gazed out of the window at the murky sky, drizzle smattering the glass and then down at my Converse plimsolls. They'd be soaked through in a matter of minutes, but it hadn't occurred to me to dress for a chilly late October evening back in the UK. Around this time, I'd be sitting down to devour a cassoulet and a glass of red wine, followed by a walk along the beach, bathed in the warmth of the setting sun. The woman in the next seat in her bright orange jumper clearly had thought ahead.

My stomach gurgled and I wrapped my flimsy cardigan tighter around my middle, standing awkwardly to retrieve my suitcase from the overhead compartment. The decision to return home had been a hasty one, spurred on by an argument with my mother. As I'd thrown my clothes into my tiny suitcase, I hadn't considered the autumnal weather, leaving for the airport while she slept, as I imagined her berating me about running away from my problems yet again. She wasn't wrong but I didn't feel safe there. I never would.

I shuffled off the plane along with everyone else, contemplating the temperature of my flat, wishing I had one of those apps where I could put the heating on remotely. At least I didn't have far to go. Where I lived in Crawley was only a ten-minute drive from Gatwick Airport, once I'd got through passport control. I hadn't checked in a bag, so theoretically I could be home by eight o'clock and, if I was lucky, tucked up in bed by nine.

Five months ago, leaving hadn't been an option but a necessity. I'd sunk into a downward spiral since losing my best friend in an accident and was barely functioning. We'd both been looking forward to the annual awards ceremony organised by Cardinal

Media, a top brand advertising company that worked on bespoke projects. Once the formalities were over, the party had moved on from a hotel to a club in Brighton, where drinks had flowed and class A drugs were passed around like sweets.

Livvy and I never touched the stuff, both of us having no interest in gurning the night away like we'd witnessed our colleagues do. Consequently I was shocked and appalled after a toxicology report confirmed she'd had ketamine in her system. She'd fallen in the toilet, hitting her head and causing a massive bleed on the brain. When she was eventually found, she couldn't be revived. My gorgeous friend, who I'd only known for a year, had died alone inside a cubicle on a dirty toilet floor.

I was beside myself with guilt and grief, but no one wanted to talk about it. Drugs were a dirty subject and her death was brushed under the carpet. Hushed up to stop any bad press associated with Cardinal Media. The others there that night were reluctant to admit to any drug-taking in case they had the finger pointed at them. Neither me nor Livvy's parents could comprehend her taking anything illegal, especially when, like me, she'd always been against it. We were in complete denial.

I felt responsible. While I'd been dancing, I hadn't noticed Livvy leave the crowd. If I'd searched for her sooner, instead of creeping off to snog Jayden in a dark corner, I could have saved her life. Livvy was twenty-two when we met, a year younger than me, and we'd clicked as soon as I'd joined the company, both of us starting on the ladder as junior executives. She'd had a great sense of humour and was fun to be around. It was a work-hard, play-hard atmosphere at the company and we poured ourselves into it. Striving to meet each target, grab every bonus available and climb the corporate ladder.

After Livvy's death, work had become impossible. I was always late, rolling in looking like I'd just got out of bed. Most of the time I had. My budding relationship with Jayden, an account executive, had fizzled out and I became so anxious I barely left my flat. The image of Livvy's pale, sweaty face, her blue lips and limp body slumped on the floor stayed with me constantly. It drove me slowly mad.

I hadn't contributed anything to the company in a month. The fountain of creativity had dried up along with my ideas and Chris Lightfoot, who owned the up-and-coming advertising agency, was well within his rights to sack me, but he suggested a sabbatical, some time out to get my head together. He'd assured me I wouldn't have to worry about the rent whilst I was away and my job would be waiting for me when I got back, so in June, I'd booked a ticket to Seville. I'd planned a hedonistic few months doing some soul-searching and trying to get over my loss. But it hadn't worked out that way.

I ran out of money sooner than expected and ended up working at a bar in Malaga throughout August and September, spending my wages on alcohol and hostels. In the end, I decided to put a stop to the cycle and visit Mum and her boyfriend, flying first to Paris to soak up the Parisian life until the money was gone, then reluctantly moving on to my Mum's in Nice with my tail between my legs. Asking for another handout. I only managed two weeks before we were at each other's throats. My turning up was an inconvenience to her much older French-Algerian boyfriend, Tarek, he'd made that plainly clear up until the last night at least.

It wasn't the first time my mother had put Tarek before me. In January, she'd decided to relocate to Nice with him after he'd been lured back with a job offer, and suddenly I was homeless at twenty-three. Yet again, Chris had come to my rescue. In what was supposed to be a temporary measure, he'd put me up in the company-owned flat. A lovely two-bedroom modern place less than five minutes' walk from the office in the centre of Crawley. I paid rent, of course, but as I was doing well, it allowed me to save for a deposit for a place of my own, but now it was all gone. I was back to square one and needed to return to work and replenish my savings.

Tired and deflated, I made my way through passport control, calling a taxi when I reached the exit to take me home. Shivering and taking shelter from the persistent drizzle, I wished I was back in France. Time had seemed to stop there, it was like a parallel universe, one that no longer existed.

When Commonwealth Drive came into view and the flats with their illuminated windows blinked through the darkness, relief flooded my veins. In a matter of minutes, I could be inside, taking a nice hot shower, washing the stink of travel from my skin and climbing into clean pyjamas.

I lugged my suitcase up the stairs, avoiding the queue for the lift. There was always a queue, so many parents with buggies or people with shopping, and it was only two flights to climb. As I reached number twelve, digging out my keys, my skin prickled and unease slid over me. Something was off. I checked I had the right door number, shaking my head at how stupid I was. Of course, it was the right number.

Pushing the door open, I froze. Sounds of laughter carried from inside the flat. All the lights were on, heat blasting from the hallway radiator and the background noise of a television. My television.

I crept inside, quietly lowering my suitcase by the door which I left open in case I had to dash back out again. Who the hell was in my flat? Did I have squatters?

'I think that's the one we should go for, it's so vibrant.' A plummy voice floated through from the living room and I edged closer until a pretty platinum blonde came into view. She turned to gape at me, her steely eyes narrowed to slits before she uttered, 'Who are you?'

2

'Ria?' Jayden's face was a picture, his eyes wide as I took a few more steps inside to see the both of them sat in front of the sofa on the rug. Seemingly going through documents scattered on the coffee table, a glass of wine in hand. Perfectly at home in *my* flat.

'This looks cosy,' I smirked, unable to stop the irritation radiating off me. 'What are you doing here?'

The blonde's eyes had changed, no longer were they clouded in confusion. 'You're Ria,' she said, as if she knew all about me.

'Would someone like to tell me what on earth is going on?' I snapped. It was like I'd walked into an episode of the twilight zone.

Jayden got up and hastily gathered the papers together, sliding them into his satchel. 'I'm sorry, I didn't realise you were back today,' he said, his voice overly jolly, avoiding my eye.

'I'm Amanda,' blondie said, standing in front of me and holding out her hand to shake as if stating her name explained everything.

My temples thrummed with an incoming headache. 'Okay, *Amanda*,' I said, enunciating every syllable, ignoring her outstretched hand, 'why are you here?'

'Oh,' she giggled and I had to resist the urge to slap the smirk off her face, 'I'm your new flatmate.'

Her voice was annoyingly trill and I couldn't work out if it was that making my eye twitch or the fact a minute ago she was cosying up with *my* ex-boyfriend in *my* bloody flat.

'What do you mean you're my new flatmate? Says who?' I frowned, forehead creasing, intensifying the thudding in my brain.

'Amanda is the new junior exec, she's moved back to Crawley from Broadstairs, so Chris offered the other bedroom in the flat until she finds something else.' Jayden flung his coat over his arm, keen to leave the awkward confrontation, but I was blocking the exit.

Amanda was Livvy's replacement at Cardinal Media, the realisation a knife in my side. I glanced at the sideboard, the photo of us celebrating my birthday still in pride of place. It hurt to look at her.

'I'll see you at the station at half seven, Amanda,' Jayden said, clearing his throat in a signal for me to move.

I stayed rooted to the spot.

'We're going to see a client in London, nine o'clock meeting,' he continued, as if he needed to explain their spending time together on a Sunday night over a bottle of wine.

I raised my eyebrows and Jayden's face flushed.

'It's good to see you back,' he said, squeezing past me and out the door.

'Bye, Jayden, see you in the morning,' Amanda called over my shoulder before resting her gaze on me. 'I'm sorry, it's been a bit of a shock. I'll get out of your way.'

'It's fine,' I sighed, knowing I had no right to cause a fuss, it wasn't my flat after all but it still felt like an intrusion. 'I'm just tired, it's been a long day. I'm going to have a shower and go to bed.'

Locking the front door, I carried my suitcase through to my bedroom, relieved to find it looked exactly as I left it.

'Well, there's milk in the fridge if you want a cuppa and I'll be up and out early tomorrow,' Amanda said, rolling onto the balls of her feet outside my room.

'Thanks,' I replied, mustering a weak smile before closing the door and slumping down onto my bed.

I'd longed for the creature comforts of my own home, not to mention the peace and quiet I hadn't had at Mum's. I didn't want to share the flat with anyone and it put a damper on my return. It was my space and I was used to living alone. I knew nothing about Amanda, although sharing the flat with her would no doubt give me a crash course. She looked about my age, maybe a little older. Her hair had to be bleached, it was practically white-blonde, and I was already envious of her full lips and the dimples in her cheeks.

I guessed Jayden might find her attractive. Had he been hitting on her when I'd rudely interrupted? We were polar opposites in every way, my stomach hardening as the stab of jealousy came. I was short and petite, whereas Amanda seemed to tower over me, nearing Jayden's height. My hair was shoulder-length dark and curly, hers poker straight and long with a middle parting, like a nineties Kate Moss. We couldn't have been more different. But what did I expect? I was hardly going to come back after five months for Jayden and I to pick up where we'd left off. Everyone had moved on and I couldn't hold it against them. It was only me still reliving Livvy's death on a daily basis.

I had to get back to the old routine, and fast. Tomorrow I'd go into work, have a chat with Chris about my return and see if I could resume the life I'd left behind.

I couldn't believe he hadn't warned me I had a new flatmate, although after a quick check of my phone and a cursory search of my emails, which I'd been deliberately ignoring, I saw he had. He'd sent a message weeks ago, letting me know Amanda would be moving in. Unfortunately, it looked as though I was stuck with her and she was stuck with me, especially as all my savings for getting my own place had gone. Beggars couldn't be choosers.

I listened to the sound of her moving around in the kitchen, the chinking of mugs and kettle boiling. I rolled over, groaning into my pillow, unable to fully relax, almost wishing I'd stayed the other side of the Channel, but I couldn't, not after Tarek. I stroked the tender skin on my wrists and shook his leathery face from my mind.

This wasn't the return I'd visualised. I didn't want to live with a complete stranger. In my head, I heard Livvy's voice chiding me, *she doesn't have to be.*

Livvy had been much more fun than I was, she was outgoing and approachable, taking me under her wing immediately when I started at Cardinal Media. If she was in my situation, she'd make the best of it. Amanda could be a new drinking buddy or ally at work. One thing she'd never be, though, was Livvy's replacement.

I busied myself unpacking, piling clothes in the corner to wash tomorrow, already missing my nightly visits to the beach in Nice, where the waves rolled gently and the breeze felt cool after the warmth of the day. But I had to move on, especially after how things ended with Mum.

It wasn't a surprise; Mum had always been selfish. Throughout my childhood, she was so desperate to find a relationship, a replacement for my father, men came and went like a revolving door. Most of them only after her inheritance, left by my grandfather, but she was blind to it. Mum was young when she had me, only seventeen, and although I knew she tried to be the best mother she could, it was hard. I was an accident, a blip, and although she never voiced those feelings, I heard her loud and clear. I mourned the relationship we should have had. The bond my friends had with their parents. Girls and their mothers were supposed to be close, but I guessed my mum never got the memo.

Angry at the sour end to my sabbatical, I grabbed a towel and headed for the bathroom. The living space was open plan, a large lounge and kitchen with doors to the bedrooms and bathroom leading off the one room. The colour scheme was typically neutral and inoffensive. Vanilla and beige striped wallpaper and beige carpets. Boring, Livvy had insisted when she'd suggested I paint the kitchen a sage green over the insipid paper.

Amanda was leaning against the oak worktop, a mug of steaming tea in one hand and her phone in the other.

'I made you one, just in case,' she said brightly, awarding me a smile with annoyingly straight teeth.

'Oh thanks,' I said, sounding a little more petulant than I'd intended. What was I, twelve? I hurried into the bathroom to hide my embarrassment. Amanda was only trying to be nice and I was acting like a brat. We had to live together for the short term, whether I liked it or not.

Turning the shower to as hot as I could stand it, I stepped beneath the stream of water hoping to wash the tension away. There was no lock on the bathroom door. It hadn't occurred to me I needed one before now, but knowing I could be burst in on at any moment made me rush. I hadn't brought my toiletries bag in and Amanda's bottles of shower gel, shampoo and conditioner lined the shower surround where mine used to live. All of the toiletries I'd not taken on my travels had disappeared. I used a tiny amount of the body wash, knowing if it was the other way around I'd be annoyed at the overstep, but it was either that or not wash at all.

When I got out, I checked the mirrored cabinet on the wall, but nothing of mine remained? Amanda had a gift set from Lush, hair serum and tampons stashed inside. Had she thrown all of my stuff out? Mildly irritated, I intended to ask the question, but Amanda was no longer in the kitchen. Clutching my towel to keep it in place, I turned to find the door to my bedroom wide open, a rustling noise coming from inside.

3

'What do you think you're doing?' I asked curtly, finding Amanda bent over the bed holding my mobile phone.

'I'm sorry, it kept ringing. Someone's obviously desperate to get hold of you,' she said, her brow furrowed, holding the phone out to me. 'I knocked on the bathroom door and shouted, but I don't think you heard me.'

'Let's stay out of each other's rooms okay?' I replied, taking the phone from her.

'Of course, I'm sorry.' Amanda looked crestfallen, her shoulders slumped and she hurried from the room as I checked the call history.

Mum had called, three times in quick succession. Had it taken her all day to realise I'd packed up and gone or had she waited for Tarek to be out to get in touch? My shoulders shuddered at the thought of him. His patchy beard like a sunburnt lawn, yellow tobacco stains on his fingers. I rubbed at the tiny bruises starting to develop on my wrists and pushed the memory of last night from my mind. I was in a different time zone, only an hour behind but over 800 miles away, however I still didn't feel safe.

I knew Mum would be remorseful at how we'd left things in the cold light of day. We weren't conventional, but deep down she cared, so I sent her a text to let her know I was safely back in the UK, but I wasn't ready to talk. My phone ringing was still no reason for Amanda to be in my room. I wouldn't dream of walking into hers to answer her phone. We'd just met half an hour ago. I clenched my jaw, gnashing my teeth together. I'd have to set some ground rules if this was going to work.

* * *

I woke to the noise of the front door slamming, rolling over to see it was quarter past seven. The sound an instant reminder of what I'd arrived home to last night. A house guest I wasn't prepared for, that I didn't want. I groaned, I hadn't slept well at all despite being back in my own bed. Nightmares plagued me and the presence of another person in the flat, although irrational, made me uneasy. I'd have to get over it. What choice did I have?

Shrugging out of the duvet, I padded to the kitchen and stuck the kettle on. The tea Amanda had made for me last night was still on the counter, a white film now floating on the top. It was a guilty reminder of my sullenness.

Impatiently, I searched through cupboards, trying to find teabags which weren't where they usually were, in the cupboard above the kettle. Everything had been moved. The cups were in the cupboard the plates had been in, the cereal and tins were where I'd put biscuits, crisps and snacks.

'Jesus Christ,' I muttered under my breath. Amanda clearly had no problem making the place her own, even down to labelling which cupboards were mine with Post-it notes. Except it wasn't her place, it was mine. Well, more mine than hers anyway. I'd have to sound Chris out about how long she was intending to stay. I hoped it wouldn't be long.

* * *

When I approached the glass-fronted Cardinal Media office, trepidation at going back inside made me skittish and I managed to push the revolving door the wrong way, almost squashing Fiona Hutchison, the HR manager, on the way out.

'Ria!' she exclaimed, pulling me into a hug when she reached the pavement. 'You're back!' She grabbed me by the shoulders, holding me at arm's length to look at me. She was every part the executive in her high-necked cream blouse, emerald-green trousers and ankle-length camel coat. Her highlighted hair perfectly coiffed in an elegant chignon twist.

'Hi, Fiona, how are you?' I said, heat radiating from my face under her intense gaze.

'I'm fine, but never mind that. How are you? You look so well, lovely tan.'

'I'm sure it won't stick around long,' I replied mournfully. 'Do you know if Chris is in?'

'I've just left him actually, he's got a meeting soon though, so best get in quick. It's wonderful to see you.'

Fiona finally released me, nudging her Kate Spade handbag up her arm and giving me a wave goodbye before heading towards the shops. If she hadn't seemed in such a rush, I would have asked her about Amanda, but I'd save that conversation for Chris.

Watching Fiona hurry out of sight, I pushed my way through the doors, smiling at Michelle on reception who was on the phone. She waved, her eyes widening at my unexpected appearance as I hurried through the glass double doors and down a corridor to where the office was.

The area was mostly open plan, in a large L-shape. Desks were in clusters of fours and sixes, partitions separating them. The account managers and junior executives sat together on one side and around the corner were the finance and human resources team, although they mainly kept themselves to themselves.

The air smelled of strong coffee and cinnamon. A reminder of Monday morning meetings with warm pastries to start the week and Livvy arguing passionately about which logo was better suited for the up-and-coming menswear brand in the meeting room.

Heads began to turn at the sound of my name being called and before I knew it I was surrounded by colleagues, asking about my trip. I tried to talk as though it had been a holiday, a chance to get away rather than a desperate need to escape for the sake of my mental health. Everyone chipped in how lucky I was to have five months in the sun and away from work. The mood was buoyant and no one mentioned Livvy. She was the elephant in the room and my every nerve was on edge waiting for someone to bring her up.

'Ria, welcome back.' Chris came out of his office, roused by the commotion, and leaned in to grasp my hand in an awkward shake. I inhaled the familiar Dolce & Gabbana aftershave. It was an anchor and incredibly comforting.

'Hey, Chris,' I said, giving him a watery smile as he looked down at me, his face an array of emotions.

Cardinal Media had been built from the ground up by Chris and he was the father figure for many of his young employees. A role he took seriously despite only being in his early forties and yet to have children of his own. It wasn't often you could say a manager genuinely cared about his staff, but there was no doubt he did. I was sure he could be ruthless when he needed to be, but I'd never seen that side of him.

'Shall we have a quick chat? I've got a little time before my next meeting,' Chris said, checking his watch and gesturing for me to go ahead into his office.

Inside, I perched on the bright orange chair, it was the only colour injected into the monotone office scheme. My pulse accelerated as he sat in front of me, steepling his fingers.

'It's so good to see you. How are you?'

'I'm doing okay, actually,' I lied, although I was surprised to feel better being back in the office I was dreading returning to.

'When did you get in?'

'Last night.'

'Ah,' he pursed his lips, 'I guess you've met Amanda then. Did you get my email about her being your flatmate for a while?'

'About that,' I began, palms sweating, but Chris raised his hand, interrupting me.

'It's a temporary roof over her head. Like you, Amanda just needs to get on her feet.'

I nodded, a strained smile on my lips. It seemed it wasn't up for discussion.

'Has she replaced Livvy?' The words were out of my mouth and sounding bitter before I could stop them.

Chris frowned. 'You know no one could do that,' he sighed, 'but, yes, she is our new junior executive. We limped along as long as we could, but without you as well, the account managers needed support. We've taken on four new clients in so many months, big ones. Amanda started with us in July, almost four months now.' Chris rubbed at his beard, waiting for a response.

'That's great,' I managed, my stomach in knots.

'So, do you feel ready to come back to us? You've been sorely missed.'

I was still shaken up after bolting from Mum's and wasn't really in the best head space, but it would be good for me to focus on something. Having too much time on my hands wouldn't be wise, I had to keep my brain busy. Forcing a smile, I tried to inject some enthusiasm into my voice. 'How does tomorrow sound?' I suggested and Chris clapped his hands together.

'Fantastic!'

I grinned, a real one, brought on by Chris's eagerness at my return. He was welcoming me back into the family and warmth spread through my veins.

'Will I be working with Jayden again?' I asked, watching Chris's smile fade.

'Well, Amanda is working on the accounts you had with Jayden, she's doing well, so I think I might pair you with Aaron.'

It was my turn to frown. Aaron used to work with Livvy.

It seemed Amanda wasn't so much Livvy's replacement, but mine.

4

I stepped out onto the pavement after my chat with Chris, shoulders looser than when I went in. I feared I'd see Livvy everywhere inside the office, around every corner and in the reflection of every pane of glass. Her absence there would be a stark reminder of what I'd lost. My best friend. But it was different. The atmosphere had shifted, almost like she'd never been a part of Cardinal Media. Life had carried on without her and I had to too.

I couldn't help but be disappointed I wouldn't be working with Jayden again, but perhaps it was for the best. Too much time had passed, our fledgling relationship had ended the moment I'd booked my ticket for Seville. Chris didn't have a rule against dating colleagues, as long as any drama was kept out of the office, and it had been early days between Jayden and me. The drama had been Livvy's death and Chris was as devastated as the rest of us.

He'd been good to me, giving me the opportunity for a sabbatical and offering to keep my job open for when I was ready to return. I owed him a lot and I was going to throw myself back into the role and prove to him he'd made the right decision, I was worth waiting for.

Chris had taken a chance on me right back at the beginning. Most employees had a degree of some kind, graphic design or marketing, but I'd rocked up with my portfolio and some relevant experience at a local magazine, asking for an entry-level role.

I'd got the job at *Sussex Life* straight out of school at eighteen after doing my A levels in English Language and Media. Initially, I was employed to write film and book reviews before branching out to cover local events. I hadn't wanted to leave and go to college once I'd started earning my own money. By the time I approached Cardinal Media, I was designing my own features for the magazine and practically running the small website, but I wanted more. At the interview, Chris been swayed by my 'buckets of enthusiasm' and ambition for a twenty-three-year-old, hiring me for barely over the minimum wage, promising I could work my way up.

In less than three months, true to his word, I'd been awarded two pay rises and a chance to work with Jayden on some specific client requests. We'd been a good team, spending time outside of the office, working on designs and marketing campaigns. He'd looked pretty cosy with Amanda yesterday and I wasn't sure whether, like us, work had spilled over into something more, but I couldn't let jealously cloud my judgement. I had to get back on track.

On the way home, I picked up some shopping, stacking it in my designated cupboards. I wasn't used to being told where to put my things and I couldn't deny it irked me. Two loads of washing later, I looked around for something to fill the time, but the place was spotless. There was no tidying or cleaning to be done and I hoped Amanda wasn't obsessively neat. I wasn't messy but I didn't want to it to be like living with my mother, who tutted every time I put a cup down without a coaster.

Settling on the sofa, Amanda's closed bedroom door was in my eyeline. Flicking through the television channels, my gaze kept falling on the door, although I tried to ignore the urge to look inside, attempting to concentrate on a programme about couples finding new homes abroad. The compulsion gnawed at me. I was alone, Amanda wouldn't be back for a while. It wouldn't hurt to take a peek, would it? Just to find out some more about my new flatmate.

Before I could talk myself out of it, my fingers were around the doorknob, twisting it slowly. It sprang open and I jumped backwards, expecting to find someone on the other side, but it was only tightened hinges that made the door pull. Chuckling at the scare, I looked around the room, which looked the same as it had before I'd left – a typical guest bedroom. Despite it now being occupied, there was no personalisation. No photos on the mirror or make-up left on top of the dressing table. It was still bland and uninviting, nothing to give me any idea who Amanda was. In fact, it barely looked lived in.

As I turned on the spot, surveying the ordinary room, my phone rang. I jumped out of my skin at the shrill sound coming from the lounge and hurried to answer it. It was a withheld number, so I declined the call, likely a double-glazing salesman, but seconds later it rang again. This time I answered it, the phone barely at my ear before I heard Livvy's voice calling my name.

'Hello?' I managed, the word sticking in my throat.

There was a delay, as though it was a call centre in India trying to get through.

My heart leapt into my throat as Livvy's unmistakable voice called out again. 'Ri-Ri,' she giggled. I clamped my hand over my mouth, unable to believe what I'd heard. Ri-Ri was Livvy's nickname for me. 'Ri-Ri,' she said again and, shrieking, I launched phone across the room and watched it skid to a stop on the kitchen laminate.

I didn't believe in ghosts. I knew Livvy was gone, but it had been her voice calling my name. I sank down onto the sofa, my entire body shaking, unable to take my eyes off the phone, which had landed face up, still illuminated, on the floor. Someone was still on the line. After a few seconds, the screen darkened, the call had been disconnected, but I couldn't move. It had to be a recording or something, either that or I was losing my mind. Livvy was not calling me from beyond the grave.

'I told you not to go in the lift,' Jayden's voice came from the front door, followed by Amanda's girlish giggle. Both of them coming to an abrupt stop at the entrance to the lounge when they saw me.

'Oh hi, Ria. I just got stuck in the lift, the bloody doors wouldn't open.'

'I told her about the lift. Remember when we got trapped inside?' Jayden laughed, putting his satchel on the counter.

With my heart still racing, I mustered a smile at the memory, recalling how we'd spent the ten minutes until the lift had got going again.

'Are you okay? You look like you've seen a ghost?' Jayden asked, frowning at me.

'I'm fine,' I managed, my throat like sandpaper as I tried to shake off the lingering unease.

'Is this your phone?' Amanda bent and picked up the handset, putting it beside Jayden's bag.

I nodded.

'Want a tea? I'm gasping!'

'No thanks,' I replied, watching Amanda and Jayden move around the small kitchen. 'You're back early,' I said, the tremor still in my voice. It was only just four o'clock.

'Jayden said we should sneak off, we haven't been back to the office,' Amanda said conspiratorially.

'Chris won't mind, not with the business we've brought in

today,' Jayden remarked.

I remembered they had gone into London for a client meeting. Amanda looked stylish in a dark red calf-length skirt and blazer, a slick of red lipstick was the pop of colour against her platinum hair and creamy skin. She was striking and today she wore black rimmed glasses which made her look even more professional. I had no doubt she fitted in well at Cardinal Media. Smart, but trendy.

They joked amongst themselves, easy in each other's company, as if I wasn't there and I did my best to concentrate on the television and still my shaking hands. I hadn't had time to process hearing Livvy's voice. If Jayden had been alone, I might have told him about the call, but Amanda didn't know Livvy, she was a stranger and I wasn't about to let my guard down in front of someone I barely knew. Hearing Livvy's voice was like being struck by a cattle prod. Who would pull such a hurtful stunt like that, and why?

'You haven't been in my room, have you, Ria?' I turned at the sound of my name to see Amanda staring at her open bedroom door. Shit, I'd forgotten to close it.

'No, sorry, I knocked it with the hoover and it sprang open. It's a bit feisty that door, isn't it,' I said, plastering on a smile and watching her eyes narrow for a second before mirroring my expression.

'It is, isn't it. Frightened me half to death when I moved in, seems to have a mind of its own.'

'I could take a look at it for you if you like. I'm quite good with a screwdriver,' Jayden offered, already rolling the sleeves of his blazer up.

'Would you, that would be great. I don't have a screwdriver though, maybe you could come back another time with your tool-box,' she sniggered, nudging him provocatively with her elbow.

Oh please, get a room. I rolled my eyes and got to my feet, turning off the television.

'So the client meeting went well then?' I asked.

'Brilliantly, they loved our ideas and are keen for us to develop one further,' Jayden said.

'That's great, and how are you settling in, Amanda?'

'Oh fine, it's been months now, it's like I've always been there!'

Her saccharine tone went straight through me. I couldn't put my finger on why she irritated me so much. It had to be a territorial thing. She was living in my flat, working with my ex-boyfriend and coming on to him too.

'I think we should go out and celebrate, what do you think? Ria, are you in?' Jayden said, draining his tea and putting his mug in the sink. He pulled his tie down and unbuttoned his collar, giving me a wink that once would have melted me.

'On a Monday?' I said, my tone betraying a hint of disapproval.

'Yeah, nothing massive, just one or two. Come on, it's team bonding. I'll message the others.'

'I'm skint,' I replied glumly, Amanda's eyes on me like a hawk.

'I'm sure I can stretch to a couple of gin and tonics,' he said, giving his hips a jovial wiggle.

'Okay, okay,' I said, getting to my feet to retrieve my bag, phone and jacket, apprehensive to see everyone again in a social setting but glad it wouldn't just be the three of us. I didn't want to play gooseberry.

'I'll meet you in the pub, I'm going to get changed,' Amanda said, her tone a little icy. Was she annoyed Jayden had invited me?

'We can wait,' I offered.

'No, it's fine, I'll see you there,' she replied, dismissing me with a wave.

Jayden met my eye and shrugged. 'You can tell me all about

your trip,' he said, guiding me out the door with his hand pressed between my shoulder blades, heat resonating through my jacket. As we left, I was aware of the prickle of Amanda's eyes on me, burning a hole in my back.

5

The Kings Head was in stumbling distance of both the flat and the Cardinal Media office, making it the pub of choice for after-work drinks. It had recently had a refurb and gone was the sticky once-burgundy carpet, revealing a hardwood floor that had been sanded and stained. The paisley wallpaper had been removed and the replastered walls were freshly painted a light magnolia, allowing the dark wood beams to shine.

When we walked in, our favourite corner was already taken. Aaron, Rav, Cassie and Grace, members of the sales and marketing team, huddled around the table, glancing up as the door opened and waving us over. Jayden didn't hesitate to pull up two more chairs while I loitered behind him. My chest fluttering, partly from hearing Livvy's voice, partly because I wasn't sure I'd be welcome.

I needn't have been apprehensive as our arrival was received with cheers and raised glasses. Warmth hit my cheeks as Aaron patted the free chair next to him as Jayden headed to the bar.

'I hear we're going to be the new A-Team,' he said as I sat, his toothy grin expanding, showcasing his wide-set jaw.

I didn't know him really well, although Livvy had, because of how closely they'd worked together. She'd thought he was hilarious and told me he had a dry sense of humour. It was obvious when they were together he had a thing for her. Usually he was macho, but she'd seen a sweeter side of him no one else saw.

'That we are,' I replied, sounding more confident than I was. Surely I hadn't lost my creative abilities in the five months I'd been away, but it wasn't going to be easy to get back in the saddle. Fake it until you make it would have to be my new motto.

'Looking forward to it,' he said, turning away and taking a gulp of his pint. I wasn't so sure he was telling the truth.

Jayden returned with a pint of lager and a gin and tonic for me, the rest of the group declining his offer to get a round in because they'd not long arrived.

'So, where's Amanda?' Aaron said, giving Jayden a look that had obvious connotations.

'She's on her way,' he replied, glancing at me sheepishly. We hadn't yet spoken about what my return would mean, if anything, for us, sticking to the safe topic of my travels on the short walk to the pub. If he wasn't going to bring it up, then neither was I. He didn't owe me anything and was free to do whatever he pleased.

'How was your meeting?' Aaron asked, wiping a foam moustache away from his top lip.

'She knocked it out the park, honestly, Brewdog loved her. I barely got a word in edgeways.' Jayden shook his head, eyes wondrous.

I simmered in my seat and took a large gulp of gin. Brewdog had been my client – or rather *our* client, before I'd left.

'Hi, everyone,' Amanda trilled, arriving at our table as if she'd materialised out of thin air at Aaron's mention of her.

I gawped at the change of outfit. Gone was the smart suit in favour of skinny black jeans she'd poured herself into, with a green top and leather jacket. Its plunging neckline showcasing an impressive cleavage I could only dream of owning.

'I just had to run through the shower. Urgghh, being on the tube makes me feel so dirty,' she said, wrinkling her nose.

Aaron and Jayden both jumped up to get her a seat and I rolled my eyes.

Grace sniggered and accompanied Amanda to the bar.

'Christ, she is something else,' Aaron said, rubbing his chin, eyes lingering on her behind as she waited to get served.

'Oh, jog on, she's out of your league, mate,' Cassie laughed, slapping him on the shoulder.

'No one is out of my league,' he replied, running his hand through his hair as we all laughed. Aaron did like to pretend he was a ladies' man, but we all knew it was rubbish.

Conversation turned to my sabbatical and when Amanda returned, she listened with interest, asking questions about Paris, a place she said she'd love to visit. Aaron preened whenever he got the chance, but she barely noticed him, her focus was on me, and I found it a little intimidating, although it was nice to be distracted from the phone call I'd had earlier.

Eventually, Grace and Cassie made to leave and I decided it would be a good idea to get an early night. Tomorrow would be a big day for me, returning to the office properly, and I wanted to be ready.

'I'm going to head out too,' I said, getting to my feet, surprised to see a flash of disappointment on Jayden's face.

'Anyone fancy Chinese?' Amanda ventured, but there didn't seem to be much interest.

I shook my head and said my goodbyes.

'She's nice, isn't she,' Grace said, linking her arm through mine as we left the pub, the evening damp and miserable.

'I guess. I don't really know her at all,' I admitted.

'But you're living together, aren't you? Didn't Chris put her up in the flat?' Cassie chipped in.

'Yep, but I literally got back from Nice yesterday,' I said, rubbing my wrist, 'and we've barely seen each other, to be honest.'

'You should make the effort, have a girls' night in or something. She knows she's got massive boots to fill,' Grace said, her words sticking in her throat.

'She'll never be able to fill those boots,' I said, forcing a smile.

We said goodbye at the corner and I headed back to the flat, which was strangely too quiet. I kept staring at my phone, waiting for it to ring, to hear Livvy call my name. It made the hairs on the back of my neck stand on end and I put the television on for some background noise. Not wanting to jump out of my skin if it rang again. I had no idea who would have made the call earlier. Whoever it was must have known the pain it would cause to hear my best friend's voice out of nowhere.

Pushing it from my mind as much as I could, I chose my clothes for tomorrow and hung them on the wardrobe before microwaving a meal for one, settling to eat on the sofa in front of the television, ruminating Grace's words. I should make the effort with Amanda, there was no point in forcing a friendship but equally no reason to block one either. Uneasy being alone, I hoped she'd return, but at nearly ten o'clock she still wasn't back. She must have still been with Jayden. I tried not to let the thought irk me, but my insides coiled with a jealousy I had no right to feel.

Climbing into bed, I pulled the covers up to my chin, propping up a pillow and scrolling through Jayden's Instagram account. His most recent posting a selfie from lunchtime of him and Amanda on Tower Bridge, grinning inanely at the camera after their client visit. With a flick of the finger, I scrolled back over the months I'd been gone. Photos I'd pored over already from across the Channel when I was homesick and missing him.

The photo on Tower Bridge hadn't been the first one he'd posted that included Amanda. There was another group shot of the team a month ago, in front of the Cardinal Media offices, the logo above everyone's heads. Likely taken for promotional material, Jayden had his arm around Amanda's waist, the two of them looking like they'd known each other for years. Not willing to torture myself any further, I closed the app, set an alarm for tomorrow morning and put the phone on my bedside table.

Rearranging my pillow and shuffling down in the bed, I stopping moving when I heard the sound of the front door open. Footsteps crept into the lounge, then a clatter, followed by a giggle. Amanda was finally home and seemed to be far from sober. Perhaps I'd go and see if she was okay. Offer her a cup of tea, a pint of water or aspirin to help with the imminent hangover, but as I swung my legs out of the bed, Jayden's unmistakable gravelly voice carried through the door.

'No, not here.'

6

I gripped the mattress so hard, the sheet puckered as more sniggering and footfalls followed, then the sound of Amanda's bedroom door closing.

With our rooms a wall apart, I had no choice but to listen to the sound of the two of them having sex in the next room. Amanda's moans of pleasure as I squeezed my eyes shut, the knowledge of what was happening mere feet away unbearable. It didn't seem like it had been that long since I'd been wrapped in Jayden's arms and I'd be lying if I said it didn't sting.

Listening to the two of them was the nail in the coffin for what Jayden and I might have had. He'd moved on and I could hardly blame him. Bar the odd comment on an Instagram post, we hadn't been in touch while I'd been away. Jayden hadn't wanted me to leave, but I was out of my mind after Livvy's death and couldn't get past the tragic circumstances. I refused to believe she had taken those drugs of her own accord and had accused everyone, even him, of spiking her.

With Jayden now wedged between us, I wasn't sure how friendly

Amanda and I could be, watching him fawn all over her, when months before I'd been the object of his affections. My stomach sank at the notion of having to suffer listening to them through the wall every night if it wasn't a one-off.

Getting back into bed, I rolled over and pulled the pillow over my head, considering the purchase of noise-cancelling head-phones. Curling up with my knees to my chest, I wished I was back in Spain or France, anywhere would do.

Thankfully, the noise stopped around ten minutes later, after a crescendo. Amanda had some lungs on her and Jayden must have done the job, unless her making all that racket was for my benefit. It wasn't long before the only sound I could hear was the oh-so familiar sound of Jayden snoring, which I found strangely comforting, eventually falling asleep myself.

* * *

The next morning, I was up and out as early as I could manage. I didn't want to be there for any awkward exchanges as we hung around the kettle for our morning coffee. I opted for a latte and croissant from Nero's across the street, deciding to eat at my desk.

Chris was already in his office when I walked in at eight, although the rest of the desks were empty. He waved me in.

'Join me, it'll be nice not to eat alone,' he said, indulging himself in a pain au chocolat, pastry flakes raining onto his desk. 'Nice outfit,' he commented, pointing to my jumper dress, tights and chunky boots, something I'd thrown on in haste to get out of the door. Most of the staff wore casual clothes unless there were clients in, although Chris nearly always wore a suit.

'Thank you,' I said, taking a bite of my pastry, leaving it half in the bag to catch the crumbs as I considered how to say what I needed to. 'Chris, I, umm, might need a couple more months in the flat than I initially thought.'

He smiled, an eyebrow raised as if he'd been anticipating the conversation.

'I used a lot of my savings whilst I was away.' I grimaced.

'Ah I see, well, it's no problem. Amanda thinks she'll be there six months, tops, while she saves for a deposit. How are the two of you getting along?' Chris brushed his beard free of crumbs and took a sip of his coffee.

'Fine, we've not really seen much of each other, to be honest,' I admitted. Whatever happened between me and Amanda, I didn't want to rock the boat with Chris. I needed the job and the flat to keep my head afloat.

'I think you'll get on,' he said as though it wasn't up for debate.

'I hope so,' I replied, although the fact she'd shagged Jayden had already put paid to that.

'Did you visit your mum while you were away?' Chris asked.

'Yeah, that didn't go so well,' I admitted, my hunger evaporating.

'Families, eh! I hear you, nothing but trouble sometimes,' he said with a small shake of the head. 'I'm sure you'll work it out. We're nothing without our roots.'

Once we'd both eaten, the office began to fill up. I checked with Chris that my desk was the same one I'd always had, in the corner, around the back of the office looking directly out onto the walkway between us and the small car park. On it lay an envelope addressed to me, inside a welcome back card signed by everyone, which was a nice touch considering the hell I'd put them through before I'd left. I wouldn't have been surprised if not all of the team embraced my return. Smiling as I logged on, I began to trawl through the hundreds of emails from the past few months.

Just before nine Amanda and Jayden arrived together, greeting everyone the moment she was through the double doors. Her voice unnaturally loud, it carried through the office.

Does she think she owns the place? I scowled, glancing over my shoulder into Chris's office, but he didn't even raise his head, either having not heard her or used to her entrances.

'Hi, Ria, you left so early this morning. I thought we were late,' she said, from a few desks away, a sly grin on her face. Jayden wouldn't meet my eye.

'I thought I'd get in and catch up on what I've missed, leave *you both* to it. You must be exhausted after that Oscar-winning performance last night,' I said, matching her grin with a smirk. My overly polite response seemed to catch her off guard and she carried on around to her desk, ignoring my jibe, as inwardly I scored a point for team Ria, however petty.

'How's about I run through what we're going to be working on,' Aaron popped up behind me, making me start.

'Christ, you're jumpy!' he said, taking a step back.

'Still half asleep,' I smiled weakly, 'Let's crack on.' I said, following Aaron into the meeting room.

A footwear brand specifically made for hiking wanted a winter spread mock-up advertising their boots. I suggested getting some action shots along one of the many local hiking trails, perhaps some puddle jumping, which he was keen to develop. We also had to tackle a tricky customer who was trying to break into the men's underwear market.

'Couldn't we do something around Men's Health Awareness Month? That's November, isn't it? Would we have time? It might be a great tie-in?'

'Excellent idea, Ria, I'll pitch it to them. If we can come up with a strapline, that would be great.' Aaron nudged my arm as we sat side by side, my notepad full of details I'd scribbled.

'Leave it to me, I'll have a think,' I said, excited the creative juices were flowing again.

Aaron gathered up his papers and headed out as I spotted Jayden loitering by the door, joining me as soon as I was alone.

'About last night,' he began before I cut him off.

'Don't worry about it, it's none of my business,' I said brusquely, watching his shoulders sag.

'It was a... mistake, I was really drunk,' he said, eyes imploring.

'Perhaps you need to tell Amanda that.' I squeezed past him out of the door, internalising my annoyance. What was I supposed to do with that information? Did it make it okay because he'd decided a one-time roll in the sheets was enough with her?

I wished Livvy was around to talk to about it. She'd know what to say, how to act. As terrified as I was when that call came through, I longed to hear her voice again. Her death had left a massive crater I couldn't fill. Perhaps I'd see if Cassie wanted to go for a drink after work, she might have some words of wisdom for me. I caught up with her at lunch, bumping into her as she came out of the toilets.

'Hey, Cass, fancy a quick one after work?'

'I would, but Amanda and I are going to try that new Turkish restaurant. Why don't you join us?'

My face must have said it all as Cassie laughed.

'Come on, I'm sure you'll like her if you give her a chance, she's cool.'

I grimaced, Cassie's personality was as spikey as her hair and it normally took her ages to warm to anybody. The fact she'd befriended Amanda already made my eyes pop out on stalks.

'Cool? You don't *like* anybody, Cass,' I laughed, trying to keep our conversation light-hearted despite the sinking in the pit of my stomach.

'I know, it's weird isn't it, but I guess we've just clicked.'

'Oh God, you don't fancy her too, do you?' I nudged Cassie with my elbow, knowing Amanda wasn't really her type. She liked edgy girls and Amanda had no facial piercings to speak of.

'No, but I think everyone else does. The lads are practically foaming at the mouth every time she's around.'

'Tell me about it,' I grumbled. She'd already managed to steal my flat, my job and my man.

7

At that moment, we were interrupted in the corridor by Michelle from reception, who wanted to let me know I'd had a package arrive.

'We'll have that drink another time,' I called to Cassie as I followed Michelle back to the front desk.

'I wonder what it is?' I mused, making conversation as we walked.

Michelle always had a cheery disposition, no matter what time of day it was. It was rare not to see a smile on her lips, which made her the perfect face for anyone coming into the Cardinal Media office.

'No idea, looks like an Amazon package. I would have brought it round but wasn't sure if you wanted to leave it to collect when you go home.'

'That's weird, I haven't ordered anything,' I replied. It would be unusual for Mum to send me something, unless she was apologising for how we'd left things.

The box was around half a metre long, and relatively slim. What was inside, a baseball bat? I ripped off the packaging as Michelle resumed her seat behind the desk to answer the ringing phone.

'Cardinal Media, Michelle Forster speaking, how may I help you?' she trilled into the handset.

I carried on tearing the cardboard box, revealing an ominous bunch of black roses tied with a ribbon. Breath hitching, I took a step back, wrapping my arms around myself. Who on earth had sent me roses? Not pretty pink or romantic red but artificial black roses with silk petals and plastic stems. Was it Tarek trying to get his own back? How had he got the address of where I worked? Beneath the bunch lay a slip of paper, the Amazon logo printed at the top. I reached in and lifted it out. What was typed in the block font made my mouth drop open, pulse accelerating in my throat.

Missing me yet? Livvy xxx

Vomit surged upwards from my chest and I clamped my hand over my mouth, edging further backwards. Michelle looked at me quizzically, still fielding the call that had come through moments before. Heart hammering against my ribcage, initial fear morphed into white-hot rage. Someone was messing with me. First the phone call, now flowers. Whoever they were, they were sick!

I grabbed the flowers from their packaging, the note too, leaving the box for Michelle to dispose of. Storming back into the office, I saw Aaron, Jayden, Rav, Grace, Cassie and Amanda gathered around the table inside the glass-panelled meeting room.

'Ria, are you ready?' Aaron waved me in.

I'd forgotten I was supposed to be attending. It wasn't a formal meeting, more of a team catch-up, sharing what everyone was working on and the exchange of ideas across the department, which was often helpful.

Rav was chattering away about his plans for the Diwali celebrations that night when I rudely interrupted.

'Who the fuck sent me these?' I slammed the flowers down on the table where there was an empty spot.

Grace and Cassie both jumped in their seats, their mouths gaping as I leaned over, glaring at each person in turn. Accusing them with my stare.

'Here we go again,' Aaron muttered under his breath.

'No one did, Ria,' Jayden said, furtively glancing around the room. His voice was calm, and he was already on his feet, making his way around the table to me, hands raised in a placating gesture.

'Are you okay, Ria? Do you want a glass of water?' Amanda's sickly-sweet voice came from my right.

'Oh fuck off,' I spat as Chris appeared in the doorway. Poor timing on my behalf.

'Ria, can I see you in my office.' It wasn't a request.

He lingered outside, waiting for me to join him before walking ahead in long strides. I had to quicken my pace to keep up.

I sank into the same chair I'd been in hours before, a wave of shame washing over me. Tears pricked my eyes as Chris assumed his position behind his desk, picking up his phone and dialling.

'Fiona, can you pop into my office please for a sec?' He put down the receiver, clasped his hands and waited for me to speak.

'I'm sorry. I shouldn't have shouted. Someone is messing with me and it's doing my head in.'

'Who's messing with you?' I could tell by the tone of Chris's voice he was exasperated. He'd been through this with me before when I was hurling conspiracy theories around about Livvy's death. Accusing the team of knowing what really happened to her and being responsible for spiking her drink. I couldn't comprehend Livvy had taken ketamine willingly not when it was something we were so vehemently against.

'I don't know. Someone pretending to be Livvy.'

The crevice between Chris's eyes deepened and he seemed momentarily at a loss for words.

'Someone sent me flowers,' I blurted, 'from Livvy. They're in the meeting room.' My eyes burnt with tears.

He opened his mouth to speak, but a tap came from the door and Fiona slipped inside, perching on the chair next to mine. It worried me Chris had invited Cardinal's human resources manager to join us. Was I about to get fired?

I quickly wiped at my eyes, trying to gather myself.

'Hi, Fiona, thanks for joining us. I'm having a chat with Ria and wanted you to sit in,' he smiled at her, her face acknowledging something unspoken before turning to back me, his tone more professional in her presence. 'Ria, I'm worried. Before you left, you were, understandably, very upset about Livvy and what happened to her. You were quite manic, accusatory even, to some of the staff—'

I cut him off mid-sentence. 'I still don't believe she took that stuff willingly.'

'Okay, I understand, and that's your opinion. However, we can only go on what the police told Livvy's parents about what was in her bloodstream.' He sighed. 'I thought you getting away for a while might make it easier. Because the crux of it is, Ria, we all need to move on. I can't have you shouting and swearing in the office. It's not professional.' Chris's tone had softened. It was almost a plea.

'I know I'm sorry,' I replied, the tears falling freely now. I swiped at them with the back of my hand.

'I know it's hard, but you've got to work with me here. I want you to stay, but if you carry on, it's not going to be an option.'

'Have you had any counselling?' Fiona piped up, crossing her legs and smoothing her olive skirt down her thighs.

I shook my head.

'Because there's a service available to you, through the company, called LISTEN. It's independently run and they aren't allowed to share any information with us. It's all confidential. Maybe you might find that useful?'

I nodded, sinking further into my seat. It was something they'd suggested before I left, trying to get me to talk to someone about what was going on. I'd refused at the time, adamant there was nothing wrong with me. All I wanted was justice for my friend. Now, I was backed into a corner. If I didn't sort myself out, I'd lose my job. Chris's generosity and his patience had its limit.

'I'll send the details over to you,' Fiona said.

Chris nodded. 'We want to help you. You're a valuable member of our team, but you need to focus now on getting back to where you were before.' Before Livvy's death Chris meant, which stung. Everyone else had managed to get over it, why couldn't I, was the insinuation, but they weren't the ones receiving little reminders.

'I'm sorry, I'll sort myself out,' I said, telling them what they wanted to hear. In the meantime, I'd find out who was messing with me. 'I'm sorry for swearing,' I added, 'I was angry, I thought one of them had sent them.'

'The flowers?' Chris asked.

Fiona raised an eyebrow, puzzled.

'Yeah, like a stupid prank.'

'I'm sure it's a misunderstanding, but if it is one of them playing a prank, there'll be consequences. I'll have a chat with the team, and don't worry about the flowers, I'll get rid of them.'

'Thank you,' I sniffed.

'Okay, you can go. Have an early day and we'll see you back, firing on all cylinders, tomorrow.' Chris stood to see me out and I went on shaking legs back to my desk to retrieve my bag, ignoring the whispers and glances I received as I left the building.

Knowing I'd have to face Amanda later made my stomach

churn. I'd have to apologise, play nice until I found out who had it in for me. She was my immediate guess – after all, she was the one I knew the least. Although why she would do such a thing escaped me.

Back at the flat, I googled the meaning of black roses, knowing what I'd find. They were a symbol of death and mourning. I shuddered, remembering the silky gleam of the petals, glad I'd let Chris dispose of them. Was it a prank or a threat? Whatever it was, I'd have to hide my suspicions from Chris if I was going to carry on working at Cardinal Media. I had a couple of hours at least before Amanda returned to the flat. Enough time to do some digging, if only to put my mind at rest.

8

Systematically, I moved through Amanda's room, searching each drawer and obvious hidey-hole, making sure to leave everything as I found it. I couldn't be discovered rooting through my flatmate's room and had to ensure I'd left no trace of being there. I was over-stepping the mark, infringing on Amanda's privacy again, but I had to know if she was up to something.

The weird thing was Amanda had hardly any stuff. Other than clothes, many items still with the tags on suggesting she'd splurged on a whole new wardrobe, there wasn't much in the way of personal things. Had she put her belongings in storage until she found a bigger place or was she averse to clutter?

Amanda had some jewellery stashed away in a little box, a couple of necklaces and a bracelet, but other than that and her toiletries, there was nothing that told me who she was. No clue to her background, or where she'd come from. I didn't even know Amanda's last name. In fact what did I know about my new flat-mate? I'd hardly tried to befriend her. An hour ago, I'd told her to fuck off, not the best of icebreakers.

Pacing the room, I decided if there wasn't anything physical to go on, perhaps I'd see what I could glean online. Double-checking her private space hadn't looked as though I'd invaded it, I retreated to my bedroom and booted up the laptop stored under my bed. From there, I was able to log in to my work emails remotely. Fiona's email about LISTEN, the counselling service she'd mentioned, with their contact details supplied, glared accusingly at me from my inbox. Ignoring it, I opened up a new email and typed Amanda into the recipient box. I waited for Outlook to fill in the rest. It popped up immediately. Amanda Dowd. Her name seemed familiar.

My phone pinged through with a WhatsApp from Jayden.

Hey, you okay?

I shifted the laptop off my knees onto the duvet and tapped a reply.

I think so. The flowers were a shock. Did you see the note?

I waited for Jayden to reply, the bubble came up to let me know he was typing.

No, Amanda took them to Chris and he threw them away.

I frowned. Was Amanda getting rid of the note before Chris saw?

Did Chris see the note?

I didn't want Chris to think I was lying.

Yeah, he came and asked us, but there has to be a logical explanation as no one sent them, Ria.

Well someone did!

I shot back, unable to help myself. I wished now I hadn't got Chris to throw them away, perhaps I could have used what was on the note to track the delivery and find out who sent them. I waited for Jayden to respond, but he took his sweet time.

Maybe contact Amazon, see if you can get the sender's details???

It wasn't a bad idea, although I doubted they'd be able to give out the information due to GDPR rules.

I watched the screen as Jayden typed again.

I'm here if you want to talk. X

Snorting, I tossed my phone and retrieved the laptop. Opening Google Chrome, I typed Amanda's full name in. Not much came up other than a professor with the same name at the University of Warwick.

It was time to check social media and I quickly found her. Amanda had profiles on Facebook and Instagram, although the Facebook one was limited to friends only. I'd have to do some groundwork before I sent a request, considering I'd sworn at her that afternoon. I cringed as I imagined being the topic of the meeting. Everyone questioning whether I should have come back at all.

Amanda's Instagram was open to the public and I scrolled back as far as I could, although there weren't many photos. It appeared to only go back five months, a little after I'd left for Seville. Something seemed off about the photos, but I couldn't put my finger on what it was. Like I'd seen them before, although Amanda and I had never met. There were the standard poses before going out – grinning at the camera, all glammed up, the occasional sunset and yoga pose, as well as photos of cocktails. I guessed most women's Insta accounts looked similar these days.

Most of the photos were pretty ordinary, except there were no pictures featuring other people outside of the Cardinal crew, which, when I considered it, was a little odd. Where were her friends?

I jumped as the front door clicked open, closing the lid on my laptop and pushing it under my pillow.

'Ria?' Cassie's voice came before she appeared at my bedroom door.

'Hey, Cass,' I said, mustering a smile. Over her shoulder, I could see Amanda moving around the kitchen, putting the Tupperware she used for her lunch in the sink.

'Are you okay?'

'I'm fine, sorry about earlier,' I said, heat rising in my cheeks.

'It's not me you should be apologising to,' she whispered, gesturing over her shoulder.

'I know,' I conceded. 'I will.'

'Who do you think sent the flowers?' Cassie's nostrils flared, her nose ring twitching. I looked at her intently, her expression, her body language. She seemed as outraged as I was.

'I don't know. Someone called me too! Played Livvy's voice down the phone,' I whispered.

'Holy shit, that's fucked up.'

'I know, it's like they are deliberately trying to send me mad.' I peered up at her, chin wobbling.

'We'll get to the bottom of it,' she said, giving my shoulder a reassuring squeeze. She smiled before saying loudly, 'I'm just going to use the loo,' winking at me before disappearing.

Taking my cue, I heaved myself off the bed and joined Amanda, standing the opposite side of the counter, pulling at the sleeve of my jumper dress as I wished the ground would open up and swallow me whole.

'I'm sorry for what I said, I didn't mean it.'

Expecting Amanda to glare at me stonily, instead she leant back against the sink, her face lighting up. 'Oh God, don't worry about it. I know what happened to... your friend. It's awful and I hear you've had a rough time.'

I gritted my teeth. Knowing my colleagues at work had been talking behind my back incensed me. 'Yeah, it's been tough,' I admitted, easier to play along.

'Let's call a truce, eh? We have to live together after all.'

'Of course, I'm sorry, I guess it was just a surprise, you know, when I got back and you were here.'

'I get it, I'm used to my own space too, but it won't be for long. It's a stopgap for both of us.'

I nodded, the tension leaving my body. She was bending over backwards to be nice to me. Why was I being such a bitch?

'So why don't you come out with Cass and me, we're going to Baraka's, that new Turkish place?'

My stomach hardened at the shortening of Cassie's name, but I quashed the desire to correct her. Did Amanda even know Cassie well enough to be so familiar? But I reminded myself I'd been away for months and it was ridiculous of me to think time had stood still. Jayden had moved on and who was I to deny Amanda being welcomed into the fold.

'No, honestly, it's fine. Enjoy. I'm going to catch up on a bit of work and I've got loads of ironing to do.' The last part was true, the pile of dirty clothes in the corner of my room had been replaced with clean creased ones.

'Your loss,' Cassie's cheeky voice came from behind me. She nudged me in the ribs and I chuckled.

'Have fun,' I said as they headed out the door.

9

I put the ironing board up, berating myself for the rising jealousy. Amanda was my co-worker, my flatmate, not my rival. Just because she was maybe seeing Jayden, working on my old accounts and now hanging out with my friends shouldn't make her a target for my animosity. I imagined Livvy, rolling her eyes and laughing at my petulance. She'd tell me to grow the fuck up. The more the merrier was pretty much her motto.

I'd managed to iron one T-shirt when Grace messaged me.

I'm late leaving work, are you okay? Shall I stop by for a cuppa?

I replied, inviting her over and stuck the kettle on.

When she arrived, looking a little windswept, I made tea.

'Is it raining?'

'No, but it's blowing a gale out there!'

'You've left late today,' I said, placing two mugs on the coffee table.

'I know, I was working on something with Rav and we kind of looked up and everyone had gone,' she laughed, taking off her coat and sitting on the sofa. 'Were you in the middle of some ironing?' Grace pointed to the board.

'You've given me a reprieve from the mountain of clothes I brought back from Nice.' I sat next to her, shifting my body around so we were face to face.

'No Amanda?' she asked.

'Gone for dinner with Cass. They popped in and invited me,' I added, not wanting to sound surly.

'I just wanted to check you were all right. I was worried as you disappeared after the meeting.'

'Chris wanted me to go home, I was so mad about the flowers.' I tucked my legs beneath me and reached for my tea, handing Grace hers.

'That was dark! Who sent them?'

'I have absolutely no idea, but now I'm worried everyone is going to think I've lost it.'

Grace peered at me over her mug, as if choosing her words carefully. 'Are you sure you're ready to come back?'

I blanched at her question, my stomach clenching. Did she not think I was ready? I knew what had happened with Tarek had been weighing heavily on my mind but I believed I was holding up well. I had been about to mention the phone call I'd received too, but perhaps it wasn't a good idea.

'Yeah, I'm ready,' I said, jutting my chin forwards, 'but after that delivery, it feels like somebody doesn't want me there.'

Grace sipped her tea contemplating.

'Were there concerns, within the team I mean, when Chris said I was coming back?' I asked, knowing Grace would give me a straight answer.

'I mean Aaron had something to say, but doesn't he always,' she said, rolling her eyes, but I couldn't help being wounded. We'd been working well together, but Grace saying that made me all the more inclined to prove myself. 'I think we're all worried,' she continued, holding my gaze, quickly adding, 'but it's because we care about you.'

I knew what she meant, I couldn't afford to go down the same rabbit hole I did when Livvy died. Back then, I wasn't sleeping, barely eating and taking out my grief on everyone.

'I know, and I've come to terms with it now.' I was bending the truth. Livvy's death was something I could never truly accept, but hopefully it would get back to the rest of them I was better, or, at the least, stable.

Grace went on to fill me in on Amanda joining Cardinal and how long it had taken for her to settle in. All the time, they were trying to get used to Livvy's absence. It seemed my presence and erratic behaviour had only compounded their loss and Grace admitted, albeit a little shamefaced, it had been easier to deal with once I'd gone. I wasn't surprised by her admission, although it stung. She meant no harm and was only speaking truthfully, but it emphasised I had to work harder to resume my standing within the team.

'Right, I better get back, otherwise Mum will feed my dinner to the dog,' Grace said, getting up to put her mug in the sink.

'Thanks for popping round.' I stood to see her out.

'I really am glad you're back,' Grace said by the door, pulling me in for a hug and squeezing me tight. 'I've missed you.'

'Missed you too,' I said, surprised to find I was a little choked.

The silence of the flat was all-consuming once Grace left and I carried on ironing with her words bobbing around my head. If Grace was right, there could be friction surrounding my return and perhaps not everyone was happy about it.

Then I spied Amanda's laptop bag on the floor by the sofa. She must have dropped it off when she'd come back with Cassie. I chewed my lip, trying to resist the temptation, especially after having found nothing of interest in her room.

On top of that we'd called a truce, but no matter how hard I tried to ignore it, the bag seemed to call to me. I debated for as long as it took to finish the ironing before I gave in and peered inside.

10

Amanda's laptop bag didn't contain a smoking gun. No receipt for the flowers or a tape recording of Livvy's voice. Still digging inside the bag in case there were any hidden compartments, I found nothing other than the MacBook, charger, a few pens and a notepad. Pressing my hands to my temples I leaned back against the sofa. Maybe Amanda wasn't trolling me after all. I mean, she didn't even know Livvy. They hadn't worked together, Amanda had arrived at Cardinal after the fact. It didn't make any sense it would be her, was I singling her out because I was jealous?

I cleared my throat, putting the laptop, pens and charger back in the bag. The notepad was blue, leather-bound and had Great Ideas in a cursive script embossed in gold. I flicked through the pages, finding what I'd expect, notes on Jayden's projects in neat handwriting. A slip of folded paper fell into my lap. It was a recent printout taken from Cardinal Media's intranet site. An organisational chart of the sales and marketing team, including the account managers and marketing executives with our pictures above our names.

I snorted at the photo of Amanda, it looked like a professional headshot, slightly turned to the side, hair pulled over one shoulder.

It was in the spot Livvy's photo used to be, which made me flinch. I frowned when I got to my photo, seeing it had been circled numerous times with black biro. Stomach fluttering, I squinted, bringing the paper closer to my face. It looked like someone had coloured in my eyes in too. I dropped the sheet to the floor, the air around me seeming to chill. It was weird. More than weird.

Placing it back inside the pages of the notebook, I returned the bag to where I'd found it. I stewed on the circling of my photo as I put the ironing away. Why had Amanda marked me out? I wasn't even at Cardinal Media when she'd joined. And the eyes, that gave me shudders. My mind played devil's advocate. Maybe Chris had done it, printed out the chart to run Amanda through the team and highlighted me as I'd be her flatmate when I returned. Alternatively she could have mindlessly doodled in the eyes. It was a possibility.

I tried to force my attention elsewhere, putting *Firefly Lane* on Netflix, something gentle to distract me, but my mind kept coming back to the circling and seeming disfigurement of my eyes. As though the image was seared in my mind.

A message came through from Aaron around seven o'clock, checking in to ask if I was okay after 'losing my shit' earlier.

They'd all seen me at my worst before the sabbatical and after what Grace had told me were likely wondering why Chris had let me back. We were a tight-knit group, before Livvy died and everything changed.

I sent a short message back to say I was fine, thanking him. I didn't want to say too much, reluctant to blur the lines of professionalism. I had to ignore whoever was playing mind games with me and focus on the job because if I lost that as well as the flat with it, I didn't know what I'd do.

Half an hour later, Amanda arrived home carrying a polystyrene takeaway box. She handed it to me before she even took her coat off.

'Leftover lamb shish,' she explained, 'still warm too.' She gave me a bright smile and my stomach growled appreciatively at the smell. My mind had been so occupied, I'd forgotten I'd missed dinner.

'Thank you,' I said, peering inside the box and salivating.

'Want me to microwave you some rice? I've got one of those pouches in the cupboard?' Amanda shrugged off her coat, hanging it behind the door, and kicked off her heels, flopping down next to me on the sofa.

'No thanks. Was the restaurant nice?' I asked, sinking my teeth into the meat, which tasted divine.

'It was so good. Cassie had marinated chicken wings. We ordered way too much. She took some home to have tomorrow. What are you watching?' Amanda's gaze fell on the TV and she answered before I had a chance. '*Firefly Lane*, oh I love it.'

We chatted comfortably as I ate and I made us cups of tea afterwards. The edginess from before seemed to evaporate. Grace and Cassie were right, she was nice and it was hard not to warm to her, despite the weird printout I'd found playing on my mind.

After two episodes of *Firefly Lane* back-to-back, Amanda asked if she could put her pyjamas on and take her face off before we embarked on a third. I agreed, and we headed off to our bedrooms. Reconvening, awkwardly at first, in fleece pyjamas, now make-up-free.

'I hate people seeing me without my war paint on,' Amanda admitted and I noticed she had some acne scars I hadn't seen before.

'I'm a bit the same,' I said, offering solidarity, although it wasn't strictly true.

About ten minutes into the episode, Amanda broke the silence.

'What happened to your friend?'

I recoiled as though I'd been punched.

'I'm sorry, you don't have to talk about it if you don't want to,' she added.

'No, it's fine.' I paused to take a breath, summoning the words. 'Livvy died while we were out at a works do. It's an awards ceremony Cardinal puts on every year in Brighton. They rent a conference room in a posh hotel. It's recognition for the staff, who brought in the most money, that kind of thing. We'd moved on to a club and towards the end of the night I found Livvy collapsed in a toilet cubicle.'

Amanda gasped, her face grave, absorbing my every word.

'It was awful.' Tears welled up in my eyes. 'I couldn't rouse her and we called an ambulance.'

'What happened to her?' Amanda asked, propping herself up on the sofa.

'They said she'd taken ketamine, the hospital found it in her bloodstream, but Livvy didn't do drugs. She hated them.' I sniffed. 'The doctors believe she fell in the cubicle and hit her head, which caused a massive bleed on the brain.' A tear escaped down my cheek and I batted it away, too consumed with grief to be embarrassed. 'I think she'd already passed when I found her.' The emotion was still so raw, Livvy's death didn't make any sense at the time and it still didn't now.

'Do you think she was spiked?' Amanda's eyes widened, boring into mine.

'I do,' I said simply, getting to my feet and collecting our empty mugs to take to the sink.

'I'm so sorry. I didn't mean to upset you,' she said.

'It's okay. I don't talk about it much. I'm not sure I'll ever get the image of her slumped on that toilet floor out of my head. It haunts me,' I admitted.

The silence stretched out between us and I spent longer than necessary washing the cups out in the sink.

'I've really dampened the mood haven't I, I'm sorry.'

'It's fine. I just miss her, that's all,' I said, suddenly desperate to retreat to my room. 'Listen, I'm really tired, thanks so much for the food. I had nice evening. We'll do it again, okay?' I managed a smile through blurry eyes. Once the tears started, it was hard to quell them.

'Sure,' Amanda said, getting up to turn the television off. It was almost ten o'clock and I was drained. 'Night then.' Amanda gave a little wave as I disappeared into my bedroom, the door clicking shut behind me.

Sighing, I pulled my hair out of my scrunchie and shook it, curls falling in front of my face. I wished I could shake off the gloom with it. Everything had been fine until Amanda had brought Livvy up, although I guessed it was only natural. Why shouldn't she want to find out what happened and who she'd replaced at work. It wasn't as if Livvy had left Cardinal, moved on and got another job. Replacing someone who died must be weird. I still found it hard to talk about though. No one else saw Livvy in the toilet, they'd been spared that vision. Livvy's cold lifeless fingers as I'd squeezed her hand, trying to inject the life back into her that had seeped out before I got there. How I'd screamed and wailed for help. Amanda had no idea how traumatic it was, and I hoped she never would. I wouldn't wish it on my worst enemy. Not that Amanda was my enemy. I had to push aside my insecurities because there was a tiny possibility we could even become friends.

11

A stabbing pain in my stomach woke me as I pulled my knees up to my chest, wincing as it struck again. It was still dark outside and I wiped the sleep from my eyes to see it was only four in the morning. Groaning, I sat up, nausea hitting me like a tidal wave. The room spun and I fought to hold back the vomit in my gullet. I stumbled to the toilet, just making the bowl before I threw up.

I panted on the cool tiles, fighting the urge to heave again. I didn't even have time to wipe my mouth before the retching started. Shivering in my pyjamas, cold sweat collected on my top lip as I remained on the floor in the dark, waiting for it to be over.

Eventually, when I deemed it safe and my stomach was empty, I slowly got to my feet, pulling the cord to turn on the light. My reflection in the cabinet mirror was like that of a ghost. So pale, my skin seemed translucent, with a glowing sheen of perspiration across my forehead. I washed my hands and scooped water into my mouth, swilling it around to get rid of the acidic burn.

It must have been the kebab. My stomach gurgled at the thought, although thankfully the purge seemed to be over. Cleaning my teeth at speed, I flushed the toilet and stumbled back to bed, pulling the covers up to my neck, although it didn't help my shivers. My stomach continued to cramp no matter what position I tried, it was impossible to get comfortable.

I seemed to blink and the alarm went off, the room bathed in sunlight through the curtains. My cramps had been replaced with by a dull headache suggesting dehydration. Fighting the urge to turn off the alarm and go back to sleep, I sat up with a grunt to get in the shower. The idea of tea or coffee repulsive. I needed water, and lots of it.

I didn't see Amanda until I was dressed. She came into the kitchen as I was rummaging in the cupboard for some Alka-Seltzer to drop into the pint of water I was drinking.

'Were you ill last night?' she asked, grabbing a cereal bar from the cupboard.

'Yes, it was awful. Were you?' I rubbed at my clammy forehead.

'Yeah, about two. I'm surprised you didn't hear me.'

I narrowed my eyes, taking in Amanda's perfect appearance, the glow of her skin in comparison to how washed out I looked.

'No, I didn't hear anything,' I admitted, a little brusquely. Amanda looked a little too perky for someone who'd been throwing up, unless she bounced back quicker than I did.

'You do look rough, why don't you stay home today?' she suggested.

'I'll be fine,' I said, giving up the search for anything in the makeshift medicine cupboard that would settle my stomach. I'd pop to the chemist on my way in.

'Okay, I'm going to meet Jayden for a quick coffee. I'll see you in the office,' she said, applying some lip gloss before tossing her hair over her shoulder. I had to resist the urge to roll my eyes.

'Bye,' I said sweetly instead, ignoring the pinch of jealousy.

Doing the best I could with my appearance, I made it to the

chemist to get some Alka-Seltzer, aware I was sweating despite the wintry temperature.

When I got into the office, Michelle frowned.

'You don't look so good,' she said, leaning over the desk as I hurried past.

'I'm fine,' I said as chirpily as I could manage, not wanting to stop and talk. The fresh air and the motion of walking had made me nauseous again and I had to spend a few minutes in the ladies' to steady myself. I couldn't go home sick, I'd only just returned to work. How would that look.

In stark contrast, Amanda breezed past my desk in her tight shift dress, carrying her takeaway coffee cup as I logged on. I looked like death and she looked like she'd had a blissful eight hours of uninterrupted sleep and woken up as fresh as a daisy. I scowled into my water, listening to the fizz of the Alka-Seltzer tablets work their magic.

'Rough night?' Aaron said, smirking at my glass bubbling away.

'Food poisoning, I think.'

'Sure,' he sniggered, rubbing his chin, backtracking when I shot him daggers. 'You had a tough day, that's all I meant, no one would hold a little drink against you.'

'Is there something I can help you with?' I replied.

'I've got a call with High Point about their hiking boots, I think you should sit in.'

Minutes later, I was on a Teams call, frantically dabbing my forehead with a tissue to reduce the shine which the camera seemed to highlight. Aaron presented a mock-up he'd created with the ideas we'd talked about yesterday, the focus on splashing in muddy puddles.

'I think we go for a green and black theme, with a bolt of neon yellow.'

I watched as the two employees from High Point, Jessica and David nodded along.

'We can tinge the backdrop to complement the scheme, like this.' Aaron clicked the picture to change the mountain background to a steely grey.

I wanted to contribute, but every time I opened my mouth to speak, I was worried I was going to throw up.

'I love the strapline,' Jessica leaned forward towards the camera.

'We do too,' Aaron agreed. The strapline 'For the road less travelled' wasn't something I'd seen before. Had Aaron come up with it?

Eager to offer something, I steered them towards the copy I had put together. They agreed it was the right length and suggested using some specific terminology which they would send across.

Once the call was over, Aaron leaned back in his seat.

'That went well,' he said.

'It did,' I replied, although my stomach was in knots. 'Great strapline.'

'Awesome, isn't it. Amanda came up with it.'

My throat immediately tightened. What the hell was she involved for? She had her own projects with Jayden.

'It was in the meeting yesterday, after you... left,' Aaron said diplomatically, sensing me stiffen at Amanda's encroachment.

'It's good,' I admitted, pasting on a smile.

'She's just what we need, a real team player.' Aaron got up and disconnected his laptop from the console at the centre of the table that operated the smart monitor.

Was he insinuating I wasn't a team player or was I being paranoid?

'I'll let you deal with the copy when Jessica sends it through,' he said, pushing open the glass door and beaming at Amanda, who strode past. She gave me a little wave through the glass and I had to fight the urge to throw back an obscene gesture. Christ, did she have to get involved in everything?

I leaned back in the chair, raising my face to the ceiling and momentarily closing my eyes.

'Sleeping on the job?' Chris's voice broke through the fog and my lids snapped open. Thankfully, he was smiling.

'No, Aaron and I have just had a meeting with High Point.'

'I saw the mock-up, looks great, well done. Love the strapline.'

I gritted my teeth, but instead of correcting him I nodded, taking the compliment. 'Thanks.'

'Are you sure you're okay?'

'A touch of food poisoning, it seems,' I explained, patting my stomach.

'I thought you looked a little green around the gills. Take it easy, okay.'

'Will do.' I smiled and sighed with relief when he carried on down the corridor, stopping to talk to Amanda, who was returning from the opposite direction.

I watched with interest as he squeezed her shoulder. She let out a giggle and they fell in step until I could no longer see them. I sat, my jaw slack, shocked at what I'd witnessed. We all knew Chris was a great boss, he genuinely cared about his employees but he always maintained professionalism. In today's society, everyone was super careful, especially in the aftermath of the #MeToo scandals. Chris never crossed the line except to offer a firm handshake. He never touched us but somehow Amanda seemed to have everyone fawning over her. What was it about her that had them all so enamoured?

12

The rest of the afternoon dragged, but I tried to get as much work done as I could. My brain wasn't sparking and every idea I came up with, seemed to fall flat. Some days were like that, but Amanda's presence in the office irritated me, she seemed to be everywhere I went and when I couldn't see her, I heard her sugarcoated tone. Something about her voice pierced through the membranes like tiny stabbing needles. It was torture, but I wasn't particularly tolerant today.

With my stomach still tender, I skipped lunch and headed around to Cassie's desk later that afternoon to find her shovelling down a bag of prawn cocktail crisps.

'I take it you're feeling all right then?' I commented.

She looked at me quizzically as she chewed. 'Fine, yeah, why?' she asked, folding the empty packet into a tiny triangle and popping it in the bin.

'I think the kebab Amanda bought home was a bit dodgy,' I said, rubbing my stomach.

'Oh no, that sucks. I'm all right, but I've got iron guts,' she laughed, 'plus I had the chicken wings. You should have come with us.'

'Maybe next time I will,' I replied. 'A different restaurant though.'

Cassie's desk phone rang and I nodded I was off before she answered it.

As the minutes ticked past, I longed to leave. The office was too crowded. I couldn't help thinking Amanda had purposefully given me food poisoning, although how I had no idea. Was it my overactive imagination?

I longed for space, some peace and quiet to collect my thoughts away from Amanda. Although there would be no escape at home, so I decided to put off going to the flat and when five o'clock came around, I headed out into the bitter air wishing I'd brought my gloves, deciding to go in the opposite direction, towards the library.

Pleased to find one of the computers in the business section free, I logged on to see what I'd be able to afford in the rental market locally, but every flat was out of my price range. Whilst killing time and enjoying the peace, I had a quick search for jobs as well, to see what was out there.

I'd be mad to leave Cardinal when Chris had already told me he could see me as an account manager in a couple of years. That was if I sorted my shit out. Considering my history, to have Chris still believe in me meant a lot, although I wasn't sure how long I would be able to put up working with Amanda.

My phone beeped with a message from Jayden.

We're in the pub for a quick one, where are you?

I ignored it. I knew *she* would be there and my tolerance level wasn't up to it. I'd been sure to dash out of the door at five o'clock, without waiting to see what any of the others were up to. At least knowing Amanda was in the pub with Jayden meant I could escape and go home. I'd taken having the flat to myself for granted. There was a lot to be said for lazing around in your pyjamas without anyone there to judge you. Despite hating sharing the space, I reminded myself the flat wasn't mine and I shouldn't moan. I was lucky Chris let me rent it from him so heavily subsidised. I wouldn't be able to afford anywhere half as nice in town by myself.

I got ready to log off, before an advert popped up on Total Jobs, which gave me an idea. I opened LinkedIn and I tried to recall my password. It was a site I rarely used, although everyone was on it for networking purposes. I typed in Amanda Dowd and a few hits came up. I scrolled through them, but there appeared to be nothing of note until further down the page my mouse froze.

On the screen below the list of Amanda Dowds was a Mandy Dowd. What caught my attention was the mention of Cardinal Media. It was listed as where Mandy Dowd currently worked and had done since 2020. Her title was payroll administrator, but there was no further information. I clicked on her profile, aware she might be notified I'd looked, but I had to know more. Unfortunately, there was no photograph or personal information to be gained. Surely Amanda and Mandy had to be the same person, it was too much of a coincidence not to be. However, I knew if the employment history wasn't updated on LinkedIn when moving companies, the current position listed could easily be old information.

Intrigued by my finding, I logged off and made my way home. Back at the flat, thankfully Amanda hadn't yet returned. Not wanting to chance a repeat performance with my stomach, I had a couple of slices of toast, hoping to eat and disappear to my room before she got back. Unfortunately, I wasn't quick enough and still at the breakfast bar, motoring through the second slice, when the front door opened and Amanda's voice called out.

'Ria, are you here?'

'In the kitchen,' I called back, through a mouthful of crust.

Amanda appeared with Jayden in tow and I visibly deflated on the stool.

'How's the tummy?' Amanda asked.

'Better, thanks,' I said, holding up the toast to show I was eating.

'That's good,' she replied, turning to Jayden. 'Want a drink?' Her hand was firmly planted on his arm.

If I wasn't mistaken, I was sure I saw a flicker of irritation sweep across his face at her touch. Our eyes met, but I looked away.

'No thanks.'

'I'm off to bed,' I announced, keen to get away as Amanda rustled in the fridge.

'Already? It's early!' Jayden said, following me towards my room.

'I'm tired, and I feel crap, I just want to sleep,' I replied over my shoulder.

Jayden stood at the threshold of my bedroom. 'I came back here to see you, you know, not her,' he whispered, gesturing over his shoulder, where I could see Amanda's eyes penetrating his back.

'Sorry, should I be grateful?' I hissed, before shaking my head. 'I didn't mean that.'

I sank onto the bed, Jayden stepped inside and pushed the door to, coming to sit beside me.

'I'm sorry, I know I've been a twat,' he reached over and rested his hand on mine, 'but I care about you. I want to make sure you're okay.'

Hot tears stung my eyes, but I blinked them away, sliding my hand out from under his. I didn't want to get into it, not now. 'Thank you, but I'm fine.'

Jayden sighed, his jaw clenching and unclenching, frustration evident.

'How are you finding working with Amanda, I hear she's great,' I said as he stood to leave.

'Yeah, she's good at the job, but she is driving me around the bend.'

I laughed before saying, 'That's your punishment.'

We smiled at each other, the tension broken.

'Dickhead,' Jayden replied, sniggering. It was easy slipping into our old banter.

My phone rang and Jayden turned towards the door.

'I'll let you get back to it, take it easy.'

'Night,' I called after him before turning my phone over to see who was calling.

Livvy's name flashed onto the screen and I dropped the phone onto the carpet as though it had burnt my fingers, the toast I'd eaten crawling its way up my throat. In the kitchen, I could hear Jayden and Amanda talking, the ringing stopped, the caller sent to voicemail because I hadn't answered. I prayed there wouldn't be a message. I couldn't cope with hearing Livvy's voice again today. It was too painful. I picked up the phone and switched it off, not wanting it to ring again.

I had no idea who was torturing me, or what they wanted. Could it be one of my colleagues? The thought was like a knife to my side; they weren't only colleagues, they were my friends. My mind swirled with numerous possibilities, but I was clueless to who it was or what was their motivation. Unless Tarek was the caller? Mum knew everything about Livvy's death, I'm sure she would have told him the reason for my sabbatical. Was he trying to get to me from across the Channel?

I slipped underneath the covers, not bothering to remove my clothes, pulling the duvet up like a shield. The toast sat in my stomach like a brick, making me bloated and a little queasy. Was Amanda behind it all? She already had Livvy's job, what more could she want? I remembered Chris's hand on her shoulder, something I'd never seen him do with anyone. Did she intend to sleep her way to the top, and if so, what did that have to do with me. I was hardly standing in her way.

Minutes later, I heard Jayden say goodbye and the front door close. Perhaps he had been genuine when he said what had happened between them was a mistake. Maybe Amanda was too much for him. Too perky, too professional, too friendly and too loud. Someone who was overwhelming and exhausting at the same time.

I put on a Netflix documentary to distract myself, but my head was full of Amanda, or Mandy if that was what she used to call herself. And if she was the Mandy I'd found on LinkedIn, why would she change her name, not to mention her profession? Surely I would have bumped into her in the office. Also how on earth would no one have mentioned she'd worked there before?

13

'Shit!'

'Oh God, I'm sorry, my fault,' Amanda said, dabbing at the once white sleeve of my shirt that was now a brown mess of coffee. The skin of my hand on fire.

'Doesn't matter, I'll go and get changed,' I said through gritted teeth as I unbuttoned the shirt, knowing I'd have to leave it to soak if I was going to get the stain out.

That morning, I'd decided the best way to find out about Amanda, if there was nothing to be gleaned online, was to simply get to know her. Leaping out of bed early to get into the shower, desperate to wash off another nightmare about Tarek, I'd distracted my brain by playing One Republic through my phone as I got ready.

Thankfully, there had been no voicemail left when I'd checked as soon I woke up. My mysterious caller obviously hadn't wanted to leave any proof of the call. It was disconcerting, someone portraying to be my deceased best friend. How the hell were they doing it?

'Oh, I love this band,' Amanda had said, coming out of her room and poking her head into mine as I'd applied mascara to my lashes.

'Me too, they're fab, I'd love to go and see them.' I'd sounded eager and told myself to dial it down a notch. Although all I was doing was matching her enthusiasm. 'Coffee?' I'd offered, putting down the mascara and following Amanda out into the kitchen.

'Sure.'

I appeared plain standing next to her in my grey trousers and white shirt when she'd poured herself into a khaki leather skirt, knee-length boots and a black fine-knit polo neck.

As the kettle had boiled, we'd talked about music. Amanda loved Lady Gaga and Taylor Swift, declaring them as empowered women with amazing voices. Once I'd got her talking, I'd decided to ask a more personal question.

'Chris said you moved from Broadstairs, that's Devon right?' I'd asked, pouring coffee into plain white mugs, bringing the milk and sugar to the breakfast bar and sliding onto a stool.

'No,' she'd giggled, sitting beside me, 'it's in Kent. I moved in with my aunt for a while, to get away from things. My parents have had a few issues.'

I'd poured milk into my coffee, but Amanda had left hers black, blowing the steam off the top and taking a sip. Her trademark red lipstick staining the porcelain.

'My geography is rubbish,' I'd admitted, hoping she'd elaborate on the reason for the move, but she didn't. 'Just you and your aunt, was it?' I'd pressed on.

Amanda's back had seemed to stiffen, her mouth pulled into a tight line.

'Yes. My parents are here in Crawley, but it's complicated, we don't all get along. What about you, any family locally?' she'd said, swiftly directing the question back to me.

'My mum is in Nice, with her boyfriend. I think I was a mistake and not one she was going to repeat, so no brothers or sisters for me.'

Amanda's eyes had widened at my pragmatic tone and I'd chuckled.

'She's never kept it a secret, it must be why we're so close,' I'd said sarcastically, watching as Amanda's lips turn upwards despite herself.

'That's rough.'

'How about you, any siblings?' I'd asked.

With a jerky hand, Amanda had nudged her cup, managing to right it, but not before coffee sloshed over the edge and onto my sleeve. Liquid seeped up the cuff, turning the fabric brown as she'd apologised profusely. My favourite Zara shirt would be ruined.

By the time we left for work, once I'd changed and left the shirt soaking in bleach, the conversation had moved on to friends and Amanda admitted she didn't have many in Crawley. I was about to ask why exactly she'd moved to Kent, but Jayden joined us at the entrance to the office.

'Ladies,' he said, greeting us with a wide smile and a twinkle in his eyes.

'Morning,' Amanda said, managing to make the simple word sound flirtatious.

'We've got that meeting in a bit, updating Chris on our projects, but perhaps we can grab some lunch later?' Jayden's eyes searched mine, but before I could answer, Amanda piped up.

'Ooh yes, Greggs sausage rolls are calling me today. What about you, Ria?'

'Sounds good,' I said, watching as Jayden stifled a laugh. I knew he'd been talking to me and not Amanda, but she'd blithely invited herself regardless. She either had zero self-awareness or there was no way she was letting Jayden out of her sight.

At my desk, I logged on, pleased with the progress I'd made with Amanda. While I waited for my emails to load, I took the opportunity to follow her on Instagram, as well as sending her a friend request to her Facebook account. She accepted quickly and I had no doubt she would be scrolling through my posts and photos as I raced through hers.

Disappointingly, there wasn't much to see. It was mainly the photos I'd already viewed, ones she'd uploaded to her Instagram account. The feed on her Facebook going back around six months, as if she'd only discovered social media then. It didn't make any sense. Almost everyone I knew was on Instagram, Twitter, Facebook and Snapchat, but Amanda had such a limited online presence, it was odd. Perhaps she was a private person, although that didn't reconcile with the loud, brash Amanda I'd met in real life.

At half past nine, all of the account managers and junior executives gathered in the boardroom to give Chris an update on the projects they were working on. Grace and Cassie had a Christmas-themed spread for a healthy baked crisp company they were pitching for. Jayden and Amanda took the next slot, showcasing their campaign for Brewdog. I focused on Chris when Amanda spoke. He stared at her intensely, fiddling with his tie and hanging on her every word. It left a bad taste in my mouth and I looked around the room, but no one else looked as though they'd picked up on it.

When it was Aaron's turn, I joined him by the screen as he showed a similar presentation he'd delivered to High Point.

'Here's the new copy,' Amanda purred, sliding a sheet across the desk.

Before Aaron could get to it, I snatched it up, skimming the lines. It was a revised version of what I'd produced.

Aaron's ears tinged fuchsia as my face hardened.

'You asked Amanda to revise it?' I snapped, unable to control the incredulity in my tone as the room fell silent.

'It's no big deal, they just wanted it a little punchier, like the strapline, so I gave it to Amanda to look over.' Aaron's words came out fast and he pulled at the collar of his shirt as though it had suddenly become too tight.

'It's our project, Aaron. Amanda is working with Jayden.' I tried to keep my voice calm, but my toes curled in my boots. Was this because he fancied her or was he deliberately trying to undermine me?

'Okay, let's move on. Aaron, I'm sure Amanda is busy with her own projects. Ria is perfectly capable,' Chris stepped in, trying to defuse the situation, but my nostrils were already flaring.

'I'm sorry, it's my fault, I offered to help.' Amanda, the picture of innocence, lowered her eyes to her mug, wrapping her fingers around it.

Aaron scowled, annoyed at being caught out and publicly admonished. He tried to carry on but had little input from me. I was fixated on Amanda's red painted fingernails, covering the slogan of the pink mug I knew so well. I'd bought it as a gift.

'That's Livvy's mug,' I said too loudly, interrupting Aaron as he continued the pitch. All eyes in the room fell on me.

'Is it?' Amanda said, her voice breaking.

'You can't use it,' I snapped.

'For goodness' sake, Ria, it's just a mug,' Chris shot back, exasperated.

I couldn't focus for the remainder of the meeting, my temples throbbed as I tried to hold in an eruption. I dug my nails into my palms as the rest of the account managers presented in turn. Aaron wouldn't look at me and neither would Amanda, who had discarded Livvy's mug as though I might slap her if she touched it again. I couldn't deny it wasn't a possibility.

Who did she think she was? Was she trying to muscle in on my projects and show me up? Trying to make out I was incompetent and she was better than me? If it was a genuine mistake and Aaron had coaxed her into it, then fine. But if she wanted to step on my toes, the question was why?

14

Indignation burned in my chest and I was desperate to get out of the claustrophobic room, to get some air and walk off the rage that consumed me. It was no surprise Chris asked me to stay behind when the meeting was over. Everyone left quickly and I sat on the edge of my seat, too annoyed to be anxious.

'I understand why you're upset,' he began. 'I'm sure Aaron won't ask Amanda to work on your projects again.'

He just wants to sleep with her, that's all, the voice in my head piped up, *like you*, because Chris was obviously fawning over Amanda too.

'Maybe they think I'm not up to it,' I said, Grace's words from the other day a rock in my stomach.

'I'm sure that's not the case, we all know how capable you are,' he frowned. 'Listen, about Amanda, go easy on her, okay, she's had a rough time.'

My eyebrows shot up. 'What do you mean, a rough time?'

'I'm not going to discuss her personal life with you, it would be unprofessional, however I'm letting you know she's had some difficulties lately and doesn't need you jumping down her throat about a mug.'

I recoiled at his stern tone, but there was no point arguing, Chris obviously had a thing for Amanda, she was the new firm favourite, the teacher's pet.

I nodded and gathered my things, stung, glancing at Livvy's mug, which had been left on the table.

'Just be kind, that's all I'm saying.' Chris's voice had softened and he stood to open the door for me.

'Sure,' I said as I walked out, my tail firmly between my legs.

I went straight to the toilet to splash some cold water on my face, letting the droplets run down my skin, all the time berating myself for not handling things better. I'd overstepped the mark. My issue with the mug was petty, a cheap shot aimed because of my annoyance at Amanda infringing on my project.

As I returned to my desk, I overheard Aaron, Grace and Rav in the kitchen, pausing out of sight to listen to what they were saying.

'I'm not being a dick, but maybe she came back too soon,' Aaron whispered.

'She'll be fine, give her a break,' Rav replied, his voice muffled by a teaspoon chinking against a mug.

'I don't want her pointing fingers,' Aaron scowled. 'Everything has just got back to normal without her stirring it all up again.'

'Aaron, you're being a bit harsh. I mean, someone sent her those flowers. We all saw them,' Grace said, adding, 'it's not as if she sent them to herself.'

'Maybe she did!' Aaron snapped, no longer whispering.

Grace tutted before coming back with, 'That's messed up.'

Not wanting to hear any more, I scurried away, taking refuge at my desk, where I intended to stay for the rest of the day. At least it sounded like Grace and Rav were on my side.

Amanda and Aaron both gave me a wide berth, in fact everyone pretty much avoided me. They went out for lunch without me, my invitation from Jayden seemingly revoked. When I passed the meeting room to go to the toilet, Livvy's mug still sat there accusingly, waiting for someone to remove it. I decided to leave it for the cleaners who came in each morning. At least Amanda wouldn't be touching it again. I knew it was ridiculous, but no one had used that mug since Livvy died. Out of respect.

Once I'd worked through Amanda's revised High Point copy more out of principle than because it needed changing, I arranged the muddy puddles photo shoot for a day it was supposed to rain next week.

Wanting a break, I stretched my legs to where finance and human resources lived. Fiona waved at me from her office as I passed, her phone pressed to her ear. I waved back and carried on. That was the thing with glass walls and partitions, there was no privacy. Offices were nothing more than display boxes.

When I got to finance, everyone looked to be engrossed in their work, eyes focused on their monitors, tapping away at keyboards. I found Karen Brackstone by the water cooler. She was a bubbly woman in her forties with wavy auburn hair and an infectious laugh that at times could be heard down the other end of the office.

'Hi, Karen.'

She looked up from filling her bottle and gave me an easy smile. 'Hello, stranger, how are you?'

'I'm good thanks, you?'

Karen nodded, 'Not too bad, wish they'd bloody turn the heating up though, I'm freezing!' She wrapped her fluffy cardigan tighter around herself to emphasise the point. 'How were your travels?'

'Great, it was nice to have a break.'

Karen's sympathetic eyes made me want to bolt. Instead I got to the reason for my visit.

'I've got a bit of a random question for you,' I said.

'Intriguing... shoot.'

'Did you used to have a Mandy Dowd work in your department?' I asked, rolling back on my heels.

Karen's brow furrowed, before recognition dawned on her face. 'Yes, we did. She was in payroll, only here a few months. Quiet as a mouse.'

It was my turn to frown. Quiet and Amanda didn't go together at all.

'Do you remember what she looked like?' I asked, hopefully.

'Ummm, mousy hair, a bob, I think. Glasses. Plain, I'd guess you might say,' she chuckled. 'Brad used to call her Velma, you know, from *Scooby-Doo*.'

'Oh yeah, I know,' I said. Although Amanda was definitely more Daphne than Velma.

'Why do you ask?' Karen lifted her bottle of water and took a sip.

I stalled, twiddling my hair around my finger, trying to think on my feet. Why hadn't I prepared myself for this question?

'No reason, really, her name came up on LinkedIn and I thought I knew her.' Quickly, I added, 'Not from here, from before, umm, college.'

I was a terrible liar, but Karen didn't seem to notice me wringing my hands as she commented, 'She was only here a few months, it was a bit weird really. One minute she was here, the next she was gone.'

'Strange,' I agreed, hoping Karen would elaborate.

'Yeah, Fiona said she'd not passed her probation period, but Brad, who was her line manager, said he was satisfied with her work. It didn't really make any sense, but the following week, Jamie came in from an agency to replace her and it was kind of forgotten.'

'I wonder what she's doing now,' I said, more to myself than to Karen.

'Who knows, she didn't really fit in, I'm not sure why Chris took her on to be honest, perhaps she came highly recommended,' Karen mused.

'It can't be the Mandy I used to know, I must have been mistaken.'

'Oh okay,' Karen fiddled with her locket, sat in the deep v of her blouse, 'no worries, lovely to see you round these parts.'

Amanda and Mandy obviously weren't the same person. If they were, someone would have noticed. Wouldn't it be odd for Mandy to leave payroll and turn up as Amanda in the sales and marketing team? And according to Karen's description, Mandy couldn't have been more different from Amanda. It had to be a coincidence, although the names were too similar for me not to be convinced something was off.

On the way back to my desk, Fiona called out as I passed. Now off the phone she beckoned me in with a wave. 'How are you, Ria?'

'I'm fine,' I said, a little defensively, rolling my shoulders back, 'how are you?'

Fiona shook her head, grimacing, gesturing to the metal filing cabinet behind her desk. 'Can you believe someone's broken the lock on my filing cabinet!' she said, incredulous.

'What's in there?' I frowned.

'Personnel files. It's so annoying as I can't get it to lock any more.' She huffed, crossing her arms. With no one having spoken of an external break-in, it had to mean an employee had been nosing around. 'Anyway, how's it been settling back into the fold?'

'Okay, I guess,' I replied with a half-hearted shrug.

'Good. Here's that leaflet on the counselling service I promised.' Fiona pushed it across the desk to me, the words LISTEN in large yellow capital letters branded on the front. 'It's got a telephone number and there's a chat function on their website which I believe is manned twenty-four hours a day.' Fiona was talking like she feared I was minutes away from a breakdown.

'Honestly, Fiona, I'm fine and thank you, I got the email.' My smile stretched thinly across my face. I debated with the idea of asking Fiona about Mandy Dowd, but now wasn't the time. I didn't want to give her any reason to think I was having a wobble.

'I hope so. Please remember, we're all rooting for you. My door is always open.'

'Thank you,' I replied, itching to leave. I couldn't decide if Fiona was genuine or just worried about Cardinal Media's reputation.

I edged towards the door, shuffling backwards. Fiona's intense stare penetrating right through me until I turned my back, catching her parting words.

'Because, you know, we wouldn't want to have an incident like last time, would we.'

15

I steadied myself on the wall when I got out of sight of Fiona's office, neck mottled with the shame of remembering *that day*. It was ten days after we had buried Livvy and I was in limbo, unable to reconcile the fact that my best friend had gone. Not in those awful circumstances. I was like a ticking bomb, ready to go off as the anger swelled in my stomach with each day passing.

Livvy's cause of death had been declared accidental which I'd refused to accept. It was caused ultimately because Livvy had ketamine in her system and she didn't *do* drugs. We never had, even when the rest of the team indulged now and again and it was offered, we'd always said no. Why would Livvy have had a change heart and done something so out of character without telling me? It couldn't have happened the way they'd said.

I'd ditched work that morning to visit Livvy's parents. They were exhausted, consumed with grief at losing their only daughter and were still trying to comprehend how their world had fallen apart. Her mother, Lynn, had asked me politely to leave after a heated exchange.

I'd turned up at their door and demanded they push to have the case reopened. Hire a private detective, get CCTV examined, anything that would make sense of Livvy's death. Instead they had accepted the inevitable. Their daughter was gone and she wasn't coming back. I had to accept it too. But I wouldn't, I couldn't, and instead of the verdict crushing me like it had them, a spark ignited in my chest.

On returning to work, I had burst into the sales meeting like a tornado, accusing each of them of spiking Livvy's drink. Swiping documents from the table in an uncontrollable rage and tossing them to the floor, I demanded to know who was guilty of causing her untimely demise.

I was met with silence, gawping faces at my meltdown. Of course, no one admitted anything. Why would they? If it was one of them, they were home free. No one was going to be held account-able and the knowledge burned inside of me like lava.

Fiona and Chris had to practically manhandle me out of the boardroom. He had berated me and my wild accusations. It couldn't go on, I had to stop. Cardinal Media could not live under the shadow of Livvy's death forever. I knew he was trying to protect the business, shield Cardinal from bad press that so far he'd managed to avoid.

I was a loose cannon, uncontrollable, and I threatened to go to the newspapers, to force the person responsible to panic and reveal themselves. Someone knew more about what happened that night, and they worked at Cardinal Media. Someone I would call a friend. Whoever it was had blood on their hands. All I wanted was justice for Livvy. I'd sworn to myself I would make it right.

Looking back, I saw how wild I'd become. Without Chris's inter-vention, I would have driven myself mad. He was kind to me, not judging when others had made up their minds. I'd heard the whis-pers. I was unhinged, potentially guilty myself and projecting it onto the rest of the team, some had said. So I'd agreed to leave and come back with a clean slate.

But now I had, someone wouldn't let me forget and they were trying to push me down the same path as before. I couldn't let that happen.

The leaflet Fiona had given me was a lead weight in my hand. Perhaps it wouldn't do any harm to ask for a little help. My mind continued to whirl, thoughts disjointed, scattered all over the place. I didn't want to lose control again. I had to rein myself in before it went too far and Chris washed his hands of me. For good this time.

I got to the corner of the L-shape, my neck and chest still burning. From there, I was able to see into Chris's office, the right side, where the glass wasn't frosted. He and Amanda looked to be having a heated discussion about something. She was gesticulating wildly and Chris was fanning with his hands, trying to calm her. What on earth was she ranting about?

My gut wrenched and I leant against the wall. Was it about me? Could she be issuing him an ultimatum? I couldn't lose my job or the flat. With no money, I'd be homeless. I had to do better. Fake being civil if I had to, but it was difficult when I was slipping again. On the edge, one misstep and I'd fall.

Chris always had my back, but was Amanda poisoning him against me? He cared about me, but if he was looking to screw Amanda, I was done.

The idea of it made my stomach turn, not so much the age difference, but because I had a different image of Chris. He was up on a pedestal for me. Happily married and a firm but fair employer. I couldn't reconcile him having another side. One that had Amanda work late for secret trysts over his desk.

The office door opened and Amanda strode away, swinging her arms as she went. She was angry, that much was obvious. Was it about me making a scene over Livvy's mug? That was an overreaction, I admit, but it was the icing on the cake. I had every right to be cross over her muscling in on my project. Amanda could play innocent all she liked, but she'd been trying to show me up in a room full of my peers.

With my head held high, I went around to Aaron's desk. He was a little sheepish but grateful I'd booked the photo shoot and seemed satisfied with the copy I'd tweaked again.

'As long as the client is happy, that's all that matters. Just use me in future please, Amanda has her own stuff with Jayden,' I said.

'Sure, will do... sorry,' he added as an afterthought, rolling his shoulders back. Aaron was a bit of a Neanderthal, but his heart seemed to be in the right place.

'Hey, how are you doing?' Jayden appeared behind me at Aaron's desk. His hand brushed against my back, sending sparks up my spine. He'd always been unapologetically tactile. It was one of the many things I liked about him.

'I'm okay,' I said, forcing a smile, hoping he wouldn't mention the meeting in front of Aaron.

'Missed you at lunch today.'

I bit my tongue to stop myself pointing out he went without me.

'How about I cook us dinner tonight at mine?' he added easily.

The onset of tears pricked my eyes and I quickly blinked them away. Jayden was the closest thing I had to a friend right now and I could use one. Plus, any excuse to stay away from my flatmate was a bonus.

'That sounds nice,' I agreed.

'Christ, you do get about, mate,' Aaron sniggered, punching Jayden on the arm.

'Fuck off, Aaron,' Jayden snapped.

The reminder of his and Amanda's escapades left a sour taste in my mouth. News travelled fast. Did everyone know they'd slept together?

I went back to my desk and the rest of the afternoon flew by as I tried to come up with a gimmick for the healthy crisp company to help Cassie and Grace. I didn't see Amanda when Jayden and I left together, climbing into his car to make the journey across town back to his maisonette. He lived by himself, the maisonette owned by his parents and rented to him cheaply. It was just outside of the town centre, not far from the local leisure centre, and was only a short journey by car.

The windscreen was steamed up and a trickle of apprehension peppered my skin as we sat in the dark car park, blowers on full blast, waiting for it to clear. We hadn't been alone and in such a confined space since before I went away and I had to remind myself. As much as I wanted to trust Jayden, I couldn't say for certain he wasn't the one messing with me.

Jayden rubbed his hands together, blowing into them and wiping the windscreen with a sponge. 'It's freezing today!'

'It's going to be cold this weekend,' I offered.

'Thank God, it's Friday tomorrow,' Jayden said and I agreed. The first few days back at Cardinal had been eventful, to say the least. It had hardly been the smooth return I'd hoped for after what went down in Nice.

We chatted about Jayden's weekend plans as he drove us back to his. He was going to play rugby if the pitch wasn't frozen on Saturday and maybe have a few beers with his teammates afterwards. Other than that he wasn't up to much. I remembered our long Sunday lie-ins before venturing out for brunch. Eggs Benedict at the café on Main Street, my favourite. The memory like a stitch in my side, I sucked in air to dispel it.

Jayden pulled up outside a small Sainsbury's Local around the corner from his house. 'Right, what do you fancy?'

'Anything,' I replied.

'Okay, I'll be right back.' He disappeared inside, returning a few minutes later, a lopsided grin on his face.

'Sorted?' I asked.

'Yep, right home.'

When we got inside, the maisonette was as I'd remembered it. Jaden had the top floor, so everywhere was carpeted to minimise noise below, bar the laminate in the kitchen and bathroom. I loved the plush shagpile under my feet. The one at the flat needed replacing, but I was hardly going to moan to Chris about it when I was living there for a pittance.

'Relatively tidy,' I commented with a grin, 'did you know I was coming?' I asked, my face flushing as Jayden shrugged off his grey blazer and draped it across the back of the sofa. Had he planned to invite me round?

'Maybe subconsciously. I've missed hanging out with you,' he admitted before adding swiftly, 'I bought hunter's chicken, that okay?'

'Sounds great.' I was sure Jayden only knew how to cook pasta, it was all he ever ate so this was a turn-up for the books.

He opened a bottle of wine for us to share and moved around the kitchen, sourcing oven trays, plates and cutlery, laying the table and lighting a candle to set the mood. I watched as he rolled up the sleeves of his shirt to wash his hands, coarse dark hair wrapping his forearms, the glimpse of skin sending heat to my face. Sipping the chilled chardonnay, I wished I could go back to before. Jayden had been the closest thing to love I'd had until I'd ruined it.

16

'Are you really okay?' Jayden said, laying his fork down, the remnants of a few chips left on his plate. I'd only managed to eat half of mine, my stomach knotted. Even as I tried to relax I couldn't stop my mind running through the events of the week.

'I'm still finding it hard to let go,' I admitted, knowing Jayden would immediately understand what I was talking about.

'I thought you might find it difficult coming back. Lots of memories.'

I didn't want to go into why I came back so soon. I pulled my sleeve down, the tiny bruises now fading. They were disappearing quicker than the memory of that night.

'She's on my mind all the time, the injustice of it and everyone is happy to look the other way,' I said bitterly, bile rising in my chest.

Jayden sighed, grimacing before he spoke. 'You need to move on, Ria, we all do.' Had he invited me round to pacify me? Jayden nominated as the Cardinal Media spokesperson? But then he reached around the candle and put his hand on mine, warmth spreading from his fingers.

'I guess.'

'And obviously Amanda being Livvy's replacement has to be hard. I know how much you loved working with her.'

I scowled at Jayden, annoyed he'd brought *her* up, but she was the elephant in the room. I pulled my hand away before he could tighten his grip.

He leaned back, his legs spread wide apart taking a mouthful of wine. 'I'm really sorry about... what you heard. I don't know how it happened. I was wasted and she kind of threw herself at me. I don't remember much about it at all.' His words came out in a rush, as though it was going to be less awkward if he said them quickly.

My throat constricted as I recalled the noises I'd heard through the wall. I bet Amanda remembered every second.

'We aren't together, Jayden, you're a free agent. You can snore with anyone.' Despite trying to be light-hearted, my voice had a hard edge to it.

'That's the thing, I don't want her and I don't want you thinking I do.' He rose out of his seat, propping himself up on the table, looming over me.

'It doesn't matter,' I said, although it did. He couldn't turn the clock back.

'Did you meet anyone else, while you were travelling?' He'd tried to make his question sound light, but his features betrayed him.

'No. That wasn't why I went.'

'I know, I just...' His voice trailed off.

I stood and collected the plates, scraping mine off and putting them both in the sink, Jayden's breath ruffling my hair behind me. Standing so close yet barely touching. He buried his face into my shoulder and I closed my eyes, resolve draining out of me. I didn't protest when he turned me around and pressed his lips to mine.

'I've missed you,' he whispered.

'I've missed you too, but I don't know how to do this... now,' I said, unable to shake off the betrayal.

I left soon after, whilst I still had some semblance of self-control. It would be easy to pour everything into Jayden, but I was hurting and reluctant to trust anyone. I ordered an Uber, paid for with my credit card. It arrived quickly, the driver chatty, which took my mind off going back to the flat and having to see Amanda.

When I got there, it was empty. Amanda must have been out with Cassie or Grace, or even Chris. For all I knew, or cared, she could be sprawled across his desk right now, shagging her way up the corporate ladder.

Leaving the lights off, I retreated to my room, flopping onto the bed. I'd not checked my phone all afternoon and saw there were multiple missed calls from Mum. With a sigh, I called her back.

'Ria, I've been worried. Why haven't you called?'

'I'm fine and I did text to let you know I got back okay.'

It was her turn to sigh. 'Tarek has gone for a golfing weekend,' she said and I rolled my eyes. That was why she'd called, she could talk with him not around.

When I didn't reply, she filled the silence.

'Ria, you just rushed off and we didn't get to—'

'There was nothing to say. What you thought you saw was something completely different and I can't believe you jumped to that conclusion before anything else,' I snapped, unable to stop the words spilling out.

'Tarek wouldn't...' Her voice caught in her throat.

I shook my head, it was pointless. 'Mum, I've got to go, someone is trying to call me,' I lied, hanging up before she could say any more. The last thing I needed was to revisit our argument and what she'd said that had caused me to pack my bags and flee France. All I wanted to do was forget what happened.

I scrolled through my notifications, a text from Cassie and

Grace earlier, both asking if I wanted to join them in the pub. I replied quickly, saying I was sorry to have missed them, but I'd had dinner with Jayden. Hopefully that wouldn't feed back to Amanda, although why should it matter? It didn't seem as though Jayden wanted to be with her, but I didn't know if I wanted to rekindle things with him either, not now she'd had her paws on him.

Amanda had posted on her Instagram account, blood-red acrylic nails, her ring finger had a spiderweb painted on it. #Halloween. I'd forgotten that was next week. My heart panged as I remembered Livvy and I having a horror movie marathon last year. Her hiding behind a cushion watching *It Follows* as we munched our way through a bowl of sweet and salty popcorn. I missed her so much my chest hurt.

Unable to avoid the temptation, I opened up Livvy's account, something I'd deliberately not looked at for months, knowing there were photos and reels of the two of us, in happier times, out on the town or chilling in our pyjamas. We were two peas in a pod. I wished she was still here so I could talk to her about Tarek. She'd understand and believe me without question. As I scrolled, I smiled through tears I couldn't stop from falling. Weirdly, some of the photos looked familiar, although they were old. Where had I seen them recently?

Flicking back to Amanda's profile, at first I was adamant she'd stolen Livvy's photos. But when I compared the sunsets, the yoga poses and one of some cocktails we'd bought at Turtle Bay, I saw they were similar but not identical. Amanda had recreated some of Livvy's posts. I looked at each of them, one by one, comparing them to Livvy's. My jaw dropped. The most recent one of her nails was so similar to the design Livvy's had chosen last Halloween, even the Pandora ring was the same.

I swallowed, my throat bone-dry. Why would Amanda copy Livvy's photos? Jayden said Amanda had replaced Livvy – and she had at work, but what if she was trying to replace her in life too? I shook my head, thoughts strangling me. Amanda hadn't known Livvy, she'd have no cause to check her social media let alone copy it.

I flicked back to Livvy's posts, the last photo one that still haunted me. It was a group shot of the team – Aaron, Jayden, Cassie, Grace, Rav and Chris in the background, Livvy and I at the forefront. I remembered Michelle taking it when we first got to the club and Chris had bought a round of shots before he'd bowed out gracefully. He rarely stuck around after the formalities were over. Aaron had a bottle of champagne he'd received as he'd been awarded account manager of the year. He'd snuck it into the club under his jacket and was drinking straight from the bottle.

My heart throbbed as I looked at the photo, knowing that less than two hours after it was taken, Livvy was dead. I pinched at the screen, my fingers dragging the photo wider, looking at everyone's faces. In the background, other revellers milled around, a guy even trying to photobomb, two fingers raised in a peace sign.

I squinted, zooming in even closer at a seemingly familiar face. Just able to make out some glasses and a bobbed haircut. The girl was looking over, her full lips parted, a sense of longing in her eyes.

We were oblivious, in the middle of our night, buzzing from the awards ceremony and eager to carry on partying. Unaware disaster was looming.

I stared at the face again, my breath catching as the front door slammed in the flat. She looked like Amanda.

17

I squinted, zooming in again at the face until the pixels blurred. I couldn't be sure, but if it was Amanda, she'd had a major transformation. Gone was the mousy bob, the thick framed glasses. Amanda's face was thinner, sharper, like she'd lost weight, but there was a likeness that couldn't be denied.

Through the bedroom door, I could hear Amanda shuffling around the flat, moving from the kitchen to the bathroom. Then the shower running. It made me uneasy, cohabiting in such close quarters with a stranger. Just who was I living with? Someone who possibly knew me better than I knew her.

My shoulders clenched, tension already building in my neck. Had she been watching us before she'd started working at Cardinal Media? Or was it a mere coincidence she was there the same night Livvy died?

That night, I struggled to sleep with so many questions roaming around my head. Every sound made me start, a floorboard creaking, or imagined footsteps padding around the flat, positive I'd wake up to find Amanda looming over my bed. Instead it wasn't Amanda or my alarm clock that woke me, it was a nightmare I'd had before, not featuring Tarek this time, but one from shortly after Livvy had died.

I woke screaming, thrashing in the duvet. Fighting to sit up, as sweat dripped down my chest, dampening my pyjama top. Yelping again as Amanda burst through the door in a panic.

'Ria!' she said, her hair sticking up in all directions, lines from her pillow ingrained into one of her cheeks.

'It was just a bad dream,' I said, trying to steady my breathing.

She stood in the doorway, awkwardly, her arms wrapped around herself.

In the nightmare, I'd been under the duvet, stewed in sleep but vaguely aware I had company. The bedroom had been draped in shadows, the snapshot of a pre-dawn thunderous sky could be seen through a gap in the curtains. Jayden's body next to me was cold and I'd shuffled away, pulling the covers up to my chin. Trying to drift back to sleep, curling my body into itself for warmth.

Terror had hit me like someone had flicked a switch inside my brain. My body had reacted instinctively, going rigid. I couldn't breathe or make a sound as the realisation flooded in. Jayden hadn't stayed last night, but someone had been there, beside me. In my bed. I could sense their weight, the slight dip in the mattress. Knowing a body was inches away had made my skin crawl like ants were scurrying up my limbs.

Bracing myself, I'd rolled over, coming face to face with Livvy. Her mouth was open as though she was mid-wail, eyes wide and piercing their way through me. Her skin had a blue sheen to it, an egg-shaped lump on her forehead looked angry. In the dream, she'd reached out her hand and, like last time, I'd woken up before her fingers touched me.

'I'll make us a coffee.' Amanda rubbed sleep from her eye before leaving for the kitchen.

I glanced at the clock on the bedside table, it was 6.37 a.m. Twenty-three minutes before my alarm was set to go off.

I wanted to roll back over, lay there until the nightmare had been banished from my mind, but not wanting to be rude, I joined Amanda at the breakfast bar. Both of us shivering in our dressing gowns, waiting for the radiators to warm up, fingers wrapped around mugs of hot coffee.

'Do you often have bad dreams?' Amanda probed.

'Sometimes,' I admitted.

She stared down at her mug as the silence stretched out between us.

'You?' I asked. Something about how her shoulders curved into her body made me sense she knew the horror of waking up drenched in sweat.

'Yeah, sometimes.'

I wanted to ask more, find out what her nightmares were about, but she spoke first.

'I'm sorry about using Livvy's mug. I wasn't aware it was hers.'

I nodded, not believing her for a second, but also not wanting to get drawn in.

'I feel like we've got off on the wrong foot, what with Jayden and then Aaron asking me to look at the High Point copy.'

'What do you mean Jayden?' I asked, narrowing my eyes, my spine arrow-straight at the mention of his name.

'Cassie told me you two used to go out, before you went travelling. I never meant to step on your toes.'

'You haven't,' I said brusquely, then remembered Chris's words about being kind. That Amanda had gone through hardship, although what, I couldn't imagine. She seemed far more together than me. 'It's fine,' I continued. 'Jayden and I aren't a thing any more and Aaron should have known better.'

'I feel like I've been walking on eggshells,' her cheeks flushed.

'Please don't. I'm sorry about the mug, that's my hang-up, it wasn't about you,' I said through gritted teeth. Amanda and I were playing a game of cat and mouse, neither of us trusting the other. 'Have you worked at Cardinal before?' I asked, changing the subject, my gaze fully on Amanda's face, ready to detect any lies.

'Me? No,' she chuckled, her hand resting on her chest. 'It's my first job in a marketing role, totally different to what I used to do.'

'Finance?' I suggested, watching her like a hawk.

'Telesales,' she replied, her face pinched. She stared at me quizzically. 'Why do you ask?'

I'd already prepared myself for the question and my answer rolled off the tongue. 'Oh, just you get on with everyone so well, I kind of assumed you'd met them before.'

'No, but generally I get on with everyone,' she simpered, emphasising the word 'generally' as though it was a direct dig at me.

I smiled serenely, taking a drink of my coffee as the conversation stilted. Perhaps I had it wrong. She was nothing to do with Mandy Dowd. Maybe it was all a coincidence, although I didn't believe in them.

'We're all going to Shocktober Fest at Tulley's Farm on Sunday night, you know, for Halloween. I hope you're going to come with us?' Amanda said, her voice suddenly bright again.

'Sure, why not. Have you ever been?' I asked.

'No, is it good?'

'Prepare to be scared,' I chuckled, sliding off the stool and putting my cup in the sink. Shocktober Fest was an annual affair at local farm where they put on various scary attractions with actors dressed up, jumping out on you as you walked around. The first time I went, I was terrified and Livvy vowed never to return. She'd almost given a guy dressed as a mummy a black eye, automatically swinging for him as he'd stepped out from the darkness in front of her.

'Oh, I don't get scared,' Amanda said nonchalantly.

I raised my eyebrow. 'We'll see about that,' I winked. 'Mind if I jump in the shower first?' I asked, eager to wash away the sweat my nightmare had left behind.

'Sure, go ahead.'

A few minutes later, once I'd lathered up and was washing the shampoo out of my hair, the water turned from blisteringly hot to ice cold, which only happened when someone flushed the toilet or ran the kitchen tap. Scowling, I stood out of the spray, waiting for the temperature to return to something I could withstand. A full minute later, it was still cold and I visualised Amanda smirking at the kitchen sink watching the water pour out of the tap, knowing I would be freezing.

'Bitch,' I hissed under my breath, forcing my head under the icy stream and suppressing a howl.

Although, when I got out, Amanda was nowhere to be seen. The flat was empty, her bedroom door left open, bag and coat gone. She'd vanished into thin air.

18

When I got into the office, my bones still chilled from the freezing shower I'd had to endure, I expected to find Amanda at her desk. But she wasn't one of the few employees who'd arrived early. Chris was deep in thought in his office and didn't even acknowledge my wave as I walked by.

The first thing I noticed as I got closer to my desk was the scent hanging in the air. It was like being transported back in time. Paco Rabanne's Lady Million floated in the atmosphere, like it had recently been sprayed. It was Livvy's favourite perfume. I stopped and closed my eyes, inhaling deeply, wanting to savour every second. Not caring what I might look like to the others arriving. It was like Livvy had walked by, talking animatedly like she always did, wafting her perfume as she waved her hands around.

When I opened my eyes, I saw a polaroid of me and Livvy sellotaped to my monitor. One we'd asked a passer-by to take of us on the London Eye. A tick on her bucket list, she'd said. Not realising she'd have such little time to fulfil it. Red biro was scribbled on the white part at the bottom. *Why did you do it?*

The hair on the back of my neck stood to attention as I lifted it from the screen. Why did I do what? I hadn't done anything to Livvy, although someone clearly thought I had. I shoved the photo into my drawer, sniffing the air, but Livvy's perfume had evaporated. Had it even been there in the first place, or had I imagined it?

Wanting to get away for a few minutes, I found Cassie and Rav in the kitchen, talking about Halloween.

'Are you coming, Ria?' they said as I rounded the corner heading for one of the water coolers.

'Shocktober? Yeah I'm up for it,' I replied and watched Cassie clap her hands together with glee. I needed to get back out, start socialising more and work my way back into the group again. Especially if someone was targeting me. What was the saying: keep your friends close and your enemies closer.

'Cool, I've heard it's going to be a good one this year,' Rav added.

When I eventually returned to my desk, I logged on and opened up my emails. Jolting back in my chair and knocking the desk, sending my water flying everywhere.

Why didn't you save me?

The email had been sent from *oliviameadows@cardinalmedia.com*

Livvy's email address.

I watched, unable to move as water dripped over the edge of the white surface, pooling on the carpet. With legs like jelly, I forced myself up, looking towards Chris's office. I couldn't storm in there, not after all that had happened this week.

Who was doing this?

I made my way around to IT. Cardinal Media had one guy who looked after all the systems, a friendly man with pitted acne scars on each cheek. Tim was in his mid-forties with floppy Hugh Grant hair and a penchant for Metallica T-shirts he thought gave him some kudos with the kids.

'Ria, you okay?' Tim frowned as I darkened his door. 'You don't look well.'

'I'm fine, can I borrow you a minute, it's a bit... delicate,' I said.

He raised an eyebrow.

Without giving him a chance to speak, I turned to go back to my desk. Tim followed behind, humming.

'Can you find out who sent this?' I pointed at my screen, keeping my voice low. Causing a scene wouldn't get me anywhere and I wasn't going to give whoever had sent it the satisfaction of getting a rise out of me.

Colour drained from Tim's face, his Adam's apple bobbing as he swallowed.

'I should be able to, I'll go and look. Shit, I'm sorry, Ria, I should have deleted Livvy's account ages ago. It slipped my mind.'

He rushed off and I mopped the water left on my desk with a tissue.

'Hey, all good?' Jayden asked, striding towards my desk. His timing was impeccable. Had he been the sender of the email?

'No, not really,' I replied, the beginnings of a headache at my temples.

'What's up?' He looked handsome in a green round-necked jumper, the collar of his checked shirt resting over the top.

'Someone is fucking with me.' Before I even finished my sentence, he frowned. 'Look!' I snapped, pointing at the screen.

'Shit,' he said, cracking his knuckles while I squirmed. He looked genuinely surprised.

'I'm telling the truth, Jayden, it's not me going mad or overreacting. Someone has it out for me. First the flowers, now this. I've had two phone calls as well, both from Livvy,' I hissed, keeping my voice low so I wouldn't be overheard.

'That doesn't make any sense,' Jayden said.

'I know it doesn't!'

'Have you told Chris?'

'He knows about the flowers, but not about anything else. I've almost burnt my bridges as it is.'

The desk phone rang, an internal call. It was Tim. As soon I answered, I could hear his fingers tapping his keyboard.

'I can only see what PC was used with Livvy's log-in.'

'Okay, which one was it?' I asked, irritation growing at Tim keeping me in suspense.

'Ria, it was yours.' My head swam and I was at a loss for words.

I glanced at the screen, the email was sent at seven thirty. Who would even be in the office that early other than the cleaners? I hadn't sent it to myself.

'Thanks, Tim,' I replied.

'I've deleted her account now.'

I thanked him again before hanging up.

'Hiya,' came a voice from behind me and I quickly shrank the email until my screen displayed my desktop.

'Hi,' I said, overly friendly to Amanda. 'Where did you go this morning?'

'Well, we were up so early, I thought I'd get a gym session in,' she beamed, her face still glowing from a post-workout shower.

'Putting us all to shame,' Jayden said.

If Amanda had been to the gym, she couldn't have come into the office to send that email. Unless she did it before she went? Chris was usually the first in, arriving before eight every day, but he'd have nothing to gain from sending an email like that. I knew at least Cassie and Rav were in before me this morning, maybe Jayden too.

'Earth to Ria,' Amanda chuckled, nudging Jayden as she sidled up next to him.

'Sorry, miles away. What were you saying?'

'I was saying you're going to come to Shocktober on Sunday,'

Amanda purred and my eye twitched. It was so obvious she fancied Jayden, it made me cringe.

'Are you? That's brilliant. We can all go together, I'll book a seven-seater to pick us up from the pub at eight,' Jayden said, oblivious to Amanda's seductive tone. 'Should be a right laugh.'

'You may need to look after me, I've never been before and Ria's warned me it'll be scary.' Amanda looked at Jayden with big doe eyes and I wanted to vomit into my bin. A bit of a leap from the girl who, only a few hours ago, said she didn't get scared.

Jayden looked uncomfortable but smiled weakly, such as the gentleman he was, before making his excuses to return to his desk, saying he'd catch me later.

'Oh well, I better get started. Don't want Jayden cracking the whip,' Amanda giggled and I smiled tightly before she walked away, her high ponytail swinging.

After going through my emails and dealing with the ones that needed answering straight away, I spent a moment looking at Instagram. Perusing Cassie and Grace's accounts, scrolling back to the night of the awards. Grace hadn't posted anything, but I remembered she was so drunk she'd lost her phone for part of the night down the leather seats of the booth we'd commandeered in the club. Cassie had posted a few photos. A selfie of her and Livvy in the toilet that gave me chills. Cassie's mascara was already making its way down her face and Livvy's eyes were glazed, despite her laughing during the picture. Was Cassie the one who had spiked Livvy?

The next shot was a photo of the dance floor. Aaron and Jayden were throwing some shapes as the lasers lit up the chequerboard floor. The last one was a wide-angled shot of Rav, Grace, Jayden and me. I remembered the weight of his arm around my shoulder, the smell of Armani's Acqua di Gio mixed with perspiration from dancing. I scanned the background again, the bar behind us, and there she was.

The bob, the glasses and a frumpy dress in an unflattering salmon colour. Jayden's elbow blocked out half her face, which was partly turned, as though we'd caught her attention taking the photo. I was sure it was the same girl. Mandy, or Amanda? Which one was it and why was she watching us?

19

LIVVY – BEFORE

There is a girl in the office toilets, dabbing her eyes with a tissue. Neck blotchy, she sniffs, one hand on her glasses resting on the counter. I haven't seen her before. She is the new girl in finance and we don't mix with them much. Mainly because they are around the other side and our paths don't cross often.

I think about heading straight into a cubicle, minding my own business, but then experience a pang of shame that makes me stop in my tracks. She looks young. What if it was me crying in the toilet at work? How would I feel being ignored?

'Are you okay?' I ask gingerly, not expecting to get much of a response.

'I messed up, it's my first day and I made a mistake,' she sniffs again, holding her tissue to her nose.

'Don't worry, everyone makes mistakes. It's what makes us human,' I smile reassuringly. 'I'm sure they'll understand, especially if it's your first day.'

The girl gazes at me, her huge grey eyes looking like the world has ended.

'Honestly, don't worry. It will be fine,' I say, resting my hand on her shoulder before going into the cubicle and locking the door. Smiling to myself, knowing I might have made a tiny difference to this newbie's day.

'Thank you,' she squeaks, her voice the other side of the cubicle door as if she's pressed her face against it. I jump at the proximity, sat on the toilet seat with my trousers down by my ankles.

'It's okay,' I say, watching the shoes beneath the door linger for a second before leaving.

20

On Saturday morning, I agreed to wander around the shops with Cassie as she searched for something to wear to Shocktober Fest the following day. I kept questioning the photo she'd taken in the toilets, both her and Livvy looked out of it. What if she'd been the one to talk Livvy into taking ketamine? I knew she partook, casually, around the others.

Cassie lingered on a rail of black sequinned mini dresses, lifting one off to hold it up against herself.

'Cass, it'll be freezing and muddy, why are you bothering to dress up?' I snorted.

'Because you never know who you'll meet, Ria. Mrs Right might be one of the roaming vampires on the Haunted Hayride.'

Cassie carried on perusing the rails in New Look, before selecting some black ripped jeans and a cropped black polo-neck jumper.

'Come with me to try this on,' she instructed and I followed her into the changing room, sitting on a pouffe outside her cubicle.

'Cass, do you remember a girl who used to work at Cardinal called Mandy?' I asked, through the curtain.

Cassie grunted as she pulled on the jeans. 'God, these are tight!' she wheezed. 'Mandy? No I don't think so.'

'She used to work in payroll,' I added.

'Ria, you know we don't hang out with them, they are so boring, bloody number-crunchers,' she said flippantly.

'Karen's not!' I said indignantly in Karen's defence. She was older than us, sure, but boring she was not.

'No, to be fair, she's all right, but the others...' She whipped the curtain back and turned to the side, modelling her outfit.

'Nice,' I said, nodding as she looked back in the mirror, twirling to appraise every angle.

'Why didn't you invite Amanda to come along?' I asked, having assumed when Cassie had text me that it would be a group shopping trip but unarguably relieved it was just the two of us. I wasn't sure if Amanda came back to the flat last night. I hadn't heard anything and her door was closed when I got up this morning.

'I did, but I think she's hanging out with Jayden.'

Her words made my chest tighten, but I didn't bite.

'I don't think he's that into her to be honest, Ria,' she backtracked after watching me deflate. I always had been rubbish at hiding my feelings.

'It's none of my business,' I said, smiling to reaffirm I was okay. 'Did you all go out last night?'

'Nah, Aaron had some Tinder date,' she rolled her eyes, 'and Grace had a family thing. No idea about the others. I had myself some Netflix and chill with the flatmate.'

I nodded, unable to help myself from wondering if Amanda and Jayden had hooked up.

Cassie bought her outfit and I picked up a similar jumper on the sale rack in a royal blue. We parted ways after sharing a panini and coffee at Costa for lunch. Cassie was going to visit her parents, something she was not looking forward to, her sexuality being an issue for them, but it gave me an idea.

I jumped on the number 20 bus out of the town centre towards Horley train station. Livvy's parents lived in a detached house on the main road from Crawley to Horley.

Livvy was buried at St Bartholomew's Church, which was a few stops before her parents' house. I got off and bought some white and pink roses from the florist further down the road before retracing my steps. Livvy's grave was easy to find, in the far right corner where the land had been extended. Her stone was a beautiful silvery grey with rounded edges, recently cleaned with bright white engraved lettering. Wind scattered fallen leaves as I crouched down to place my flowers joining more recently laid.

At one point, Livvy's mum had been coming every day, although I wasn't sure she still did.

'Hey,' I said, as if I was starting a conversation, my voice petering out. I never knew what to say or if anyone was listening. After my initial hesitation I began telling Livvy what had been happening. How I wished she was still around because who else could I talk to about it? I didn't trust anyone like I trusted her.

Eventually, lighter but extremely cold, I stood, pressing my fingers to my lips in a kiss and placing them on top of Livvy's headstone.

'Bye, babe,' I said, my voice carrying on the breeze, before I turned and made my way out of the graveyard.

I decided to walk the ten minutes to Livvy's parents' house. The last time I saw them, they were shadows of their former selves. Lynn had lost weight, the skin seemed to sag on her bones and all of the light had gone from Bill's eyes.

It dawned on me as I approached their heavy oak front door that they might not be in, they could have plans. It was Saturday afternoon and I should have called first because it was possible I could be traipsing back to the bus stop having made a wasted journey. Or, even worse, I might not be a welcome guest after last time.

The chunky door knocker sounded so loud, the vibrations reverberated through me, but then I heard Bill's baritone voice from inside and the door swung open. His face lifted at the sight of me and I knew immediately I'd be welcomed in despite my behaviour during my previous visit.

'Ria!' he said, pulling me in for a hug. Something he did whenever I saw him since Livvy's passing. It was easy to melt into his giant frame and I was never the first to pull away. It had occurred to me the first time, without any awkwardness, he might need the hug more than I did.

'Hi, Bill,' I said, when he eventually let me go, his eyes dewy. 'Sorry I didn't call ahead, it was a spur-of-the-moment visit.'

'It's lovely to see you, come in.' Relief flooded through me at the absence of any lingering animosity and I stepped off the welcome mat and followed him into the farmhouse kitchen, absorbing the smell I loved so much. Livvy had a lovely family home with an atmosphere I coveted. There was no walking on eggshells and visitors were always welcome. A stark contrast to growing up with my mother, where at times it was obvious I was a burden.

'Lynn, look who I found,' Bill said, immediately going to the kettle to start making tea.

Lynn was sat at the kitchen table, reading *Weekend* magazine. Her eyes widened when she saw me, jumping up to envelop me into another hug. She squeezed me so hard, I tried not to wince.

'Oh, Ria, it's lovely to see you. How was Europe?' Lynn led me to the table and pulled out a chair. Moments later, Bill joined us, placing a mug of tea in front of me.

'Turns out you can be lonely anywhere,' I admitted, grimacing, 'even on a beach in eighty degrees.'

'Unfortunately, grief follows you everywhere,' Lynn said with a sad smile.

'It certainly does,' I smiled awkwardly. 'How have you both been?'

'We're muddling through,' Bill said, making eye contact with Lynn, 'it's all we can do really. Lynn's gone back to work and I guess we're trying to keep busy.'

'The house is too quiet,' Lynn added, 'we're thinking about getting a dog.'

'That would be a great idea,' I smiled, imagining a Labrador puppy running around causing havoc. It would give them a focus, something to pour their love into.

'I started going through Livvy's room, I've got some bits for you,' Lynn said.

'I'd like that.'

We chatted about work and I told them how strange it was returning, the office having a different atmosphere to it without Livvy, but I was trying to get back into the groove. Lynn asked about Mum and whether I'd travelled to Nice to see her like I'd intended, so I told her about my short visit which had ended with an argument, although I didn't elaborate.

'She doesn't realise how lucky she is that mother of yours,' Lynn huffed.

'I don't think she sees it that way,' I admitted. I'd always wished we could be closer, but it was as though having me young made her resent my existence.

'Do you want to come and see what I've found,' Lynn said once I'd finished my tea and the biscuits Bill had cajoled me into eating.

Even climbing the pine staircase was strange, my feet sinking into the familiar paisley green carpet as I followed Lynn, turning right at the top to Livvy's room at the back of the house. Her bedroom walls were pale grey and she'd slept on a wooden day bed

that was still made up with bolster cushions around the frame.
Livvy also had a large oval vanity mirror and desk. Framing the
mirror were hundreds of polaroid photographs, tacked to the wall,
many of them of Livvy and the gang from work.

I ran my finger over them, absorbing the memories. She was
obsessed with that retro camera her parents had bought for her
birthday, spending an extortionate amount on film. I featured in a
lot of the snaps, despite only having known Livvy for a year before
she died.

'I've separated her wardrobe. On the right are things I'd like to
keep, but if you want anything on the left, go ahead and take it.'

I glanced back to see Lynn had opened the wardrobe door and
was running her palm across the various fabrics. I couldn't take
anything, it would be morbid to wear Livvy's clothes.

'Perhaps her scarf,' I suggested, pointing at the pink and grey
checked oversized scarf Livvy wore in winter. That was a safe choice
as I didn't want to offend Lynn.

She pulled it from the shelf, perfectly folded and I placed it on
her desk.

'The other girl who came didn't take anything either – oh, actually, she took her Pandora ring.' Lynn scratched her head, trying to
remember.

'Other girl?' I asked, coughing as saliva seeped into my mouth.

'Yes, what was her name?' Lynn tapped her chin. 'Miranda
maybe? She was at the funeral.'

'Mandy?' I stuttered. I cast my mind back, but the day was a blur
of disbelief, sorrow and tears.

Lynn raised her eyes to the ceiling, as if the name could be
found there. 'Maybe.'

She lifted Livvy's jewellery box, a pile of silver necklaces and
bracelets sat in the large compartment. The section for rings were
empty bar one, Livvy's silver onyx birthstone ring. I recalled the one

Amanda had worn in the photo of her Halloween nails she'd posted on Instagram. Was that Livvy's ring? Had she been here?

I looked back to the photographs surrounding Livvy's mirror, the absence of a couple of them now strikingly obvious. The shot from the London Eye that had been stuck to my monitor for one.

'What did she look like, the girl that came?' The words scratched my throat on their way out.

'Brunette, plain perhaps. I can't really think how to describe her.'

I nodded as Lynn turned back to the wardrobe.

'I found her notebook too, some scribbles, story ideas and thoughts. She mentions you, so I thought you might like to read it.'

'Oh thanks,' I replied, taking it from her, my mind full of Lynn's mysterious visitor. Had Mandy been to the house and if so why?

21

I left soon after, Livvy's notebook and scarf clutched tightly in my icy hands as I walked past the bus stop in the direction of home. It was too far to walk all the way and involved A roads with no pavements to get back to Crawley, but I needed air and space to clear my head.

Who was the other girl? Amanda or Mandy? And were they one and the same? Whoever it was must have known Livvy to come to the funeral. I wracked my brain to picture the faces there, in bright colourful clothing, as was requested by Lynn and Bill. But I was at a loss. If Livvy was close with someone, how could I not have known them? We'd become instant best friends almost as soon as I joined Cardinal Media. There was no Mandy or Amanda there when I started. Other than Cassie and Grace, and a girl Livvy still hung out with from her days at college, I didn't know of anyone else.

I passed two bus stops before stopping at the third, grateful when a few minutes later a number 20 arrived and I jumped on, putting my AirPods in to listen to some music. It was hard to resist the urge to start leafing through the pretty butterfly-covered notebook, but I wanted to wait until I was alone in my room. Trepidation swam through my system as to what I would find inside. Perhaps her notebook would give me some answers.

To distract myself on the journey, I scrolled through Instagram. Cassie had posted a photo of herself in the changing room in her new outfit. I was in the background, unaware my picture was being taken. Jayden's was one of the rugby pitch where he was playing, taken early in the morning, the grass covered in a picturesque layer of white frosting. Aaron's post was a photo of his football shirt hanging on a peg with his name on and the number 11.

When I got to Amanda's, she'd posted a photo of her cappuccino complete with a heart-shaped swirl on top. Next to her mug were a pair of manly hands I recognised as Jayden's. Caramel skin and nails bitten to the quick. He must have met her after his match instead of having a beer with his mates. So much for him telling me he wasn't interested in her. Was he telling me one thing and her another?

I quickly scrolled back to the photo of Amanda's Halloween nails. Taking another look at the Pandora ring I was now convinced had once belonged to Livvy.

Did the whole group know Amanda before and were keeping it from me? It didn't make any sense. Why would it be a secret? Amanda and Mandy had to be the same person though, which meant Amanda might have known Livvy. I'd have to come right out and ask her, it was the only way, and perhaps I had to have some serious words with my so-called friends.

The bus rumbled up to my stop and I got off. It was practically dark despite it being only just gone five. I considered popping into Tesco Express to pick up something nice for dinner, but Livvy's notebook itched in my hands so I hurried on. Taking out my AirPods, the back of my neck prickled as I sensed someone behind me. I quickened my pace only to hear footsteps matching the speed of mine, trying to catch me. I moved faster still, nearly tripping over my own feet as I began to jog.

When I reached the road and with one foot already off the kerb to cross, I turned my head to give a cursory glance behind me. A horn sounded, the lorry so close it practically brushed my jacket as a hand grabbed my shoulder, jerking me backwards. Spray from the tyres hit my face as I lost balance.

'Ria!' someone screeched.

I stumbled, unable to catch myself. Dropping Livvy's notebook and scarf onto the damp pavement, my backside hit the concrete with a thump, knocking the wind out of me. Amanda's tall frame towered over me as I lay crumpled on the pavement, my heart pounding.

'God, Ria, you were about to get squished!' She hauled me upright and bent to pick the notebook and scarf from the floor.

'Ouch,' I moaned, wiping the grit from my jeans, wincing as I stood upright. I was going to be bruised in the morning.

'What were you thinking?' Amanda reprimanded.

'Someone was following me.'

'Yes me, you moron. I was trying to catch up with you.'

I shook my head, biting my tongue. If that was the case, why didn't she call out, instead of scaring me into oncoming traffic?

'If I hadn't have grabbed you, that lorry would have wiped you out. Here you go,' she added, handing the notebook and scarf back to me.

'Thanks,' I replied and we began walking, me gingerly, towards the flats.

'How was your day?' she asked as we reached the entrance hall.

'Good thanks, shopping with Cassie. You?' I replied, knowing she likely couldn't wait to tell me she'd been with Jayden.

'Not bad, just errands, you know.' I was surprised at how

guarded she seemed. Surely she'd be falling over herself to let me know she'd been with him.

We climbed the stairs to the second floor, Amanda ready with her key to open up the flat when I decided to bite the bullet.

'Did you know Livvy?'

Amanda paused, her key in the door, but she turned to face me, frowning.

'No, you know I didn't. Why do you ask?'

'I guess I forgot.'

'I never met her, but I've heard a lot about her,' Amanda replied, a little stiffly, finally turning the key and opening the front door. 'Are you okay, Ria?' Amanda asked as she put her handbag on the counter in the kitchen and unbuttoned her coat.

'I'm fine, a little freaked out I almost got run over,' I said, my voice a tad higher than intended. 'What are you up to tonight?' I asked, playing nice but hoping she was going to tell me she had plans.

'It's Saturday night.' She had a twinkle in her eye and her smile was infectious despite her sarcastic reply.

'I'm aware,' I chuckled.

'Then you'll know I'll be where the cocktails are.' She grinned.

'Have fun,' I said, retreating to my room and closing the door, glad I wouldn't have to spend the evening playing happy flatmates with her. Would she be meeting Jayden? The thought made my shoulders clench and I reminded myself again he wasn't mine.

A few minutes later, I heard the shower running and Amanda singing along to Lizzo's 'About Damn Time'. I sat cross-legged on my bed, ignoring the rumble of my stomach, and opened the notebook. Livvy's curly writing was randomly scribbled across the pages. Lynn had been right, there were to-do lists, notes from work and random doodles. I flicked through the pages, trying to find something that would make some sense to me while at the same time absorbing every word. I smiled despite myself, tracing my fingers across the indentations of Livvy's penmanship.

She would always say if she didn't write something down she'd forget it and it seemed her notebook was her lifeline. Passwords were scrawled haphazardly in the margins. Telephone numbers with names I didn't recognise. I giggled at a cartoonish drawing of Chris I imagined her doing during the sales update meeting. I leafed through the pages until an image made me stop dead in my tracks.

I squeezed my fingertips into my palms at the sight of the crude heart, an arrow piercing one side and coming out the other. In thick block capitals the name JAYDEN was written in the centre.

22

I picked up my phone and put it back down again. Was Livvy into Jayden? Had something happened between them before I joined Cardinal? I picked the phone up again. What was I going to do, text him? Ask him if he was doing the rounds with every female in the office? I ran my tongue over my teeth, a bitter taste in my mouth. Had I been a fool to trust him?

Searching through the pages there were no dates, but I could tell from the projects she was making notes for, it was before my time.

I found ten occurrences of Jayden's name, absent-mindedly written, doodled in the corner of pages. Then abruptly it stopped.

Why hadn't she told me she liked him? I would never have entertained the idea of me and him together if she had staked her claim. My friendship with her was more important to me than any guy. Perhaps I hadn't given her the chance.

The spark between me and Jayden had been instantaneous. Our eyes had met across the boardroom table as I'd been brought in and introduced to the team, immediately attracted to his caramel skin and wide-set hazel eyes. It never occurred to me when I blurted to

Livvy, who I'd been buddied up with, how gorgeous he was. I didn't think to check if I was stepping on anyone's toes.

I turned over the pages, the absence of his name striking, until I reached a page where the pen had been pressed so hard into the paper it had nearly gone through.

Why won't she just leave me alone! She's everywhere. I fucking hate her.

Who was Livvy writing about? Me? My thoughts strayed to the message on the polaroid. No, we were friends. We spent hours together, nights out, shopping trips and lazy afternoons watching television. But there was someone she clearly didn't like. More than that. Someone she hated. Livvy had never mentioned feeling that way about anyone, not to me. Perhaps I didn't know her as well as I thought.

Unless she was upset because I liked Jayden, but that didn't sit right with me. Livvy was forthright, she'd tell you if you pissed her off. Office dynamics hadn't stopped her from telling Aaron where to go when he was teasing her about her grammar on some copy she'd written. Or when she found out Grace earnt more than her. Livvy hadn't hesitated to go straight to Chris and demand equal pay. She was confident and not afraid to stand up for herself, something I admired.

More notes followed over the coming pages:

She's creeping me out.
I'm being followed, I'm sure of it.
I've told her to stop. We aren't friends!
What the actual fuck! Why can't she take the hint?

More and more paranoid scribblings, until, like Jayden's name, they stopped completely. Then I saw my name in bubble writing and various plans to meet, a cinema trip where we'd been to see the latest M. Night Shyamalan offering in the summer of last year and a bar crawl for cocktails. Towards the end of the notebook, another polaroid was wedged between blank pages. One of the two of us on Brighton pier eating doughnuts during the August bank holiday weekend. The memory so vivid, I could smell the caramelised sugar.

I closed the book when the scribbles ended, stomach churning with all I'd read. Had I inadvertently stolen Jayden out from under Livvy's nose? But if that was the case, why had she never told me? Also who was the mysterious girl she couldn't stand? Was she the one who had spiked Livvy's drink the night she died? I didn't care what anyone said, Livvy wouldn't have taken anything of her own accord. Someone had caused her death. No one had owned up, but why would they? The police weren't searching for anyone. Ultimately they'd got away with murder.

'See you, Ria,' Amanda chimed through the closed bedroom door as she left. I didn't respond, too wrapped up in my own thoughts.

I needed to find out who Amanda really was. Certain it was the key to unravelling everything. Leaving it ten minutes to ensure Amanda didn't return having forgotten something, I reluctantly went to check her room again. The pull to find answers overriding my worries of intruding on her privacy.

It wasn't as tidy this time. Make-up and clothes were strewn across the bed, open and discarded shoeboxes on the floor. She had to have a passport or driver's licence somewhere and I became increasingly frustrated when I was unable to find anything, no paperwork or bills with her name on. No form of identification anywhere.

Did I believe Amanda when she'd said she'd never met Livvy?

At the time, she'd seemed genuine, but Amanda had been to Livvy's house. Lynn had gifted her the Pandora ring and I'd seen it for myself on Amanda's Instagram photo. It had to be her pretending to be Livvy, messing with me, calling and sending those flowers, but I needed proof.

Was Amanda the person Livvy had written about, the one who had been stalking her? I knew it was linked to what was happening, but I didn't know how or why. What motive would someone have now, after Livvy's death, to mess with me about it?

Giving up on my search I headed back to my room, crawling on top of my bed, my mind running in circles. Eventually I fell asleep, waking still in my clothes. The sun was just coming up and I was surprised to find I'd slept for eleven hours straight. The notebook was no longer on the bed but on the floor. Perhaps I'd knocked it off in the night. Bladder full, I crept to the bathroom, my backside tender from yesterday's fall. Glancing at Amanda's closed door as I passed, I strained to listen for any signs of life.

Was Jayden in there, spooning her under the duvet? It had taken all my resolve not to message him about Livvy, but I wanted to wait until I could casually drop it into conversation. Everyone at work seemed to think I was going to relapse every time I uttered her name. The whole group would be together tonight at Shocktober Fest, so perhaps I could ask him then.

'Oh God, sorry,' Amanda said, pushing open the bathroom door and finding me on the toilet.

'Fuck's sake,' I muttered, wiping myself and pulling up my jeans as she turned her back.

'Did you sleep in your clothes?' Amanda said when I came out of the bathroom, wrinkling her nose.

'Yep, just passed out, so tired.' I hurried back to my room to avoid any further conversation and dived back under the covers, hearing Amanda's attempts to flush the toilet after she'd been. The flat was chilly and I burrowed deep, trying to warm myself up, thrusting my arm out to reach for the notebook to look at again.

Had I knocked it off the bed in my sleep or had Amanda snuck into my room to read it when she'd returned home? If she'd been creeping around undetected while I slept, what else had she done?

23

LIVVY – BEFORE

She's turned up again at the Kings Head. Sitting at the bar with what looks like a Coke whilst trying to catch my eye. I deliberately sat side on, forcing myself not to look over. I get she's lonely but the others don't want her to sit with us.

The time she did, she hardly said a word, despite me trying to make conversation. It ended up being hard work and the others ribbed me mercilessly when she finally went home. I was only trying to be nice, but since I spoke to her in the toilets that day, she's followed me around like a lost puppy. It's unnerving.

If I go to the kitchen to make tea, she's there. When I go to the toilets, she pops up, and don't get me wrong, she's sweet, but a bit weird. I don't think she has many friends as she seems socially awkward. It was why I relented and made the mistake of telling her we often go to the local pub after work for a quick one.

Now she's there *every* time we go. Like the elephant in the room. And no one mentions it. They all seem happy to crack on and pretend she's not there, sitting at the bar, hanging on our every word, but it's not easy to do that. Especially when they whisper things and say she's a freak. I feel bad, but what am I supposed to do? I can't be responsible for her. Perhaps I'll go and speak to Karen – I mean, she works with her. Perhaps she can have a word.

24

I ditched the duvet and got up, shaking off the cold and searching the wardrobe for jogging bottoms. I hadn't been running for months, but I needed to clear my head. Put my jumbled thoughts into some sort of order. The notebook hadn't given me the answers I craved. If anything, it gave me more questions. Someone was stalking Livvy and I had to find out who.

Shoved at the back of the wardrobe, I found my joggers rolled into a ball. When I sat on the bed to put on my trainers, I pushed the notebook underneath, hiding it behind a shoebox. Visiting Lynn and Bill yesterday was lovely, but I wasn't prepared for the can of worms it would open. What if I was heading back down the same path, so consumed by conspiracy theories of Livvy's death I was slowly driving myself mad? I was positive after my time away I was ready to come back and face it, but now I wasn't so sure.

Pounding the pavements in the mist, the wind was chilly, but I soon warmed up, running against the traffic towards the town centre. Sunday trading hours meant the shops weren't yet open, so there were few cars on the road and fewer people. I saw a couple of dog walkers, wrapped up in hats and scarves, who bid me a good morning as I passed. I barely managed a wave, shockingly out of condition. The slight incline making my lungs work overtime, but it had the desired effect. My mind emptied and all I could concentrate on were my aching muscles.

Three miles later, exhausted, I walked back to the flat, determined to put everything with Livvy and Amanda behind me. It was time to move on. I had to stop digging. It was about my own mental well-being and I needed to set a course of action. Something to focus on that wasn't her. Namely saving for a deposit again to get a place of my own and searching for a new job, where I could start afresh and wouldn't be haunted by Livvy's shadow at every turn. I couldn't rely on my mother to support me. Despite her offer for me to move to Nice, I knew it wasn't something either of us wanted, and I wouldn't live under the same roof as Tarek. Especially not now.

I knew how my brain worked, that focusing on Livvy meant I didn't have to think about what happened in Nice. I wasn't ready to deal with the fallout of that night or even process my emotions about it. I'd just been avoiding the memory, another reason to put off speaking to my mother about what Tarek did. Clinging on to anything else pushed it to the back of my already fragile mind.

After a hot shower, I was ready for the day, even managing an amicable exchange with Amanda as we went about our chores, taking turns using the washing machine and tidying the flat.

'I always use Sunday for cleaning,' she said, repositioning the cushions on the sofa after hoovering the rug, the Pandora ring nowhere to be seen on her slim fingers adding to my reasoning I might have been fixated on something that wasn't really there.

'Me too, chores and chilling. That's what Sundays are for.'

'Are you looking forward to tonight?' she asked, wrapping her long hair into a messy topknot.

'It'll be good, but prepare to get cold.'

Amanda pulled a face, the idea clearly didn't suit her.

'What are you going as?' she asked.

'Going as?' I questioned, filling the sink to wash up the plates from our lunch of beans on toast.

'It's Halloween, everyone dresses up right?'

I shook my head. 'No, well, some do, but it'll be freezing. Trust me.'

* * *

I couldn't believe it when Amanda emerged from her room much later in a slinky black catsuit, complete with red lipstick, winged eyeliner and painted on whiskers.

'Catwoman?' I frowned as I shrugged on my coat and woolly hat. Our outfits the polar opposite.

'Miaowww,' she said in a mock-seductive tone.

I rolled my eyes, stifling a laugh. At least she'd gone for chunky boots and not stilettos, but I knew full well she'd be shivering later.

We met the gang at the pub for a drink while we waited for the taxi Jayden had booked. He was quick to hit the bar when we arrived, coming back with double gin and tonics.

'Ready to be scared!' he said, a wicked grin on his face.

'Nothing scares me,' Amanda grinned, rolling her shoulders back. Quite the contrast from her doe eyes in the office on Friday.

Aaron came to join us, getting up from the table, his eyes out on stalks at Amanda's choice of outfit. I was sure she'd lowered her zip on purpose, her cleavage practically spilling out.

'Very sexy,' he said and Amanda purred.

I had to fight the urge to heave, instead meeting Jayden's eye as he smirked at me conspiratorially. I looked away, remembering his name enclosed in the heart in Livvy's notebook.

Amanda wasn't the only one who'd dressed up. Grace and Rav modelled fake blood and cuts on their faces, both zombies in raggedy jumpers and ripped jeans. Cassie was wearing the outfit she'd bought yesterday and Aaron and Jayden, like me, were wrapped up in thick coats and scarves.

I drank my gin quickly, enjoying the warmth as it hit my chest.

'Cab's here,' Aaron announced after Jayden received a text on his phone and we piled out of the pub and into the waiting car.

Tulley's Shocktober Fest was heaving. The ground was frozen and uneven when we jumped out of the car and I grabbed onto Jayden for support.

After queuing to get in, Aaron bought a round of Tequila Rose shots, which we all necked before making our way to the first attraction. Amanda squealed as a ghoul ran past screaming, bursting into laughter at the shock.

'Creepy Cottage,' she mused, staring at the sign, her hands on her hips as we queued for the attraction. It was so cold our breath wafted into the air and my back tingled with a mix of fear and excitement at what was to come.

I stayed close to Jayden as we shuffled inside the run-down cottage that had been deliberately made to look like it was about to collapse. It was dark inside, sparsely lit and every surface covered with fake body parts, grime and blood splatter. It made me think of Leatherface's lair from *Texas Chainsaw Massacre*. Grace screamed as one of the actors wearing a bloody apron stomped into the room and shouted at us to get out. All of us clinging on to each other, giggling nervously, backs against the wall as we pushed through into the next room, which was more of the same.

Someone was stood in the corner, wearing a dirty leather apron. He had a blank stare and was swaying, a machete dangling from one hand. Cassie threw the guy an insult and he lurched towards her. She screamed and ran, shoving me out of the way as my hip collided with a dusty sideboard.

'Ouch,' I winced, suddenly claustrophobic. I wanted out, my chest was tight and I longed for the crisp night air.

Behind me Jayden's hands found my waist and steered me towards the next room, moving straight through as if he could read my mind. Behind us, I could hear Rav shouting, Amanda swearing and the sound of blood-curdling screams before the speakers overhead switched to the sound of chopping.

The desire to be outside intensified as I stumbled forward, tripping over something on the floor. Jayden's hands no longer around my waist.

A second later, we were plunged into darkness. I crouched in the pitch-black room trying to get my bearings until hot breath caressed my neck.

25

I shrieked, my hands flying up, connecting with something solid.

'Owww!' The lights flickered back on, as though on a timer and Jayden pulled me up, rubbing at his nose I'd swotted. 'It's just through there,' he said, his voice loud in my ear, gesturing towards the far end of the corridor. With a scream lodged in my throat I launched forward, desperate to get out of the airless space. Skin crawling from the deliberate breath upon my neck. My mind thrown back to Tarek's smoke induced rasping.

Eventually, we found the exit, bursting through the rickety door and outside into a bunch of revellers excitedly chattering. Jayden led me away, the grass crunching beneath our feet, and we leaned against a wooden lamp post as I caught my breath.

'I don't remember that from last year,' he said, grinning, and I was grateful he hadn't mentioned my freak-out.

'Must be new,' I replied, giving him a weak smile and trying to still my quivering hands. 'Sorry about the nose.'

'That was a riot!' Amanda said, bowling out of the door and towards us.

'Jesus, did you see that guy. I almost punched him,' Cassie

panted, following behind as the rest of the group spilled out into the gangway.

'Another shot!' Aaron pointed towards the bar and we headed in for round two. It was a tradition they told me last year, an attraction, then a shot, all of us getting more intoxicated as we moved around the park. It ended up being an expensive night, but the yearly event was not to be missed.

'The Haunted Hayride doesn't have much of a queue,' Grace said as we ventured back out into the cold.

'That's because it's lame,' Rav moaned.

'Come on,' I coaxed, starting towards the line of people waiting, wanting to force Tarek from my mind and get the night back on track. I remembered enjoying it more last year with Livvy. Tonight the scares were all a little too real. I wasn't sure I trusted who I'd come with. It hadn't escaped me that one of them had to be behind the messages from Livvy.

Pushing the thought aside, we jumped on the wagon, which took us through the woods, where werewolves roamed and howled. Halfway through our bumpy journey, one jumped onto the back of the wagon looking for its next meal. I screamed as a furry hand brushed mine when the monster sprang aboard, growling.

'It's teen wolf,' Jayden laughed as the monster dived off, running into the trees, chasing another actor, who had been planted in our wagon as one of the revellers.

An hour in, my toes were numb and I was exhausted from all the adrenaline rushes. Amanda seemed to be enjoying herself, although I noticed her teeth chattering on more than one occasion. She gripped Cassie's hand as we wandered through the Penitentiary, where escaped crazies roamed in their orange jumpsuits, but as the night wore on, it was Aaron's lap she sat on when we hit the bar a fourth time.

I noticed his hand travelling up the back of her coat in a caress as she laughed at something he whispered in her ear. Jayden looked on, mildly amused, until he caught my eye.

'Another one of her victims,' I said, downing my fifth shot and slamming the glass on the bar a little too hard.

We split up, most of us heading to the hot dog stand for food, Rav and Jayden went hunting for burgers. Alcohol had made us hungry. I wasn't bothered but chose hot dogs, happy to be away from Jayden for a few minutes.

I'd just about got my head around his one-night stand with Amanda, if that what it was, but throwing Livvy into the mix too, my brain couldn't cope.

'Is she after Aaron now?' Grace whispered in my ear as she watched the two of them flirt by the napkin stand.

'I think anything with a pulse is fair game,' I grumbled, not having forgotten how Chris had touched her in the corridor the other day. It didn't look innocent. Maybe she was magnetic to men.

'Now, now,' Cassie said, a devilish look in her eye, fiddling with her nose ring, 'the girl knows how to have fun, that's all.'

I rolled my eyes as she nudged me in the ribs with a low chuckle.

'Jayden's yours, anyone can see that,' Cassie continued, but I shrugged.

'Before I joined, was he going out with anyone?' I asked.

'No, I don't think so,' Cassie's brow furrowed like she was trying to remember.

'I remember Livvy had a crush on him for a while, but I think that petered out,' Grace said.

'She never told me,' I said, a wound opening up inside.

'It was before your time, don't worry about it,' Grace said, patting my arm and shrugging like it was no big deal. 'He wasn't interested.'

Perhaps Grace was right and it wasn't a big deal, no more than a passing infatuation.

'Let's do the Mirror Maze,' Grace suggested, changing the subject, wiping ketchup, or fake blood, I wasn't sure which, away from her chin. Her button nose was pink from the cold.

I blew hot air into my hands, wishing I'd remembered to bring some gloves.

'Come on, guys,' she called back to Amanda and Aaron as Cassie and Grace linked their arms through mine. Jayden and Rav were yet to return from their quest for burgers.

The Mirror Maze was exactly that, a complicated maze full of mirrors where you had to keep your hands in front of you for fear of bumping your face, or your knee into solid glass. It was tricky to navigate, made harder with the lights going out every twenty seconds or so before white strobe lighting came into effect, making everyone look like they were moving in slow motion. Every attraction at Tulley's had a variety of noises pumped through the speakers. The Mirror Maze had shrieks and gasps that made you jump when the lights were on, let alone in the dark.

I trailed behind Grace, the pompoms from her torn scarf bouncing on the back of her jacket. We weaved our way slowly through the maze, listening to the thumps and yelps as people in front of us walked into the glass believing it to be the way through when they'd been tricked. It seemed to be taking forever to find the right path. Then the lights went out and it was suddenly pitch black. I crept forward emitting a nervous giggle as high-pitched wailing blasted overhead.

'Grace?' I shouted, but there was no response. Any second now the strobes would start, at least giving a flicker of light, but when they came on all, I could see was my own reflection staring back at me from every angle. Grace was gone and I couldn't see any of the others. Had I gone the wrong way?

Anxiety began to build in my chest, wrapping its tendrils around me.

'Guys,' I called, blood pounding in my ears. Hands trembling as I held them out in front of me. 'Are you there?' I shouted, although I couldn't hear anything above the wailing.

The lights cut out again and I froze, knees practically knocking together. My heart was racing in my chest. Moving through the maze as a group was a laugh, but alone it was utterly terrifying. Every time I moved, my reflection did too and catching it out of the corner of my eye freaked me out.

From what seemed like far ahead, I could hear my name being called and I moved forward at a snail's pace, counting down in my head until the strobe lights came on. My temple throbbed in rhythm to the darting lights. *You're safe, it's just a maze. No one can hurt you. It's all pretend*, I told myself repeatedly, trying to believe the mantra.

My fingertips pressed glass and I turned to my right, shuffling forward until I reached a dead end.

'Sod this,' I muttered, pulling out my phone and clicking the torch on.

Even with light, I was disorientated and turned around again, having no idea if I was going the right way or was any closer to getting out.

'Ria!' came a shout from far away. It sounded like Amanda, but I couldn't be sure. The wailing on the speakers had switched to intermittent gasps and I couldn't decide what was worse.

I'd been inside the maze for ages. Lost and alone. I contemplated remaining where I was, waiting for other revellers to come along so I could go through with them, but the urge to get out was compelling. Panic seized my lungs, making it hard to breathe.

'Amanda?' I shouted back.

The strobes came on again, bouncing off the glass and momentarily blinding me. I turned right and the mirror ahead looked like it had blood on it. I edged closer, squinting to make out the pattern. As I neared, I saw it was writing, someone had drawn on the mirror.

Ungluing my tongue from the roof of my mouth I spoke the words aloud.

'Livvy was here.'

26

What I first thought was blood was lipstick as I smeared the words down the glass. A fire-engine red stained my palm. Amanda had to have done it, she was wearing red lipstick.

Fire burned in my belly and I forced myself forward, clenching my jaw with a steely determination to get out of the damn maze. Too enraged now to be afraid, I ignored the gasps and blackouts and soldiered on. Finally I reached the exit, bumping into Jayden who was trying to make his way in.

'There you are,' he said, 'we thought we'd lost you.'

I pushed past him, storming up to Amanda, who baulked at my furious glare.

'What's up with you?' she said.

Without pausing to think, I launched at her, shoving her hard in the chest as she stumbled backwards onto Aaron, who caught her fall. 'You wrote that didn't you? On the mirror. Livvy was here... original, but I'm not falling for it. What are you trying to do, Amanda?'

'I don't know what the fuck you're talking about,' she spat back, regaining her balance.

'She's behind it,' I shouted, pointing right at Amanda. 'She's trying to make me crazy.'

Everyone stared at me, exchanging awkward glances. I looked at each of them for some kind of support, some concern, but their eyes darted away.

'Ria, enough of this please!' Cassie sighed, rubbing her forehead.

'You're losing it, Ria,' Aaron chipped in.

'Come on.' Jayden's hands clutched my shoulders, effortlessly steering me away from the throng.

'You are crazy,' Amanda shouted after me.

I glared back to see Aaron comforting her. Her! Molten tears streamed down my cheeks, my face smouldered as I willed myself not to sob. Not to fall apart in public. I bowed my head, away from prying eyes as we walked.

Jayden took me straight to the exit, tapping away on his phone as I circled the frozen yard, staring at the sky, my fingers laced behind my head. I wasn't crazy. Livvy was gone and Amanda was tormenting me. She wasn't trying to make contact from beyond the grave. That was impossible.

'The cab should be here any minute,' Jayden said, watching me pace. 'What happened?'

'Amanda wrote Livvy was here in red lipstick in the Mirror Maze.'

'How do you know it was her?' It was only a question, but Jayden's tone got my back up.

'Because I do. It's always been her. The flowers, the phone calls and email, she's trying to make me look crazy.'

Jayden raised his eyebrows and he didn't need to speak for me to know what he was thinking. *It's working.*

'Why would she?'

'I don't know, she keeps denying it, but I know it's her, I just don't know why.'

Jayden reached for me, but I kept moving, pretending I hadn't noticed.

Seconds later, a cab pulled into the entrance and we jumped in. Jayden gave them my address as I stared out of the window, wiping the tears from my face. He squeezed my hand, trying to comfort me as we drove past houses adorned with glowing pumpkins and ghoulish decorations. Halloween was only a day away, but I refused to believe Livvy was back from the dead.

It was a short drive to the flat and Jayden paid the driver as I fumbled in my pocket for my keys. He followed me up to the second floor and inside, switching on the lights and going straight for the kettle. Tea seemed to be the British answer to everything.

'I've got vodka in my room,' I said flatly, going to retrieve it. Despite having to work tomorrow, I wanted to numb the emotions flooding through me, already woozy from the shots we'd had at Tulley's. It wouldn't take many more to make me blissfully indifferent.

'Okay,' he said, reaching instead for two glasses.

We sat on the floor in front of the coffee table, still in our coats.

'I know about the email, the photo and the flowers. What else has happened?' he asked.

I told Jayden about the calls I'd had, Livvy's voice on the end of the phone, although I had no idea how Amanda had done it. It seemed she was deliberately trying to make me look unstable, like I was imagining Livvy was back. I told Jayden about my visit to Livvy's parents, the notebook, the missing ring and Amanda's Instagram photos.

'Do you think I should call the police?' I asked.

Jayden lowered his eyes to his glass. 'I'm not sure they'd believe you.'

He was really saying, he wasn't sure *he* believed me.

I took off my coat, chucking it on the other sofa and pulled my knees up to my chest. I downed the vodka and poured another.

'Amanda hasn't worked for Cardinal before has she?'

'Not that I'm aware of,' Jayden said, scratching his forehead.

'Do you remember a girl called Mandy who used to work there?'

'Nope, was she in sales?' Jayden stared at me blankly, not a hint of recognition betraying his features.

'No, accounts. The person who visited Lynn and Bill called herself Mandy. Did Livvy ever mention her?'

'Not to me, but Livvy and I weren't close, other than the work get-togethers. We didn't hang out.'

'So you never *went out* with her?' I asked, narrowing my eyes.

'Livvy? No. Who told you that?'

I shrugged.

'We never went out, nice girl and all that, but I never saw her that way.'

Jayden's phone pinged as I emptied my glass and poured us both another shot of vodka, my muscles starting to loosen.

'Amanda is staying at Aaron's, she's not coming back here tonight,' he said, showing me the text he'd received from Aaron.

'I bet he's well chuffed,' I sneered. 'Poor guy, she's like a piranha.'

He sniggered at my comment as I threw the vodka back, shuddering. It tasted disgusting.

'Will you stay with me?' I asked, inching closer to Jayden. I didn't want to be alone knowing as soon as I closed my eyes the nightmares would come.

'Of course,' he replied, leaning in and pulling my woolly hat off my head, hair going wild with static.

'Thank you.' I put my glass down and without thinking pulled him in for a kiss. I needed to feel something other than the misery that had followed me back from Nice. I wanted Jayden's hands on my skin to remove the tarnish of Tarek's touch.

* * *

We woke at the sound of the alarm, our legs entangled, with thumping headaches and furry mouths but no regret for last night's events. I imagined it would be difficult to let anyone touch me, but being with Jayden again was like being magically transported back to before Livvy died, when our relationship was blossoming.

'I better nip home and grab a change of clothes,' Jayden said, rubbing his forehead. He sat up in bed and I smirked at the sight of his bare chest.

'I think I still have one of your shirts in my wardrobe actually,' remembering he'd left one at mine before and I'd washed and ironed it, sticking it in the wardrobe and forgetting it was there. I jumped up to check, instantly nauseous with the motion. It was a mint green Ralph Lauren shirt, still hung at the end of the rail, untouched for months. 'Here it is. Your jeans are clean enough, aren't they?' I asked, picking them up off the floor and checking for any signs of mud.

'Come back to bed,' he giggled, looking at me, naked except for knickers and one sock that had managed to stay on.

I crawled beneath the covers and laid in his arms.

'I'm going to get fired today,' I sighed. I'd taken it too far last night, shoving Amanda in front of everyone and calling her out. I regretted acting so impulsively.

'You don't know that.'

'I do.'

'Shall I order an Uber Eats McMuffin?' As though that was the consolation prize for my life going down the toilet.

'Definitely.'

The flat was home again without Amanda in it and we made coffee and showered, waiting eagerly for our breakfast to arrive. Hurriedly munching it at the breakfast bar before brushing our teeth and heading to the office together. I was numb on the walk as though heading for my sentencing.

'Don't worry, she probably hasn't even told Chris about last night,' Jayden said, linking his fingers through mine. It was nice and we stayed that way right up to the front door, stopping as Chris and Fiona came out, deep in conversation.

'I'm not sure she's stable,' Fiona said, before catching my eye. 'Oh, hello, you two,' she said without skipping a beat, her cheeks colouring slightly.

'Jayden, Ria, morning,' Chris greeted, following after Fiona, his brow furrowed. It clearly wasn't a *good* morning.

'Morning,' Jayden and I said in unison as they both hurried down the street.

'What was all that about?' I asked, pushing through the revolving door.

'No idea, perhaps they're late for a meeting or something.' Referring to them rushing away. He couldn't have heard what Fiona said as she exited the building, he'd been behind me, but I'd caught it. Had she been talking about me?

27

I didn't repeat Fiona's words to Jayden, instead they buzzed around my head like a persistent fly. Had last night's events got back to her already?

I kept my head low, trying to fly under the radar as I slinked to my desk, waiting for Chris to return. Surely I'd be packing my desk up by the end of the day.

I was copied in on a proposal sent through to Aaron for a cough syrup and I spent the morning trying to come up with a snappy by-line. All I managed was one lame sentence and I stared blankly at it for around an hour. At lunchtime, I was still full from my McDonald's breakfast and didn't want to eat but headed to the kitchen to make a cup of tea.

'Oh hello,' Aaron said flatly as I walked in.

'Hi,' I replied, mirroring his tone and considering whether to turn around and leave. Dark circles under his eyes and the faint whiff of alcohol seeping out through his pores told me the rest of the group, or at least him and Amanda, had partied late into the night.

He turned his back to me, waiting for the microwave to ping.

The silence uncomfortable. His back stiffened when the microwave timer went off, but he didn't open the door to retrieve his lunch, instead turning around to face me as I bobbed my teabag in my cup.

'What is your problem with Amanda?' Folding his arms across his chest to emphasise his point.

'Leave it, Aaron,' I said.

'No, really, what is it? Because she's been nothing but nice to you.'

'Stop trying to pretend you're a gentleman when you're anything but,' I snapped.

His eyes darkened and he took a step towards me. 'I don't know why you came back,' he hissed.

'Hey, you two.' Grace's eyes darted between us as she entered the kitchen, smile faltering as she picked up on the atmosphere in the small space.

I nodded a greeting and turned back to finish my tea.

Grace tried to fill the silence, chattering about her hangover. I didn't join in and instead slipped out of the kitchen, annoyance at Aaron's remark scratching beneath my skin. Amanda was such a perfect victim wasn't she. Which made me the villain.

In my haste to leave, I'd forgotten to add sugar to my tea and wrinkled my nose at the bitter taste as I tried to focus back on work. The leaflet Fiona had forced me to take, listing counselling services, was wedged in between two ring binders, glaring at me accusingly. *You need help.*

'Oh shut up,' I muttered, pushing it deeper into the crevice so I could no longer see it.

'Happy Halloween!' Frankenstein's head popped up over the partition and I yelped, rolling back in my chair.

Karen pulled the mask off, the corner of it getting caught on her dark waves as she fell about laughing.

'Jesus, Karen, you almost gave me a heart attack,' I wheezed.

'I've been scaring everyone today. Got to get my kicks somehow.' She peeled her hair away from the latex, her forehead shiny.

'What can I do for you?' I gave her a thin-lipped smile, not in the mood for conversation or any Halloween fun.

'Remember you asked me about that girl, Mandy, who worked for us?'

I sat straighter in my chair, interest piqued. 'Yes.'

'Well, I was passing by Brad's desk and he'd left out a printout of the payroll spreadsheet. I happened to glance at it, you know, as you do.' Karen looked sheepish, but I knew she had a nose for gossip and if she had a chance to see what everyone was earning, she wouldn't let that pass her by. 'Anyway,' she continued, tucking her unruly hair behind her ear, 'I saw the name Dowd, which is why I stopped.'

'Okay, Amanda is on the payroll though,' I replied, frowning, not understanding what Karen was getting at.

'That's the thing, it's not Amanda we're paying.' Her eyes glinted and I wished she'd hurry up and get to the point.

'Mandy?' I guessed, but she shook her head, the corner of her mouth turning skyward.

If not Amanda or Mandy, then who?

'Anna. The name on the list is Anna,' Karen said triumphantly.

'Who the hell is Anna?' I said, throwing my hands up in the air.

'I have no idea,' Karen replied, enunciating each word.

Just when I couldn't be any more confused about who Amanda was, another name had been thrown into the mix.

At that moment, Jayden approached my desk and Karen took it as her cue to leave.

'Thanks, Karen,' I called after her as she went in search of more victims to scare.

'You okay? Hardly seen you today,' Jayden said. He rested his forearms on the partition, an easy smile played on his lips.

'I'm trying to work on this cough syrup thing, but it's not going well. Have you seen Amanda?'

'Aaron said she's not in today, didn't say why.'

I had visions of her back at the flat, burning every one of my possessions. The urge to get home made my legs jiggle up and down beneath the desk.

'She's probably hungover,' Jayden continued, seeing my face fall. Amanda not being in only added fuel to her victim narrative.

'Ria, my office please.' Chris's voice carried over the partition from his office door, the tone not exactly friendly. I hadn't seen him return.

Jayden and I exchanged a worried glance. I already knew what was about to happen. I was resigned to the fact that because of a relative stranger, I was about to lose everything.

Chris's office was cold, where the door had been shut all morning. I waited as he signed into his computer before lowering himself onto the chair. My boss looked weary, like he'd aged in the past week. Had I caused it?

Fiona appeared at the door, her notebook in hand, and slipped inside, giving me a thin-lipped smile. At that moment I knew I was done for.

'Ria,' Chris began, with a sigh, 'I'm sorry, but I'm going to have to let you go. I hoped you and Amanda would get along, but that seems not to be the case. She's concerned about coming back in, something about a physical altercation last night?'

My body went rigid, feet planted to the floor as my temper simmered. It was hardly a fight and I knew full well Amanda wasn't scared of me.

I kept my voice calm and steady. 'Chris, she's been gaslighting me, calling and emailing me from Livvy's computer. She's the one who sent me those flowers. She's trying to make me look unstable.'

'You are unstable, Ria! You can't see past your grief.'

I shrank back at Chris's words, as though they'd been littered with pellets striking through my armour. He shook his head, rubbing at his temples.

'Amanda has put an official grievance in this morning,' Fiona said.

'A grievance? What am I supposed to have done?' I blurted, fighting to keep from shouting.

'She's saying it's bullying in the workplace, which, of course, we have to investigate.'

'It's not me, it's her.' My pitch rose, trying to cling on to the edge of the cliff I was dangling from.

'Do you have any proof?'

I lowered my eyes to the floor. Amanda had been clever, she'd covered her tracks, but I knew it was her.

28

LIVVY – BEFORE

I don't mean to join in when they all laugh, but I can't help it. We're in the usual catch-up meeting, Chris is out with the shareholders, so it's just us going through our projects and getting input from the other teams.

She trips up in the hallway as she goes past, unfortunately spilling her freshly made tea down her blouse and dropping the documents she is carrying. I'm nearest the door and step out to help her pick them up, noticing the tears welling in her eyes.

'Whoopsie-daisy!' calls out Aaron with a laugh.

I shoot him daggers, he is hardly helping.

'Here you go,' I say as we get to our feet, handing her the documents I've collected.

'I'm not being funny, but it has to be an improvement to that blouse,' Cassie says, her voice low but not low enough.

I wince internally and watch as she scurries away.

'I mean, there's yellow and there's melt-your-eyes yellow. You need bloody sunglasses to look at her,' Cassie carries on as I return to my seat.

'I feel sorry for her,' I say.

'And where has that got you,' Grace chips in, 'she's everywhere you bloody go!'

We carry on with the meeting, but I'm consumed by guilt at the hurt in her eyes. Cassie has a venomous tongue sometimes, she doesn't mean it, it's just the way she is. Spikey and often opens her mouth without engaging her brain first.

As I pack up to leave, I see her loitering by the water cooler, her gaze trained in my direction. I try not to make eye contact, I'm tired and want to go home.

'Pub?' Aaron says, materialising at my desk on cue.

'Hmmm,' I consider.

'You can invite your mate – what's her name?' he sniggers, gesturing over his shoulder to where she is still watching.

'Oh shut up!' I sigh, swinging my bag over my shoulder. 'Nah, I can't be bothered, I'm going home.'

'Oh I didn't mean it. Come on, gorgeous,' he says, giving me a wink. 'I'm buying,' Aaron pushes, but I shake my head and tell him I'll see him tomorrow.

Outside, the sun shines brightly, its warmth hitting my shoulders as soon as I am in the open air. Always a mood-booster, I make my way to the crowded bus stop to wait for the number 20. Pulling out my phone, I am fully engrossed in Snapchat when the bus arrives and mindlessly follow the crowd on, tapping my pass across the reader. There is nowhere to sit so I lean against the pole by the exit doors, gripping it tightly as the bus jerks away.

A flicker of yellow catches my eye at the back and I crane my neck to see, but the bus is rammed with passengers, standing in the aisles, all trying to get home. An eerie sensation creeps over me and I can't shake the idea I am being watched. It isn't until I get off and watch the bus trundle away when, out of the rear window, a spectacled face pops up inches away from the glass. The sight of her makes me jump, her almost illuminous blouse unmistakable. Has she been following me?

29

'Do you have any proof?' Chris asked again.

I showed him the call log on my phone, supposedly from Livvy. He frowned as he stared at the screen.

'There was a photo stuck to my monitor too, of me and Liv. Someone sprayed her perfume and I have an email sent from her account too. Tim saw it. Then there's the flowers, did you see the note?' I asked, exasperated.

'Tim told me about the email, he also said it was sent from your machine.' Chris said, stroking his beard.

'I didn't send it!' I snapped, balling my hands into fists.

'How do you know all of this was Amanda?' Fiona interjected, leaning forward in her seat.

'I... I just do,' I stammered, blotches climbing my neck.

'That's not enough, Ria. In addition to the grievance, you swore at Amanda right in front of me. Then there was the issue with the mug. I warned you it had to stop.'

'We're worried about you and I'm not sure being here is doing your mental health any good,' Fiona chipped in. They were like a tag team.

'I'm really sorry, Ria. Perhaps it was too soon,' Chris said, looking like all the air had been let out of him. 'You can work the rest of the week, hand over to Grace. Her and Rav are tying up their current project, she can help out with Aaron until...' Chris's words trailed off.

I'd had two warnings before I went on my sabbatical because of my behaviour. I knew he didn't want to sack me, but he was stuck between a rock and a hard place, and something had to give. That something was me.

'Until I'm replaced,' I finished his sentence for him, incredulous.

Chris cleared his throat and continued, maintaining his professional exterior. 'We'll give you three months' pay, I think that's fair, but I'm afraid after that you'll need to find somewhere else to live.' The weight of his decision was etched deeply in every feature. 'I really hope you get the help you need,' he said, with a slight quiver.

My face crumpled as the world tilted on its axis and tears clouded my vision. I wrestled internally to stop myself boiling over.

'It's favouritism, she's only been here five minutes.' I hated myself for arguing when I knew it was pointless. Chris had made his decision, he'd given me ample warnings and Amanda had sucked him in with a sob story.

Chris sighed, head bowed. He opened his mouth to speak, but closed it again.

Was I right? Was it favouritism?

My stomach swirled. Oh God, was he sleeping with her too? Jesus! Was Cardinal Media becoming a hive of Amanda's conquests with her the queen bee? What power did she wield over them? Sure, she was attractive, but didn't they realise they were being used? Manipulated for her personal gain. She'd got her claws into Jayden and Aaron, was Chris next?

'It's not favouritism, but for transparency, Amanda is my niece.'

Chris sighed, looking up at me, deep lines furrowed his brow. 'It's my job to protect her, professionally and personally.'

'What?' I floundered. Those were the last words I expected to hear out of his mouth. They were related!

'She's my niece,' he repeated, 'and I promised my brother I'd keep an eye on her. I told you, she's had a rough time and *this*' – he gestured towards me – 'isn't helping.'

I had no words, how could I argue my position when Amanda was Chris's family. There was no point. He was never going to believe me over her. She'd been one step ahead of me from the outset. I bet she knew everything, all about Livvy and the circumstances in which I'd left. Did he discuss us over family dinners? Casually dropping in my breakdown as dessert was served. I swallowed down the injustice of it.

'I'll start my handover tomorrow,' I said, unable to think about the fact I was going to be homeless.

On wobbly legs, I trudged back to my desk. Amanda had won, although why had I been the target of her hate campaign? What was her connection to Livvy? Was this about Jayden?

With tears welling, I grabbed my bag and coat and headed out into the cold. I couldn't sit at my desk crying, the whole situation was embarrassing enough without having everyone witness my turmoil. How had the morning gone from utter contentment, waking up in Jayden's arms, but turned into a shitshow so fast? It was a rollercoaster I didn't want to be on.

I made my way to the park. Sitting on a swing as the wind blustered around me. There was only one parent there with their child, brave enough to come out despite the elements.

It was there I let myself cry, the overwhelming situation taking hold as my shoulders heaved with wracking silent sobs. It all seemed so pointless.

My phone rang and I dug it out of my pocket thinking it would be Jayden, but it was Mum, calling again. We hadn't spoken since I'd ended our call abruptly. I sent it to voicemail, she was one more disappointment I couldn't deal with today.

Eventually, when I could no longer feel my toes, I got up to walk back to the flat, trepidation building with each step. Knowing Amanda would be there, revelling in her victory. I wasn't sure I could stomach it, but I had nowhere else to go and would have to return to pack up my things at some point. The situation was a mess. What was I going to do? No job and three months' wages to live on. Despite Chris not chucking me out on the street immediately, I couldn't stay with Amanda, not now. But I couldn't afford to live anywhere else either.

I slid my key into the front door, loud music pumped from the flat, and as I entered I glimpsed Amanda dancing around to David Guetta in the lounge. Yeah, she looked distraught. My lips peeled back from my teeth in a snarl. Poor little Amanda, such a victim. I loitered in the doorway until she spotted me and froze, arms raised in the air.

'You're back,' she didn't sound surprised, weirdly she seemed pleased to see my puffy tear-stained face.

'I'm going to start packing,' I said through gritted teeth, breezing past her.

'Listen, I'm sorry things have gone the way they have.' She sounded so insincere I snapped, turning back towards her.

'You're a psycho, do you know that. I mean, what did I ever do to you?'

'I'm the psycho?' she said, her hand springing to her chest, her outrage as fake as her smile had previously been.

'Oh whatever, Amanda, Mandy, or is it Anna? I mean, who the hell are you anyway?'

'You don't know what you're talking about!' she faltered, face darkening at my words.

'I don't? Really?' I laughed manically. 'I know you're Chris's niece,' I hissed, the day's rage spilling out of me like molten lava, unstoppable and unable to control. 'And I know you knew Livvy, no matter what you say.'

'I told you, I never met her!'

'Well, I don't buy it. You're full of shit. Every word out of your mouth has been a lie from the start.'

'Jesus, you're obsessed with Livvy, aren't you. It was probably you that spiked her drink! Did you want to hook up with her, is that it?'

I gritted my teeth, curling my hands into fists and taking a step towards Amanda. She tilted her chin, grinning at her provocation, enjoying goading me.

'You left the door open.' Aaron stepped into the flat, pausing at the scene before him, Amanda and I glowering at each other from across the lounge. I was minutes away from slapping the smile off her face. 'Have I interrupted?'

I scowled, but Amanda turned and went to him, giving him a peck on the cheek.

'No, Ria is just experiencing some anger issues. She really needs to get some counselling.' She smiled sweetly back at me before grabbing her coat, turning to Aaron. 'Ready to go?'

He nodded, still trying to work out what he'd walked into.

I was too livid to speak, the blood rushing to my head, flushing my cheeks.

'See you later, flatmate, have fun packing,' she trilled as she whipped out of the door, slamming it so hard, it echoed around the empty flat.

30

'Aaaarrgghhh,' I let out a scream of pent-up anger, launching my bag across the room and watching the contents spill out and scatter. That bitch! Tearing through her bedroom like a tornado, I ripped her clothes out of her wardrobe until they lay in a heap on the floor. The hangers rocking back and forth like a bizarre set of pendulums. Pulling back her duvet, I tossed that too, dragging the pillow from its case and the sheet from the mattress before shoving it across the slats until it was at an angle and half resting on the floor.

Sweat pooled on the small of my back, but still I kept going. Anger driving me on. Drawers were wrenched open, turned upside down until the room was a wreck. Slumping down on top of Amanda's diagonal mattress, I panted, exhausted. Spying her jewellery box laying on its side by the door, I crawled towards it, taking Livvy's ring and slipping it onto my finger. She'd say I was a thief, a crazy, psychotic thief, but I didn't care. A piece of paper caught my eye, sticking out from the corner of a picture frame I'd knocked off the wall in my rampage, the glass shattering on impact with the floor.

I unfolded it. It was an Amazon order print out for the black silk roses, the message to include: *Missing me yet? Livvy xxx*

I'd been right all along. Amanda had been behind it all, but why? Why did she hate Livvy and why did she hate me?

A knock at the door jolted me from my hysteria. I ignored it at first, slowly getting up to answer it as the knocking intensified.

'Ria?' Jayden's voice carried as he hammered on the door. 'What happened to you?' he said as I swung it open, a hot sweaty mess with frizzy hair appearing before him. I turned back, towards Amanda's room and he followed me, perplexed. Glass crunched beneath my feet as I resumed my position on the mattress.

He surveyed the devastation, his eyes wide. 'You did this?'

I nodded.

He put his hands behind his head, blowing out a puff of air through his cheeks, casting his eyes over the damage I'd caused.

'Look,' I said, holding out the Amazon order. He took it from me, staring at it.

'Amanda sent them?'

'Yep. It's been her all along,' I said, taking the paper back. 'I told you.'

'Christ. What is her problem?' he said.

'No fucking clue.' I let out an involuntary laugh.

'We better go, before she comes back.'

'Where to?' I mumbled.

'Mine. Obviously. Come on, let's pack.' We locked eyes, mine conveying a tidal wave of gratitude. I wouldn't have dreamt of asking Jayden for help yet here he was, showing up and offering me a way out.

He disappeared and seconds later I could hear him in the room next door, my bedroom. I knew how easy sound carried as I'd had to listen to Amanda's moans from her night with him.

I bit my tongue until I tasted blood. How low she had sunk to get to me. My head hurt from trying to figure out why. What connected us and why did she hate me so much? I couldn't think about that now, I just had to get out of the flat and Jayden was offering me a lifeline.

'I have so much to tell you,' I said to Jayden as between us we emptied my room, getting as much stuff as I could in my tiny suitcase and putting the rest into bin bags he'd found under the sink.

'Later, seriously we need to get out of here. She might call the police.'

'Oh, I doubt it,' I replied, taking a photo of the Amazon order on my phone and leaving the original on the kitchen worktop. I wanted her to know I'd found it. That I'd been right all along. She could no longer deny it.

* * *

'She's Chris's niece?' Jayden repeated, the beer bottle inches from his lips. We'd ordered takeaway and sat on the floor eating, surrounded by my life, packed in minutes into bags.

'Yep, explains the preferential treatment. He admitted it, as he was sacking *and* making me homeless at the same time,' I said, unable to keep the sarcasm out of my voice.

'You're not homeless, you can stay with me.'

I sighed, I couldn't stay permanently.

'What are you thinking?' Jayden frowned at my grim expression as I considered my options.

'I don't know, a plane ticket back to Nice with my tail between my legs.' I rubbed at my forehead before twirling some noodles around my fork and taking a bite. Going back to live with mum and Tarek was a last resort. I wanted somewhere I felt safe and mum couldn't provide that all the time he was living with her.

'You can't go! You've only just got back.' Jayden nudged my arm.

'I may not have a choice,' I said, shoulders sagging.

We ate in silence for a while.

'I wonder what she's up to,' Jayden mused, crunching a spring roll.

'We need to find out *who* she is!' I sat forward, picking up my phone before continuing, already navigating to the internet. 'And now we have a connection. She's Chris's family, which is a lead. Maybe if we can find out who she really is, it'll help us work out what she wants.'

'Does any of it matter now?' Jayden sounded deflated. 'Isn't it better to move on?' His expression morphed into one of distaste and I set the phone back down. It wasn't worth dragging Jayden into it, but I needed an explanation of her actions and why I was the target. It wasn't his life she'd blown up but mine. Reluctantly I switched the phone off ruminating Jayden's words. Perhaps he was right. After all, he'd been there for me when I needed him. Sticking around despite the chaos that seemed to follow my every turn.

* * *

Spending the evening at Jayden's was like we'd slipped into full-on coupledom. Snuggled up on the sofa watching a movie, he'd assured me I could stay as long as I liked. But being thrown together and having to be there because of circumstances wasn't the same as inviting me to move in. Things were already going too fast and I wasn't sure it was what I wanted.

My mind was so distracted with Amanda, I struggled to relax and ended up tossing and turning all night as he grumbled beside me. The result was both of us were bleary-eyed on Tuesday morning. I groaned as I got up, Jayden suggesting I get in the shower first while he made strong coffee for us. Once out, I had to iron my trousers and blouse as everything had been so hastily thrown into bags, all of my clothes were creased beyond recognition.

'How do you think it'll be today?' Jayden asked.

'No idea.' I shrugged, hiding the apprehension I had about seeing Amanda after I'd trashed her room. Not to mention Chris's reaction when he found out. But I'd seen and photographed the Amazon order slip, my actions were vindicated. She could hardly deny it now. Jayden was right, it would be better to walk away, but I was desperate to know what her problem was.

When we reached Cardinal Media's building, Jayden decided, as we were early, he was going to go to the bakery and get a bacon roll for breakfast.

'Okay, I'm going to crack on, so I'll see you in a bit,' I said, pushing the revolving door and heading inside.

The office was quiet, it was just after eight o'clock, reception empty as Michelle didn't start until nine. Chris's door was open, although I wasn't about to wish him a good morning. However, as I passed, I registered a pair of black laced brogue shoes on the carpet, then pale hairy legs poking out from suit trousers before Chris's horizontal body came into view as I rounded the door.

'Chris!' I shouted, letting go of my bag and rushing into his office, dropping to my knees beside him as he writhed on the floor.

31

Chris clutched his arm, his face an insipid grey with a sheen of sweat clinging to his forehead.

'Chris,' I yelled again, as his eyes fluttered, 'what happened?'

'My chest,' he puffed as I fumbled for my phone.

I'd never dialled 999 before, my voice trembling as I asked for an ambulance. Racing back to my desk to search through my drawer for an aspirin while at the same time handing over the address to the call handler. Once I'd confirmed he was awake and responding she told me to keep him comfortable, they were on their way.

'Chew this,' I instructed, pushing the white pill through Chris's lips. In the panic, I hadn't even thought to ask him if he was already on any medication, or whether he could be allergic. I only knew aspirin was helpful if you were having a heart attack, which I was sure Chris was. His jaw moved, crunching the pill as his eyelids flickered. I rolled him onto his side and held him, muttering assurances.

I rocked him gently, stroking his hair as he whimpered, telling him to stay with me, while looking around for my phone which I'd dropped just inside the door to the office in the rush to get back from my desk, vaguely aware the call hander was still talking, although I couldn't hear what she was saying and I wasn't about to leave Chris to get it. He was making no sense, mumbling about the past, he'd tried his best and was sorry. I comforted him as much as I could as he flinched in pain.

Eventually, paramedics came through the door and I moved aside to let them work on Chris, answering the questions they asked as calmly as I could. My heart was racing so fast, I barely registered Jayden wrapping his arms around me as Chris was lifted onto a stretcher.

'I'm going with him,' I told the paramedic. It wasn't up for discussion.

'I'll follow behind,' Jayden said, picking up my phone and handbag and holding them out to me.

In the ambulance, I held Chris's hand, trying to remember his wife's name. I believed it was Zoe, although I had no idea how to reach her.

The sirens wailed and it seemed we got to the hospital in minutes, where Chris was unloaded and taken straight into Accident and Emergency.

I lagged behind the paramedic as they drew the curtain and handed over Chris's care to the team, managing to catch the word 'stable' before Jayden appeared a few minutes later, rushing through the double doors into the corridor where I was waiting.

'Sorry, I struggled to park,' he said, pulling me into a swift hug. 'Are you okay?'

'I'm okay,' I breathed, my cheeks wet with the onslaught of tears. Adrenaline was coursing through my system, heightening all my senses.

'We need to contact his wife,' Jayden said.

'Zoe, her name's Zoe isn't it, but I don't have her number, do you?'

'No, but I know where he lives.' Jayden pulled his keys out of his pocket, already edging towards the door.

'Mr Lightfoot is conscious. He's asking for you.' A freckled-faced nurse, put her hand on my arm, and I walked back towards the bay he was in.

'I'll wait for you,' Jayden called.

'Mr Lightfoot is stable, the aspirin you gave him helped. Thankfully, the heart attack was mild, but he'll need to stay with us, at least for a few days so we can investigate the cause.'

'Of course, thank you,' I said as she drew back the curtain, revealing Chris. 'Hey,' I smiled, taking hold of Chris's hand as he reached out for me. Some colour had come back to his cheeks and his skin was no longer ashen. His shirt had been removed and it was strange to see my boss, bare chested with pads stuck to his skin to monitor his heart rate. I raised my eyes quickly to his face. It was all too intimate, the situation overwhelming.

'I think you saved my life,' he whispered, eyes damp.

I squeezed his hand.

'I've never been so pleased to have missed breakfast,' I joked weakly.

He laughed, wincing.

'Where's Zoe, how can I reach her?'

'She's in Amsterdam, on business,' he sighed. 'I have no idea where my phone is.'

'At the office probably. Give me her number and I'll call her.'

Chris reeled off Zoe's number as I typed it into my phone.

He looked at me. 'Could I ask a favour?'

'Sure, anything.'

'It looks as though I might be staying in,' he said.

'Obviously!' I scolded.

'Could you go to my house, pick me up some clothes. Maybe ask Jayden to do it, he's been there before. There's a key safe, the code is 2148.'

I nodded, knowing it would be less embarrassing for Jayden to rummage through Chris's underwear drawer. 'Of course.'

I called Zoe, passing the phone to Chris and hearing it go through to voicemail. I got up to step away while he left a message. Hearing her husband's voice would do something to quell the panic at finding out he was in hospital. When I returned, he handed the phone back to me.

'We won't be long,' I said, giving him a reassuring pat to his shoulder and leaving to find Jayden.

'I've called Amanda,' he said. 'She's coming straight to the hospital.'

I nodded, it made sense, she was family. She could call her dad, Chris's brother, to be with him in Zoe's absence. Although I knew Chris, he wouldn't want everyone making a fuss.

'How do you know where Chris lives?' I asked once we were in the car and on our way back to Crawley.

'He had a works summer barbeque once before you joined. The house is massive, he has a pool and everything.'

Soon, we were on a road I'd never been down before, where the enormous houses were set back from long gravel driveways, gardens perfectly landscaped. Most had electric gates, but not Chris's. Jayden pulled up outside a large detached white Tudor-style house with dark beams and a resin driveway. It was beautiful.

'Christ,' I muttered, taking in its grandeur.

Jayden laughed at my reaction. 'He owns his own company, Zoe has some top job in a distribution firm too. Dual income, no kids, they are minted.'

Jayden was right: Chris wore tailor-made suits with expensive shoes and I'd seen the Rolex his wife had gifted him last Christmas.

He was always groomed, immaculately dressed and he drove a brand-new Tesla. Yet he wasn't a miser with his wealth, quite the opposite. His employees were awarded generous end-of-year bonuses and treated to lavish work functions. The fact he'd let me live at the company flat for a heavily subsidised rent meant he was kind too. Sadly, I imagined no boss would ever live up to my expectations in the future after working for Chris.

'Help me look for the key safe,' Jayden said, moving the heavy spiral topiary trees in their glossy black pots.

Eventually, we found it behind a manicured hedge, drilled into the brickwork at the bottom of the house. If you didn't know there was a key safe there, you'd never find it. Once inside, I marvelled at the stylish but stripped-back décor. It wasn't gaudy at all, contemporary but with a homely feel to it.

'I'm going to grab Chris some things, are you coming?'

'No, I'll stay down here,' I replied, not wanting to infringe on Chris's privacy any more than I already had. Seeing him half naked was as up close and personal as I wanted to get.

Once alone, I wandered into the front room, admiring the enormous television mounted on one wall. There was a log burner on the other side with a stained oak beam above as a mantelpiece. A framed photo stood in the centre, Chris and Zoe laughing on their wedding day. She had long dark straight hair and wore an ivory column dress that was simply stunning. I perused the other photos of them, one on horseback, the other on the deck of a yacht. I stopped at the last one, which wasn't of Chris and Zoe at all.

Two girls, in their mid-teens, one a dark blonde, the other mousy brown with glasses, posed smiling with their heads together, cheeks practically touching. Cute pink braces attached to both their teeth. The photo had been taken at a restaurant, empty sundae dishes sat in front of them, tall spoons sticking out of the top.

I had no doubt the blonde was Amanda. I recognised her

instantly despite how dark her hair was compared to the platinum of today. Her smile was the same, her lips a perfect Cupid's bow and her slate eyes unmistakable. She looked genuinely happy beaming down the lens of the camera. Next to her was someone I recognised but couldn't place immediately. Similar features to Amanda, but her eyes were slightly smaller, her face rounder. She had a block fringe with heavy glasses and looked to be around fifteen. Amanda was the older sibling, maybe seventeen, eighteen.

Pulling out my phone, I clicked on Instagram and scrolled through Cassie's photos, back to the night Livvy died. The girl next to Amanda in the photo was the same girl in the back of the group shot Cassie had taken that night. Her face was partly obscured by Jayden's elbow and not so childlike, but the features were the same.

It wasn't Amanda pretending to be someone else. If I was right, Mandy and Amanda had to be sisters. Who named their siblings Mandy and Amanda? It was weird, but my gut told me I was on the right track. Then I recalled the payroll list Karen had seen stated Cardinal were paying Anna Dowd, was Amanda really Anna?

I pulled out my phone and took a photo of the picture, so I could study it later.

'Everything okay?' Jayden came into the room as I was slipping the phone back into my pocket, a small holdall slung over his shoulder.

'It's Amanda,' I said, pointing at the photo and waiting for Jayden to come and look.

'Oh yeah.'

'Do you recognise her?' I asked, pointing at the girl I believed to be Mandy.

Jayden shrugged. 'Nope,' he said without batting an eyelid. 'Right, let's go. Chris will be waiting.'

32

Jayden told me as we returned to the hospital that while he'd been upstairs he'd quickly phoned Fiona to let her know what had happened. We'd both received texts from colleagues as the word had spread, but I left mine unanswered. All I could think about was I'd been wrong. Amanda and Mandy weren't the same person. It tied in with Karen's description of Mandy. They had to be sisters, hence the familiar features.

It meant Mandy, not Amanda, had been there the night Livvy died. She was Chris's niece too and must have worked in payroll at Cardinal. Although it was in Amanda's room where I found the Amazon receipt for the black roses? Were they tormenting me together? Working as a team? Yet still, the motive escaped me. I had no clue what I'd done to either of them, but it was obvious they had a vendetta. I had to hope my leaving, losing my job and the roof over my head would mean they were sated. I pressed my lips into a thin line, grinding my teeth at the unfairness of it all.

Back at the hospital, I let Jayden meet with Amanda to get an update and hand over the bag. I remained in the car, it was neither the time nor the place for confrontation, or to reveal I knew what her and her sister had been up to. Plus, when I did confront her, I wanted to have all the facts, so she couldn't dismiss me as being crazy. I wanted more solid evidence she couldn't worm her way out of.

When Jayden returned twenty minutes later, I was freezing and keen for him to start the car and get the heating on. The adrenaline rush and subsequent crash was playing havoc with my internal thermostat.

'How is he?' I asked as Jayden manoeuvred out of the parking space towards the barriers.

'Stable. He's going to have further investigation to see if there are any more blood clots. He's spoken to Zoe and has his phone now, Amanda brought it from the office.'

'Did she say anything?' I asked.

'She said, "tell the bitch, thanks for tanking my room."' Jayden chuckled and I joined in. I had gone overboard, but I was angry. Amanda had cost me my job and my home and I had no clue what her vendetta was about. Still, it seemed to shrink into insignificance after the events of the morning. If I had gone for breakfast with Jayden, Chris may not have been discovered in time. It didn't bear thinking about.

'What a day,' I said, the thought of having to go back to the office making my stomach plummet. But Chris had such a strong work ethic, he'd expect nothing less from his employees. He loved the keep calm and carry on approach, wheeling it out at every opportunity, and I was sure that's exactly what he'd say to his concerned staff.

By the time we returned, it was lunchtime and we were cornered as soon as we got in the door. Everyone wanting updates on Chris and patting me on the back for acting so quickly. Fiona had told the teams separately that Chris was currently in hospital and we were to crack on in his absence.

I started my handover to Grace, who was gutted that I was leaving. I told her it was for the best, not wanting to elaborate in Aaron's presence, and we started going through the projects. He was frosty, not passing comment on my exodus as I'd expected, but eventually thawed out with the help of Grace's warped sense of humour and inappropriate jokes. No one mentioned Amanda and news of me trashing her room hadn't got back to the others yet.

The three of us spent the afternoon in the meeting room. I didn't see Amanda for the rest of the day, assuming she'd stay with Chris at the hospital. I prayed his mild heart attack was a one-off and there was nothing more sinister uncovered. I held no ill will towards him, despite the events of yesterday; he'd been a lovely boss.

As I was packing up, Karen came around to my desk to get a first-hand account of my discovering Chris. News travelled fast around the office.

'Karen, do you think you can find out how many people with the last name Dowd are on the payroll?' I asked once I'd filled her in.

'I can, but I think I only saw one on the list and that was Anna, whoever she is.'

I grimaced. 'This girl here,' I said, going through my phone and retrieving the photo I'd taken that morning at Chris's house, 'is that Mandy, who used to work in your department?'

She squinted at the photo as I zoomed in for her. 'I think so. She didn't have a fringe, but she looks similar. A bit young. Where did you get that from?'

'Oh, I just found it, online,' I lied, stumbling over my words.

Karen looked at me knowingly, a smile dancing on her lips. 'Why are you so invested in finding her?' she asked.

'I'm not,' I replied, a little too defensively.

'Sure,' she said, playfully, letting me know she didn't believe a word I'd said.

* * *

Later, while Jayden took a shower, I lay on the sofa, searching for Chris's Facebook account. He had one, but it was set to private and I couldn't even see his list of friends. I was trying to work out why his nieces had a different last name to him. He was Lightfoot, yet his brother was Dowd? It was another mystery to uncover. Perhaps they'd taken their mother's name?

Chris had a Twitter account linked to Cardinal Media, but there was nothing personal on there. I couldn't find him on Instagram and LinkedIn was again limited to professional information. If I could find out what his brother's first name was, it might help, but even searching the last name Dowd brought up no leads.

Ditching the search, I went through Livvy's journal again, page by page. Scanning every written word and doodle, searching for any reference to Amanda, Mandy or even Anna. I tried to ignore Jayden's name whenever it appeared. When I reached the page where Livvy had written *Why won't she just leave me alone! She's everywhere. I fucking hate her*, I scanned the surrounding doodles, lots of angry dark biro slashes scattered the page. In the top left-hand corner, I saw the name Dowd with a scribble through it. I turned the page over, to see if I could make out the indentation the other side. *Dowdy Dowd* Livvy had written and subsequently scribbled out.

I narrowed my eyes searching for more but found nothing. Had Mandy been stalking Livvy?

'I'm shattered,' Jayden said, yawning as he entered the room with a towel wrapped around his waist, blotting his hair with another. His toned torso making me look twice before I was aware I was ogling.

'Me too,' I yawned, closing the journal and pushing it under my leg before Jayden asked what I was looking at.

'I hope Chris will be all right.'

'I'm sure he will, he's in the best place,' I replied, a phrase I'd often heard repeated when someone was in hospital. 'Do you fancy a stir-fry, I can throw something together.' I had the urge to busy my idle hands and thoughts, needing the distraction.

'Sounds great.' Jayden went to get dressed, steam from the bathroom escaping out into the hallway.

My phone rang while I was cooking. It was Mum again. I sighed, swiping the screen to answer. I couldn't put off speaking to her any longer.

'Hello.'

'Ria, it's Mum.' She sounded weird, choked.

'Are you okay?' I asked, panic rising in my throat.

'Yes, yes, I'm fine.'

'Where's Tarek?'

She didn't reply immediately, sniffing. Obviously, she'd been crying. Had they had another row?

'He's gone.' The finality she said the words with made my breath catch in throat.

'Gone?'

'I'm so sorry, darling, I'm sorry I didn't believe you,' she sobbed, unable to hide her emotion.

I swallowed the lump in my throat.

'Did he hurt you?' I asked.

'No, but I know he hurt you.'

I couldn't answer, my chest burning. She believed me now, but she hadn't before.

'I wish you'd made me hear you,' she said, stumbling over her words, shifting the blame as she always did. Never taking responsibility for her actions.

'I told you, Mum, I told you everything. You chose not to believe me,' I spat, biting back tears, glad Jayden wasn't in the room.

'I know, I'm so sorry, I just saw the two of you and...' She tailed off, unable to voice what she had seen, while the memory would never leave me.

The night before I'd left, Tarek had come home drunk after playing poker with his friends. He'd come into my bedroom, permeating the room with stale sweat and whisky fumes. I'd been half asleep as he'd climbed on top of me, tugging at my pyjamas, sour breath in my face. He was so heavy, using his weight as leverage as he tried to undo his belt and force my legs apart. Slobbering at my neck like a wet dog and barking at me to 'lay still'. I'd been trying to fight him off when Mum had walked in, disturbed by the noise in the middle of the night.

She had appeared in the doorway, like an angel bathed in light, rubbing her eyes and tying her robe tighter around her middle. She yelled, 'What the hell are you doing?' and Tarek had got up, swaying, trying to make out he'd stumbled into the wrong room. I was crying, wide awake and shaking with fear. He'd pushed past Mum to go to bed and I hoped she would tell him to get out. Rush over to comfort me, but the look she gave me was one of resignation.

'He's just drunk, Ria, he didn't mean anything by it,' she'd said, making excuses for him. There was no doubt in my mind if she hadn't burst in, he would have raped me.

She had left the room, closing the door softly and leaving me curled up in a ball of shame to cry myself to sleep. I couldn't bear to face either of them in the morning. I was so angry at her, I'd packed my bags and headed for the airport to catch the first available flight back to London. Pausing only to slash all four tyres of his Peugeot 208 on my way out.

The phone line crackled jolting me back to the present. Mum was calling my name, fearing we'd been cut off.

'You chose to believe him,' I said, my voice carrying an undercurrent of rage. 'You chose to believe him, Mum, over me, your daughter. He tried to rape me whilst you slept!'

'Darling, I'm sorry,' she said, sobbing down the phone.

'You'd choose a man like that over me,' I said, the outrage pouring from me. 'I'm glad he's gone, but I can't forgive you, Mum.' I slammed the phone down, ending the call.

33

Dinner had been a quiet affair. My mind too wrapped up with the call from Mum. We watched television, Jayden trying to make conversation and I nodded along as best I could, before, desperate to be alone, I opted for an early night. Jayden played Xbox and the sound of machine-gun fire travelled through the wall. When he eventually came to bed and nuzzled in behind me, I pretended to be asleep.

With that night now so fresh in my mind, I couldn't bear to let Jayden touch me. My muscles tightly wound, I wanted to go for a run, something to let out the pent-up fury circling my body. But even I wasn't stupid enough to go for a run in the middle of the night without understanding the dangers it would entail. What if I ran into another Tarek, who wouldn't take no for an answer? I'd had a lucky escape with my mum waking up, but it wasn't something I could thank her for, not when her initial reaction had been so dismissive.

That was why I loathed being portrayed as a liar by Amanda. Her narrative was that I was losing it, imagining things, which everyone seemed only too happy to lap up. Mum had always done that, ever since I was a kid. I was always exaggerating, or I misunderstood when I complained, had an argument at school or if someone acted inappropriately towards her, or me. She put me second in every situation, which is why I'd distanced myself from her when I'd reached adulthood.

It might have been another reason I'd gravitated towards Chris, the father figure I'd never had. Mine had left, abandoned me before I could walk, declaring me an accident and not a good enough reason to tie him to my mum for the rest of his life. Chris's kindness had bowled me over from the outset and I bought into Cardinal Media being his family, one he looked after, cherished and watch grow. I yearned to be a part of it but look how that had turned out. I'd come second to Amanda yet again.

As soon as the sun came up, I laced up my trainers and hit the streets, burning off the nervous energy until my legs ached in complaint. Would Amanda be in the office when I got there? It was likely and despite the wrath I might face, at least I'd get a chance to get some answers.

When Jayden and I arrived, Fiona had left a Post-it note on my desk asking me to pop in. I logged on and walked around to her office, heavy-footed. She greeted me brightly, lips painted a pillarbox red, which matched her blouse. Her hair was pulled away from her face in a tight bun and she looked like a glamorous nineties Virgin air hostess.

'How's Chris?' I asked.

'He's recovering, still in the hospital, but Zoe flew back last night. He's been on the phone already this morning, so he must be feeling better.' She smiled, we both knew what a workaholic he was.

'That's great news.'

'If it wasn't for you, Ria, I dread to think what would have happened.'

I waved her away, all I did was call for an ambulance.

'That's what makes this so difficult. You leaving us, I mean.' She leaned back in her chair, sighing. It wasn't as if I'd had a choice, but there was little point bringing it up.

'It's fine, it's probably for the best,' I replied, giving her an out. No need to make it more difficult than it had to be. Chris had made his decision and even if he changed his mind, I couldn't work with Amanda any longer.

'Well, we just need to run through your exit interview, which won't take long. I see Chris has given you six months' salary.'

I raised my eyebrows, it had originally been three, but I didn't question it. The extra money would be a massive help.

Fiona ran through the prepared sheet, writing down my responses, which were measured and professional. I would need a reference at some point, so I avoided any mudslinging. When finished, I signed it and she slipped the document into a powder-blue file which had my name, employee number and address on a printed label stuck on the top. Beneath my file, another stuck out at an angle, I was only able to see three letters of the last name: owd. My eyes widened.

'I tried the counselling,' I blurted out, thinking on my feet, 'it was helpful.'

'That's great, Ria, by telephone or in person?'

'Telephone at the moment, I've got another appointment booked next week,' I lied, clearing my throat. 'But, um, I've lost my leaflet, I don't suppose you have another one, do you?'

I watched as she rummaged in her tray, scowling as she couldn't find what she was looking for.

'Bear with me, I think they are in the cabinet.' Pushing her chair back, she turned her back, opening the drawer of the tall metal filing cabinet in the corner of her office, still with its lock dangling off.

Without taking my eyes off Fiona, I nudged my file an inch and read the name on the one below. Anna Dowd, address, 67 The Rise. Committing it to memory, I glanced back as Fiona turned around, handing me another of the yellow leaflet.

'Thank you,' I said, standing.

'I wish you all the best, Ria. You're here until Friday, yes?'

I nodded.

'Great. Well, have a lovely day.'

'I will, you too, and pass my best to Chris,' I said before making my escape.

Instead of going back to my desk, I went straight to Karen's, reciting the address over and over in my head to ensure I remembered it. I found her deep in concentration, her nose practically pressed against the screen of her monitor, glaring at a spreadsheet. She held up a finger as I approached, signalling me to wait before she wrote something down.

'Sorry, I didn't want to have to count that again,' she said a few seconds later, rolling her eyes and chuckling.

'Did you find out if there was another Dowd?' I whispered, leaning closer over the partition.

'There's not, just the one.'

'Anna,' I confirmed and she nodded.

'Thanks, Karen, I owe you one,' I said, reaching over to squeeze her shoulder.

'Mine's a Prosecco,' she called after me as I left, sniggering to herself.

So Amanda was really Anna. What was with the name change? Was she running from something, or somebody?

'There you are. You ready to go over the Men's Health Awareness Month campaign for Ballers?' Aaron stood by my desk, his hands on his hips, frowning at me.

'Yes. I've been with Fiona,' I said, my hackles rising. I didn't have to explain my whereabouts to him. He wasn't the boss. A few more days and I'd be out of there. Aaron's mood swings would be a thing of the past.

'I'll get Grace and we'll see you in the meeting room,' he said stiffly, marching away.

'Twat,' I muttered under my breath before gathering my notepad. I hadn't even had time to make a cup of tea.

Grace was already waiting when I entered, chewing the end of her biro. 'Hiya,' she said, smiling.

'What's up with him today?' I asked, referring to Aaron, who was yet to join us.

'No idea, he's got a cob on about something though.'

I pulled out a chair before Aaron came in, offering no pleasantries and launching into the campaign.

'We could suggest every pair of boxers comes with a leaflet,' Grace paused, 'checking your testicles.' Her face reddened, but I nodded.

'Great idea, perhaps have some specific colour choices only available for a short period with a percentage going to a testicular cancer charity?' I chipped in.

'All good ideas, but we may be too late on that front. I'll suggest them, but for now let's get the copy down,' Aaron said brusquely.

We put our heads together, coming up with a few paragraphs.

'That photo shoot for High Point is booked in for tomorrow,' I reminded Aaron.

'Thanks, I'll pop along, although the photographer Dave is pretty good, he's had the brief.'

Amanda's platinum blonde hair caught my eye as she strode past the meeting room. My back stiffened as she paused, not taking her eyes off Aaron until he sensed someone was looking at him and glanced up. Amanda smiled darkly, looking daggers through the glass, then she gave him the finger and walked on.

34

'Fuck's sake,' he muttered as Grace burst into laughter.

'She's such a lady.'

'Lover's tiff?' I added, sniggering, surprised Amanda hadn't even glanced in my direction. It was like I didn't exist. Perhaps Fiona had warned her to stay away.

'It's none of your business. Now can we please get back to it.'

At lunchtime, Jayden popped his head around the door to the meeting room. 'King's Head?' he said by way of a question.

'Yeah, I could do with a pint,' Aaron scowled, closing his note-book and jumping up.

Jayden nodded towards me and Grace and we looked at each other, smiling, before getting to our feet.

Jayden bought a round, carrying it to the table on a tray. It was only the four of us. Cassie had some shopping to do and Rav was stuck on a conference call. Amanda had gone to the hospital to visit Chris and I had to admit I was relieved the atmosphere wouldn't be frosty. Although Aaron more than made up for Amanda's absence, grumbling about his steak sandwich, which didn't have enough mustard. Grace and I both opted for a packet of crisps, knowing the lunchtime menu was hit-and-miss.

The conversation mostly revolved around Chris until Jayden slapped Aaron on the back, almost causing him to choke.

'All's not well in paradise then, mate?' he chuckled.

'You could say that. She's bloody mental.'

'I did warn you all,' I said, unable to help myself.

'She's just misunderstood,' Grace piped up.

'*You're* just too nice!' I countered.

'Who's up for the fireworks on Friday anyway,' Aaron said, looking at each of us in turn.

We shrugged and nodded. The local rugby club put on a fantastic display, although you could watch it perfectly well from the window at the flat.

It's not your flat any more, my inner voice reminded me.

'I'm in, it can be my last hurrah,' I said, grimly.

'I still can't believe you're leaving. You'll keep in touch though, right?' Grace said.

'Of course she will,' Jayden replied before I could open my mouth, putting his arm around me and kissing the side of my head. Grace's eyes bulged with the public display of affection and my stomach swirled.

'You two back on again then?' Aaron said, pushing his plate aside.

'Guess so,' I said, forcing a smile.

'You don't sound too happy about it,' Jayden whispered in my ear as the others got up to leave. Lunchtime was over and we trundled back to the office.

'It's not that, I'm just... I don't know, nervous, I guess.'

'I won't hurt you. I promise.' He sounded genuine, but I hadn't expected him to sleep with the first attractive girl who threw herself at him either. The fact it was Amanda made it sting that much more.

* * *

After work, I told Jayden I wanted to get some shopping and would meet him back at his.

'I'm going to get a session in at the gym then,' he said brightly, giving me a kiss before we parted ways.

I called up The Rise on the map on my phone; it was around fifteen minutes' walk away from the office. Wrapped in my thick coat, I made my way through town, along with commuters who seemed to pour from every building to start their journey home. The sky had turned a fiery red as the sun sank beneath the high-rises making the air temperature plummet.

All the way there, I questioned what I was doing. Was I really going to turn up at Amanda's, or rather Anna's, home and bluff my way in? What was I hoping to achieve? *Answers*, the small voice in my head responded as a bus roared past making me jump.

When I got to the narrow road with cars parked either side, half on the kerb, I scanned the numbers until I found 67. The house was glowing in the late-afternoon dusk. All the lights downstairs were on, which meant someone was in there. I just prayed it wasn't Amanda.

I tapped at the door before realising I hadn't come up with anything to say. I'd have to wing it.

'Hello?' a slight woman answered, dark greasy hair piled up on top of her head and secured with a scrunchie. She wore faded black leggings and a long jumper with fluffy slippers on her feet. A yappy chihuahua at her heels growled through the gap at me.

'Hi, I'm sorry to bother you, I'm Stacy. A friend of... Anna's.' My neck flushed and I hoped the woman wouldn't notice.

'Oh,' she said, her eyes glazing over, 'she doesn't live here any more.'

I frowned as though it was news to me. 'I've been travelling, just got back from Europe. Sorry, I didn't realise. I don't suppose Mandy is in, is she?'

The woman in front of me seemed to shrink before my eyes.

'You better come in,' she said, pulling the door open. 'Be nice, Fred,' she instructed the dog as I smiled politely and stepped inside.

Panic rose in my chest. Was Mandy inside? What on earth was I going to say to her?

Ask her what her problem is!

'Would you like a drink?' She smiled for the first time and I noticed a gap between her two front teeth.

'No, I'm fine thank you. I just thought I'd stop by and say hello,' I said, awkward under the weight of my lie. When Mandy took one look at me, her mother would know straight away she had no idea who I was. Unless, of course, she'd been going along with Amanda's hate campaign. Either way, I wouldn't be a welcomed visitor.

The woman led me through to the dining room, where a large, polished pine table took up almost all the space. She slid effortlessly into a chair, her make-up-free face so drawn, her skin stretched over her cheekbones. There was barely any resemblance to Amanda.

I looked around the room, then at the door, expecting Mandy to come through it at any second. I tapped my foot on the carpet, legs restless.

'Who's this then?' A man barrelled through the door, startling me, wearing a Black Sabbath T-shirt and carrying a can of Tennents Super.

'This is Stacy, friend of Anna's.'

The man snorted, taking a long drink from his can before

looking me up and down. 'She doesn't have any friends!' His tone was callous and I shuddered. He had to be Chris's brother. I saw a resemblance, although he looked like he'd rolled out of bed. Chris was always well presented, yet the man standing in front of me was unshaven, his eyes sunken and skin sallow. A cigarette with towering ash was tucked in between tattooed knuckles. 'She don't live here no more,' he said.

'I've told her that! Craig, why don't you give us a minute?'

He tutted before finishing his can and eventually leaving.

'Sorry about him, we're having a bit of a tough time,' she said once we were alone, her voice low.

I waited for her to continue.

'You must not have heard.'

'Heard what?' I replied. Her eyes carried so much anguish they were hard to look at. Instantly, my mouth dried up. I bit my lip, waiting for her to speak.

'Mandy passed away in June.'

I gasped, unprepared for the bombshell. Chris had said Amanda had been having a rough time and now I knew why. Her parents looked like they'd been dragged through the mill and it all made sense.

I mentally ran through the timeline in my head. Livvy had died in May and I'd left to travel in June.

'I'm so sorry,' I said, berating myself for not responding sooner. 'What happened?'

'She hung herself.' Her words spat into the air, shifting the atmosphere instantly.

My insides hollowed, belly churning. Had Mandy hung herself after spiking Livvy's drink? I was sure whoever had done it hadn't intended to kill her. The guilt of trying to live with causing someone's death unintentionally would have been immense.

'I'm guessing you knew her?' the woman asked.

'Only through Anna,' I stumbled, trying to think on my feet.

'It hit Anna hard, she's found it hard to deal with. We all have.'

'I can imagine,' I said, although I couldn't. It was every parent's worst nightmare to lose a child. She reached for a packet of cigarettes, pulling one out and lighting it. Swirls of smoke filled the air and my throat constricted, stomach rolling. The smell was foul.

'May I use your bathroom please?'

She looked me up and down, eventually nodding. 'It's up the stairs, second on the right.'

Hurrying out of the room, I rushed upstairs, bile rising rapidly. I managed to reach the bathroom and shut the door before heaving into the toilet, the remnants of partly digested salt and vinegar crisps splashing into the bowl.

'What are you doing?' I whispered to myself in the mirror, before wiping my mouth and washing my hands. I had no business intruding on this family's grief. It was time to leave.

Exiting the bathroom, I noticed the door next to it was open, a wooden M stuck on it. Peering inside, I saw a girl's bedroom, which looked to be untouched. A pang hit my side. It was like Livvy's. Frozen in time, as though waiting for its occupant to return.

Forgetting my decision to politely make my excuses and leave, I entered the room, eyes immediately locking onto photos stuck on the pine wardrobe. Clustered together, I instantly recognised Livvy's smiling face. Some of the photos were printed from her Instagram page, some were taken of her, although she never seemed to be looking at the camera. A few I recognised as being snapped inside the Cardinal Media office.

'What are you doing in here?' came a stony voice from the doorway. Mandy's Mum had her arms crossed, a face like thunder.

'I'm sorry, I was passing and saw the photos,' I replied weakly, trying to defend the undefendable.

'I'd like you to leave.'

'I'm so sorry for your loss,' I said, squeezing past her and hurrying down the stairs.

Fred barked as I opened the front door, jogging into the street.

35

LIVVY – BEFORE

It's getting ridiculous now. She's literally everywhere I turn, usually with some sort of excuse. I popped into Sainsbury's after work at Mum's request, to grab something for dinner, and there she was skulking at the end of the aisle with an empty shopping basket, eyes trained on me. I've seen her outside my house, at the coffee shop, even around town at the weekend.

I can't even bloody go to the toilet at work without her manifesting, although I have no idea how she knows where I am. She can't even see my desk from where she sits, yet she always manages to be in the kitchen at the same time as me, trying to make conversation. What music do I like, what movies? How do I do my hair, where do I buy my clothes? I've tried to be nice, but whenever I am, she takes it as encouragement.

The constant feeling of being watched is getting under my skin. She's pushing me to my limit and I can't handle the lack of space. I'm worried I'm eventually going to lose it and tell her to fuck off. I'm not her friend, although she is clinging on to me like a life raft, always trying to make plans. She just won't get the hint!

I should tell Fiona, but what on earth do I say? I'm being

stalked. That the hairs on the back of my neck are constantly standing to attention and I'm struggling to focus on anything when she's around. It'll make me sound weak and juvenile and I can't have that.

She's made my world so small, I hate going anywhere, it's easier to sit at home in my room with the curtains drawn. It's the only time I'm ever free.

36

My body fizzed as I hurried towards home. I'd finally uncovered what had happened to Livvy. Mandy had obviously been stalking her and spiked her drink that night. She'd killed herself after being consumed by guilt. I knew she was there, the photos Cassie had taken proved it. What was she? A friend? Or did she have a crush on Livvy and was hoping for more?

Casting my mind back, I had no recollection of Mandy at all, not even her being on the periphery when we were out. I hadn't noticed her loitering in the background, watching Livvy's every move, if those photos on her wardrobe were anything to go by.

Mandy's suicide had to be why Amanda was unhinged, although it didn't explain why I was the target of such a hate campaign. I'd been asking questions about the circumstances of Livvy's death before I'd gone to Europe, but not since I'd returned. Everyone knew I didn't believe she'd taken the ketamine of her own accord, but they'd moved on, life kept going whether you were standing still or not. So it was hardly as if I was causing trouble now, pushing to uncover what really happened.

The case was closed, Livvy's death classed as accidental. Even learning the truth, I couldn't do anything about it and I didn't intend to drag her parents back through the heartache of another inquest. Not that I could convince them even if I wanted to. But I knew, and they agreed with me at the time, Livvy hadn't consciously taken drugs that night. The person responsible would never pay for what they did and the injustice of it scorched a hole right through me.

My phone beeped, interrupting my vent. A text from Mum.

I'm so sorry, Ria, please talk to me, I want to start again.

I stared at the message, imagining Mum typing it, drowning her sorrows in a glass of Bordeaux. Tarek had gone she'd said, but had she kicked him out or had he left of his own accord? We'd rowed before, many times, but she'd never apologised repeatedly, not like she'd meant it. Usually a month or two would pass and she'd drop me a line like nothing had happened. We'd carry on as before, brushing the most recent argument under the carpet, until the next time we disagreed on something, but what had happened with Tarek was something I wasn't sure I could get over and I certainly couldn't deal with it now.

I put my phone back in my pocket and lowered my face as the wind battered it, cheeks stinging like I'd been slapped. Fingers numb, I shoved my hands up into my sleeves, looking forward to curling up on the sofa with Jayden, his arms around me. At least I had some support. Knowing I could lean on him with all the chaos going on around me was comforting, even if it might not be forever.

When I got back, it was nearing half past six and I had to wait outside, realising I had no way to get in and Jayden wasn't answering the door. Less than five minutes later, his MG rolled around the corner.

'Perfect timing,' I said with a grin as he climbed out and up the steps, gym bag slung over his shoulder.

'I must get you a key cut,' he said with a shake of the head. 'Have you been waiting long?'

'No, I just got back.'

He looked down at my empty hands, rattling his keys. 'Didn't buy anything then?'

'There was nothing I fancied,' I replied, unable to meet his eye. Shit, I'd forgotten I'd told him I was going shopping.

'Ah well, I'm sure I've got something in the freezer.' He smelled freshly showered, a waft of lime hit me as he moved past, rosy cheeks glinting in the security light at the front door.

'Good workout?' I asked as he let us into the maisonette.

'Not bad, I'll ache tomorrow.'

'Doesn't count if you don't.'

We'd been inside for around fifteen minutes when there was a banging on the door. I was on the sofa, scrolling through my phone, trying to find information on Mandy Dowd, but other than a tiny paragraph in the local paper about her suicide, there wasn't much else. Jayden was pulling his sweaty gym clothes from his bag and pushing them into the washing machine, both of us freezing as the banging started. We exchanged an anxious glance before he went to see who was knocking so fiercely.

Seconds later, Amanda whirled in, her eyes wild, Jayden rushing behind her.

'You!' she shouted, pointing at me from the doorway, where she'd halted for a second before coming closer, arm outstretched. Her neck was mottled and she looked like a crazed animal about to pounce.

I stood instinctively, fight or flight mode kicking in.

'She just barged in,' Jayden said to me, coming past her and stopping in between us, sensing danger.

'How dare you go to my mother's house, how fucking dare you. Stacy is your name today, is it? I'm not stupid, Ria.'

Jayden looked from Amanda back to me, his brow furrowed, no idea what she was talking about.

The anger bubbled up and unable to contain it a second longer, I erupted.

'Oh, you want to talk about names, do you? Who's Anna then? Why are you calling yourself Amanda?'

'Who's Anna?' Jayden interrupted, perplexed but we both ignored him.

'Stay out of my business,' she screamed, teeth bared.

'Stay out of mine, you crazy bitch,' I shot back, leaning forwards onto the balls of my feet. I wasn't going to back away from this fight.

Amanda seemed to gather herself, her body retreating back into a composed stance. Lip morphing into a cruel smile, her eyes glistened with intent. 'I'd be careful where you sit.' She pointed at the sofa where I'd been moments before, raising an eyebrow. 'He fucked me right there.'

My mouth dropped open.

'And there,' pointing to the breakfast bar. 'And there,' Amanda gestured to the rug. 'In fact, in every room.' She twirled her finger around, all the time her eyes never leaving mine.

I closed my mouth, then opened it again to speak, but nothing came out. Her words were like a punch in the gut.

'Amanda,' Jayden snapped, but she eyed him pitifully and giggled.

'Told you it was a one-time thing, did he?'

All of the anger I'd held moments before leaked out of me as I looked at Jayden questioningly.

He shook his head, palms pressed together in a praying motion, fingertips touching his chin.

My throat closed up, it was another betrayal.

'He bangs like a barn door in the wind that one.' Amanda looked him up and down, her gaze lingering before directing her attention back to me, 'I'll miss that, I guess.'

'Get out,' Jayden hissed, glaring at her.

'Do yourself a favour, Ria, stop digging. You know what they say about curiosity and the cat.' She pursed her lips, gave me a wink and left before I could utter a word.

The silence was deafening, but adrenaline pumped around my body, my thudding heart loud in my ribcage.

'Ria,' Jayden said.

I looked at him, still frozen in the same spot. Shoulders rounded, head bowed, he looked like the air had been let out of him. It was obvious Amanda's words had been true.

'You've been sleeping with her all this time?' I asked, my voice flat, devoid of emotion. I had nothing left to give. That time in the flat hadn't been the first night they'd spent together, it had been one of many.

'No, not since we...' his voice trailed off. Not since we'd slept together was what he meant, but it didn't matter.

Standing straight, I collected the bin bags we'd brought from the flat whilst still maintaining what little dignity I had left.

'Ria, don't. Where will you go?'

'Anywhere but here,' I snapped. I had no car, no means of transport and no one to stay with. I could hardly go back to the flat either. Closing my eyes, I raised my face to the ceiling, counting to ten and trying to summon a solution. I'd take my suitcase and one bin bag. Everything else could stay here until I sorted something out.

Dropping all of the bags except for one, playing Russian Roulette if it had any underwear or warm clothes in, I gathered Livvy's notebook and my phone in one hand and stalked to the door.

'Goodbye, Jayden,' I said, not answering when he called out my name as I slammed it shut behind me.

37

The wind blustered outside and I zipped up my coat, walking with no real idea where I was going, dragging the suitcase behind me, the bin bag precariously balanced on top. Remnants of Halloween pumpkins had been kicked around the pavement, their orange guts spilling out across the concrete replicating my insides. I could see if there was a hotel available nearby, but being so close to Gatwick Airport they were all expensive. It would mean calling Mum to ask her to transfer me some money and I couldn't face a conversation with her right now.

Instead, I stopped beneath a streetlamp and typed out a text, keeping everything crossed the person receiving it would take pity on me. Otherwise, there was a chance I could be wandering around in the dark all night. My stomach growled, reminding me I still hadn't eaten. Not after throwing up my lunch of crisps at Amanda's Mum's house. I was cold, hungry and the number of friends I could rely on was diminishing. There was no way I could call Cassie, she was too friendly with the enemy, and Grace still lived at home with her parents.

Tears trickled down my face, blasted by the wind, which made my nose run. Once again, I berated myself for ever coming back. I could be watching the moon skip off the waves on La Reserve, warm in a cardigan with sand in between my toes. Instead, I was squelching through leaves on concrete, freezing in the chilly British weather.

Someone in one of the neighbouring roads let off a firework, the screech and loud pop as it launched into the sky making me jump. They were too early, kids messing about. I usually loved fireworks, but I'd be missing the display this year.

A text came through as I paused to reposition the bin bag and swapped arms with the suitcase. Not so much heavy but both together were cumbersome and difficult to carry.

Come now, see you soon. X

Relief flooded through me. At least now I had a direction to go in.

* * *

Lynn answered the door half an hour later, when I finally found the right bus stop to catch a bus into Horley. It began to rain as I got off, so I arrived on her doorstep looking like a drowned rat.

'Oh, poppet,' she said, taking in the sorry sight of me, 'come in.'

It wasn't long before I was at the table, a cup of tea in hand as Lynn dished up a bowl of hot stew and dumplings.

'The perfect winter fuel,' she said, smiling as she sat opposite me.

'Thank you. No Bill tonight?'

'He's gone out to play darts, got back in touch with his friends. It'll be good for him.'

'That's great,' I said, blowing the steam off the bowl and spooning stew into my mouth, my stomach groaning in pleasure.

'I've left some in the slow cooker for him, he can have it when he gets home. So, tell me what happened?' Lynn asked and I told her about my fight with Jayden, Chris's heart attack and the ongoing feud with Amanda. She listened intently, taking it all in.

'Gosh, I hope Chris is okay,' she said.

'I think he will be, it was a minor one, but they are investigating the cause.'

'Sounds like you've had quite an eventful couple of days!'

I nodded, carrying on demolishing the bowl of stew.

'I thought the girl that came here was Amanda, but I now believe it was Mandy, Amanda's sister.' I couldn't get used to calling her Anna, so Amanda would have to do.

'Was?' Lynn picked up on my use of past tense.

'She killed herself, not long after Livvy died.'

Lynn's eyes widened. 'Oh my goodness. That's awful.' Her hand fluttered to her chest.

'I think she may have been the one to spike her drink.' I paused as Lynn laid down her spoon and stared at me. 'I got her ring back though,' I carried on, flattening my hand on the table to show the Pandora ring I'd found in Amanda's room. I hadn't taken it off since.

Lynn maintained her stoic expression, as though she was carefully considering her words. I half expected outrage, or at least a rush of anger at the injustice of Mandy's suicide, the fact we wouldn't be able to push the police to reopen the case. Instead she reached over and rested her hand upon mine, her eyes searching for understanding. 'Ria, we cannot change the past. We know the truth, we know Livvy didn't take those drugs willingly. That's the most important thing.'

'But they should pay,' I said, the injustice reigniting inside of me, the unfairness of it all rearing up again.

'They won't. The case is closed. Let's not drag it up again, it's too painful.' She sighed, picking her spoon up.

I wasn't sure how to respond. The last time I'd got in a state about it, things had got heated and Lynn had asked me to leave.

'Bill and I, we're starting to breathe again, it's been six months,' she said, her eyes mournful.

I swallowed the disappointment down. The last thing I wanted to do was hurt either of them more than they were already.

'You can stay as long as you need to. The guest room has clean sheets.' Lynn smiled, changing the subject.

'Thank you, I really appreciate it, but I think I've decided I'm going to leave on Saturday.' The words were out of my mouth before the decision was fully formed in my head. However, as soon as I uttered them, a sense of calm weaved its way over me. It was the right thing to do. It was time.

Lynn drew me a bath when Bill got home, after I'd been pulled into another of his bear hugs. I sank beneath the bubbles and, ignoring the multiple texts from Jayden begging forgiveness, looked at flight times back to Nice. There was an 08:40 EasyJet flight from Gatwick, cheap at £35, and I booked it without hesitating. I had another three bin liners of stuff at Jayden's, taken from the flat, but I was sure Lynn and Bill would let me store it in their garage if I needed to.

The prospect of a new start helped ease the ache in my chest at Jayden's lie. We were never going to be anything. Let him have Amanda, especially if Aaron was done with her too. They could all have her. I was happy to disappear, put my life at Cardinal Media behind me and try to forge a relationship with my mother. She wasn't perfect and neither was I but we only had each other and that had to be worth salvaging. The quest for justice for Livvy would have to be abandoned. I couldn't do it alone and the thought of hurting Lynn and Bill was impossible to bear.

My thoughts strayed to Chris as I curled up in the warm
bedroom. Clean cotton sheets which smelled of fabric softener
pulled up to my chin as I listened to Lynn and Bill move around
downstairs. It would be strange to leave without saying goodbye or
thanking him for the gift he'd given me. Money that would help me
get on my feet in France. Perhaps I'd forge a new career, get a place
of my own. The possibilities were endless. Two more days left to get
through and then I could put it all behind me.

I fell asleep comforted by the familiar smell of Livvy's home,
remembering the nights I'd spent giggling and swapping secrets
like schoolkids in her bedroom next door. Why hadn't she told me
about Mandy? I could have helped protect her. It was a bitter pill to
swallow. No, I couldn't change the past, but I now thought I knew
what had happened.

38

LIVVY – BEFORE

I've done it. I sat in with Fiona for almost an hour today and it all came tumbling out. Even when I was in the office, she walked past three times, looking in at us through the glass. Last week in the library, I told her in no uncertain terms that enough was enough, she had to stop following me. It was creeping me out and if she was trying to make friends, she was going about it in the worst possible way.

I'd decided to hand my notice in. I can't sleep, I can't eat. The only place I am truly alone is at home and even then I've seen her outside the house at times. I can't tell Mum, she'll only worry and the others laugh it off. They call her a freak and I'm starting to think they are right. I can't work at Cardinal any more and I told Fiona it's her or me. I'm constantly on edge, looking over my shoulder because most of the time she's there. Rav calls her my shadow and even Aaron has noticed too. He told her to back off the last time we were at the pub, which was kind of chivalrous.

Even then, she followed me to the toilets and asked if I was free at the weekend. I've tried to be nice, but it's wearing me down. I hadn't realised how much until it came spilling out. Fiona was kind, supplying me with tissues for the pent-up tears I'd been holding in for weeks now. She refused to accept my resignation, she said she'd sort it, although I don't see how, and that she was going to speak to Chris because it was unacceptable behaviour. Now I'm panicking they are going to sack her and she'll be provoked into doing something crazy. What if she goes all *Fatal Attraction* on me?

I mean, she must be nuts, trailing around behind me everywhere I go, not taking no for an answer. I get the impression she's desperate for a friend and I feel bad, but she's practically stalking me. The whole situation has shaken me up, and I feel so guilty, like I've caused this. I was only trying to be nice. I wish I'd never spoken to her in the toilets on her first day. If only I could turn back time.

39

Lynn served scrambled eggs for breakfast. She twirled around the kitchen like a woman possessed, humming to herself as Bill read the morning paper.

'Bill, would you mind if I left a couple of bags here when I go to Nice? In your garage maybe?' I asked.

'Sure, no problem,' he said, straightening the paper with a flick of the wrist.

'Thanks. Lynn, this is great,' I said, shovelling another mouthful of eggs into my mouth, my appetite having returned with a bang.

'It's lovely having another person to cook for,' she beamed, wielding a spatula. 'Oh and here's a key for the house, while you're here,' she said, picking a single key off the side and bringing it over to me.

'Thanks,' I said, clearing my plate.

Despite her cheerfulness, my mood clouded over as soon as I stepped out into the drizzle to wait for the bus. I was not looking forward to going back to work. Not only was I apprehensive about seeing Amanda, I didn't much want to see Jayden either, but I knew I'd have to sort getting my stuff back.

Two days, just two days. I repeated the mantra to myself in the
queue for the bus, moving from one foot to the other to keep warm.

As the queue grew, I huddled under the shelter and pulled out
my phone. Deleting the apologetic messages from Jayden that had
carried on overnight, not bothering to respond to any of them.
Biting the bullet, I clicked on Mum's mobile number. It rang three
times before she answered, her voice groggy with sleep.

'Ria?'

'Mum, I'm coming home.'

Mum was choked with emotion when I told her I'd booked a
ticket to return to Nice on Saturday. Although it technically wasn't
my home, it was the closest thing I had to one now. She was full
of ideas, of all the things we'd do, where I could potentially get a
job and finally settle. I let her get carried away, not wanting to
spoil her joviality. Time would tell if we could build a life
together.

'And Tarek has definitely gone?' I had to ask.

'Yes, he picked his things up yesterday.'

'Wow, that was quick,' I said.

'I threatened to burn them otherwise,' she replied nonchalantly.
I stifled a laugh.

'I better go, Mum, the bus has turned up.'

We said our goodbyes and I hopped on the number 20, which
was running ten minutes late. It was hit-or-miss whether I'd get to
work by nine, but what were they going to do? Fire me?

* * *

Jayden pounced on me almost as soon as I reached my desk. I'd
barely put my bag down and switched on my computer before he
was whispering over the partition.

'I'm so sorry, Amanda means nothing to me,' he said.

I snorted at his cliché. 'Yet you so enjoy screwing her,' I smirked, voice dripping with sarcasm.

He opened his mouth to reply, but I got in first.

'Forget it, Jayden. I'm leaving. In two days, I'm on a plane out of here and this time I won't be back.'

Realising he wasn't going to get anywhere, he went back to his desk with his tail firmly between his legs.

The office was eerily silent and for a second I thought there'd been a bank holiday I'd forgotten. Amanda was nowhere to be seen, Aaron and Cassie too. Without Chris pacing in his office, or typing loudly on his keyboard, the section of desks I sat at were quiet. It was nice to get on with my work without the drama of the past few days. I spent the first hour responding to emails and sending Grace information for the projects she would be working on with Aaron moving forward.

I bumped into her in the kitchen when I decided it was time for a cup of tea. She was heating up a croissant in the microwave.

'You haven't seen Aaron, have you?' she asked.

I shook my head.

'I mean, don't get me wrong, I've got loads to be getting on with, but I thought the whole point was sorting out the handover while you're still here,' she continued.

'He's probably gone to the photo shoot for High Point.' I suggested, dunking my tea bag.

'Maybe,' she shrugged. 'I'll pop by later, but thanks for the emails.'

'No worries.'

When I got back to my desk, Fiona was waiting for me, her face grave.

'Chris has asked if you'll pop to the hospital at two when visiting hours start.'

I frowned. 'Why?'

'He wants to talk to you about something.' It all sounded cloak-and-dagger.

'Is he okay?' My pulse rising, hoping Fiona wasn't going to tell me Chris was on his deathbed, although why he'd want to see me in that scenario, I couldn't fathom.

'He's fine, recovering well actually.' She gave a small smile before making her excuses. Fiona seemed a little off, her usual cheerful demeanour absent, although I put it down to the stress of the CEO not being around. Sure she was taking on more to carry the load.

It wasn't until I was heading out of the door to catch the bus to the hospital that Jayden approached me again.

'Have you seen Aaron today?' he asked.

'No,' I said, turning to leave.

'No client meetings, or anything?' he pressed on.

'He could be at the High Point photo shoot. Either that, or I presume he's out with Cassie or Amanda.' Sometimes last-minute client engagements were called for, or a face-to-face meeting to show design boards or new concepts. Not everything could be done virtually.

'Cassie's ill, stomach bug apparently, but no one has heard from Aaron or Amanda. Their phones are switched off.' He chewed at his lip, eyebrows knitted together.

'Well, maybe they made up and decided to spend the day shagging, I don't know,' I said, exasperated. 'Look, I've got to go, but I need to talk to you later about picking my things up.'

Without waiting for an answer, I hurried out into the drizzle, irritated but intrigued as to why Chris had summoned me to his sick bed.

My hair was a mop of frizz by the time I got to the hospital and I tied it up, wiping the mascara smudges from beneath my eyes, trying to ensure I was presentable. A homely nurse directed me to the Elm ward where Chris had been moved to. The hospital was busy as visiting hours had started and people in their soggy coats trudged the corridors, shoes squeaking on the floor.

Chris's wife, Zoe, a stunning woman originally from Sri Lanka, sat by his bed, talking animatedly. Chris lifted his hand in a wave as I approached and I was suddenly aware I'd brought nothing along. I had no flowers or grapes to offer and my cheeks flushed at my empty hands.

'Hi, Ria, thanks for coming,' he gestured to Zoe, 'this is my wife, Zoe.'

'Pleased to meet you.' She was as pretty in real life as she was in her wedding photo.

'Thank you for acting so quickly when you found Chris, I understand you saved his life.'

My face turned crimson under her focus and I mumbled a 'no problem', wringing my hands as I stood awkwardly by Chris's bed.

'How are you?'

'On the mend,' he replied.

'He's been taking on too much. That brother of his is a leech,' Zoe bristled.

'Zoe, would you get me a drink, love?' Chris asked, obvious he wanted an excuse for her to leave.

She nodded, standing and brushing down her trousers. 'I'm going to get a coffee, would you like one?' directing her question at me.

'No thank you.' I smiled politely and watched as she kissed Chris's forehead before leaving the ward. I slid into the unoccupied seat, glad of its warmth. 'She's not happy,' I said.

'No, she's not.' Chris sighed, before leaning over and grasping my hand in his, palms clammy. 'Thank you again.'

'Don't be silly,' I said, resisting the urge to pull my hand away. It would take forever for my complexion to return to a normal colour.

'I'm sorry to call you here, but it's a bit delicate.' His eyes were dark and serious as he released his grip and I noticed how drawn he was.

'Okay.'

'Have you seen Amanda?'

'Not today,' I replied, unable to maintain eye contact. Talking to Chris about Amanda, knowing he was her uncle made me squirm.

'She's not turned up at work, her mum has been trying to reach her all day.' He sighed, gazing out towards the window speckled with rain.

'I saw her briefly last night, I'm sure she's fine. Aaron hasn't come in either, I think they have something going on, so they are probably at his or they've gone to the High Point photo shoot together.' I placated. I had no doubt they were holed up somewhere having a whale of a time. Amanda could look after herself, she certainly wasn't the victim everyone thought she was.

'We can't reach him either, I'm worried.'

I shifted in my seat. Why was Chris so concerned about his adult niece? He had more important things to concentrate on, like getting better.

'Have you not seen her at the flat?' he pressed.

'I've moved out,' I snapped, a little irritated. He'd called me all the way to the hospital for an inquisition. Couldn't Fiona have passed on a message? I rubbed my forehead, forcing a smile. 'Chris, please don't worry. I'm sure she's fine. You need to focus on getting better.'

'My brother is an alcoholic,' Chris went on, ignoring my attempts at reassurance, seeming to shrink beneath his T-shirt, the khaki sleeves too big for his frame. 'We've had a death in the family, and Amanda, well, she's taken it badly, she's sent her mum some weird texts.'

I almost scoffed at that. Chris painting Amanda like some poor, wounded little bird. She'd never outwardly appeared to be struggling at all. In fact, I didn't know anyone who had their shit together as well as she did.

'I know about Mandy,' I said, my voice low, respectful.

Chris blinked, staring at me before he spoke again.

'Then you know Amanda is unstable.'

40

Amanda was unstable? It was hardly news to me. I fought the urge to laugh, biting my lip to stop myself from saying 'no shit, Sherlock'.

'Her real name is Anna, isn't it?'

'How do you know that?' Chris's face darkened, but after a short pause he softened. 'When Mandy, her sister, committed suicide, Anna lost it for a while. She was all over the place and I feared she was going to self-destruct, like her father has. She spent some time living with her aunt in Kent, but it didn't change anything. My brother begged me to help, so I employed her, tried her get her back on track.'

I nodded, waiting for him to continue.

'She's a smart girl and she's proven herself more than capable, but, I don't know, I worry about her mental health. I'm sorry, Ria, I shouldn't be putting this on you. You have enough going on.'

'It's fine. I'm going back to France for a while, back to my Mum's,' I said.

Chris grimaced, guilt seeping from his every pore. He continued, 'Anna started calling herself Amanda. A combination of hers and her sister's name. I think she's looking at changing it legally.

She dyed her hair, changed her clothes. It's like she has a new persona, shedding the skin of Anna and taking on a new personality entirely.'

'Grief does strange things to you,' I said, talking from experience although Anna's reaction was something else. 'Mandy had a thing for Livvy, didn't she?' I asked, treading carefully. Perhaps what was going on with Amanda had contributed to his heart attack. I didn't want to cause him any more distress, but I had questions I needed answers to.

'She was a timid teenager, insecure, completely different to her sister. I took her on after she completed a bookkeeping course. Just an entry-level role in payroll, but she latched onto Livvy almost straight away.' He sighed, pausing for a second to scratch at his beard. 'It wasn't the first time. She'd formed an unhealthy attachment to another student at college that I had to sort out. My brother and his wife were going through a rough patch, he'd lost his job and the girls were struggling. I was the only stability they had.'

'Sounds like they are lucky to have you,' I said.

'I had no idea what was going on with Mandy until Aaron brought it to my attention, then Livvy went to Fiona to complain and I had to intervene. I tried to speak to Mandy about it, but she refused, handing her notice in then and there. It caused a bit of a rift, but from what Livvy had told Fiona, Mandy was following her all the time, wouldn't leave her alone, so I couldn't ignore it.'

'Did you know she was there the night Livvy died?' I asked softly, aware he'd been at the club long enough to buy a round before he'd left us to party.

'No,' he jerked his head back, 'are you sure?' I nodded.

'She's in one of Cassie's photographs.' Chris stared incredulously before releasing a grave sigh.

'I didn't see her at all, otherwise I would have taken her home with me.'

'Do you think she could have given Livvy the ketamine?'

Chris's eyes bulged and he coughed. 'Mandy? God no, she didn't do anything like that, she was like a little mouse. That's ridiculous, Ria.'

I sat back, shocked at how adamant Chris was that Mandy wasn't the culprit.

'It's awful what Mandy did to herself, which is another reason I'm so concerned about Amanda. My brother can't take another tragedy, it'll break him. It'll break us all.'

'Please don't worry, she'll turn up. I'll make some calls, see if we can't track her down.' I reached for his hand and watched his lids dampen. The weight of the world upon his shoulders.

'Thank you, I can't tell you how much I appreciate it.'

As I stood to leave, Zoe came back carrying a large coffee cup, the smell enticing.

'It was lovely to meet you,' I said, stepping aside so she could sit back down next to her husband, who hurriedly wiped at his eyes, trying to compose himself.

'You too, Ria.'

'Please let Fiona know if you hear anything,' Chris said and I nodded, giving a small wave goodbye and leaving the ward. The aroma of disinfectant had gone to my head and I was desperate for some fresh air, despite the rain.

Did Amanda taking on the new name mean she had some kind of split personality disorder? Was she trying to live her life for her and her sister now? It was true, grief chewed you up and spat you back out again. People did strange things to get through the pain. Some turned to self-medication, others self-harm. Some slipped into despair. Amanda it seemed was hell-bent on some kind of quest to destroy me and I still didn't know why.

Outside, I messaged Cassie and Grace to ask if they'd heard from Amanda today, both responded to say they hadn't. Then I called Aaron, but it went straight to voicemail. Next I tried Dave the photographer, who told me the photo shoot had gone ahead this morning as planned, but Aaron hadn't been present. It seemed he really was AWOL. I still had keys to the flat – perhaps it would be worth a visit in case either of them were there.

I didn't have to wait long for the bus, although my anxiety grew the nearer it got to the flat. I'd never intended to return. I would have preferred to have never seen Amanda again. It was clear she was unstable. What if she attacked me? I was safe at Cardinal Media, she was hardly going to do anything there, but would I be able to protect myself in the confines of the flat?

I climbed the stairs, listening for any signs of life, but I couldn't hear anything other than the television loudly playing from the floor below. With legs like jelly, I slid the key into the lock as quietly as I could, turning it gently and waiting for the door to pop open. Inside was dark and initially relief washed over me. No one would be sitting alone in the dark, would they? Not unless Amanda was hiding, waiting for me.

Gripping the keys tightly, the only thing I had to use as self-defence, I stepped inside, unsure whether to call out and announce my presence.

Flicking the hallway switch did nothing, despite me trying it numerous times. The power was out, but how could it be if the flat below was fine?

Swallowing hard, I edged into the hallway, leaving the front door wide open partly for light but mostly so I could make a quick escape if I needed to. Reaching for my phone I put the torch on, it beeped loudly and I dropped it, scrabbling on the floor to pick it up again.

Panic bubbled beneath the surface as I read the text message from Livvy.

Just a little closer

With my pulse smashing my throat, I clicked to dial the number. How could Amanda have Livvy's phone? Had Mandy taken it from Lynn's house when she'd gone there? It rang, and I listened to hear if anything was coming from inside the flat, the telltale vibration of a phone switched to silent, but there was nothing.

Loitering in the safety of the hallway, deciding whether to press on or leave, the phone beeped again.

You're not scared are you... bestie?

I clenched my jaw, muttered, 'Fuck this,' and walked into the living room, phone outstretched so I could pan the torchlight around the room. It wasn't pitch black, the dusky sky gave some light through the curtains, but shadows lingered everywhere.

Open-mouthed, I surveyed the mess. The place had been trashed, much the same as I'd left Amanda's room on Monday. The contents of the sideboard had been swiped onto the floor, cups and plates smashed in the kitchen. Coffee table upturned and stamped on, television smashed to pieces, even some of the wallpaper had been torn off the wall.

'Jesus,' I muttered, taking in the destruction Amanda had caused. Unstable wasn't the right word, she was unhinged. 'Come out, Anna,' I called, hoping the use of her real name might prompt her to reveal herself, but again I was met with deafening silence.

I stepped precariously over the mess and towards my bedroom. It was as I'd left it. Tidier even. Untouched by the madness in the living room, the duvet even tucked under the mattress as though the room had been made up for a new occupant. Ice flooded my veins, chilling me to the core. Strangely it was more unsettling, the clinical, clean smell assaulted my nostrils. It was like every inch of me had been wiped from the room. My torch picked up hoover lines in the carpet as I scanned the floor. I'd been erased entirely.

I backed out, moving on to the bathroom. Leaving Amanda's bedroom with its closed door until last. My hands were making the torchlight shake. The voice in my head screaming at me to get out, but I had to know for sure if she was there. For Chris, if nothing else. Every cell in my body was on high alert as I gingerly entered the bathroom, unsure whether the shower curtain twitched or it was my heightened state of anxiety causing me to imagine it.

Tongue glued to the roof of my mouth, hand outstretched and quivering, I ripped the curtain back. The cubical was empty, although a rusty-coloured liquid stained the white plastic, some of it splashed up the tiles. Its residue pooling by the drain. It was as though someone had washed themselves clean of blood.

'Holy shit,' I muttered, letting out a scream seconds later when the lights flashed on and loud music battered my ears. Disorientated and fearing my heart was about to jump out of my chest, I scrambled back towards the open front door, jumping over scattered sofa cushions to make my escape. As I ran past, I registered the ear-splitting country music was coming from the DAB radio on the kitchen side.

Dolly Parton begging Jolene not to take her man ceased as soon as I hit the off switch. Was it a message from Livvy? About Jayden? I shook the ridiculous notion from my head. Ghosts didn't exist. It had been Amanda from the start, using Livvy to get to me. I had to call the police to report the blood in the shower. Amanda had hurt someone and the whole place could be a crime scene. She was crazy. It no longer mattered she was Chris's niece.

I went back into the bathroom. Eyes burning from the assaulting bright lights. The shower tray now sparkled in the fluorescent overhead light. Kneeling down to take a closer look, I let out a mirthless laugh. It wasn't blood at all. I hadn't picked up on the spicy smell before. Opening the cabinet, I saw the Lush gift set was gone. It was a bath bomb. A dark red, gold-speckled bath bomb.

My temples throbbed. I wanted out of the flat, to be somewhere public, somewhere safe. But I still had one more room to search and I couldn't leave without knowing for sure Amanda wasn't hiding. Twisting the doorknob of her bedroom, I pushed open the door, cringing as it creaked menacingly. The room was empty. Taking a few steps in, I leaned forward to see if she could be flat on the carpet the other side of the bed, but Amanda wasn't lying in wait for me.

Her room had been put back together since I'd ravaged it. It was like I'd never been there. But something new caught my eye. The small mirror of her dressing table had a message waiting for me. In thick red lipstick 'GOTCHA' had been written in block capitals. The same shade as the one left in the mirror maze at Tulley's Farm.

'I've had enough of your games,' I shouted, half expecting a reply, although nothing came.

It was time to leave. The state of the flat told me nothing other than Amanda had lost it. Chris was right to be worried, but I had no idea where she was and she certainly wasn't my problem.

* * *

'Amanda isn't at the flat. I've just been, could you let Chris know,' I said to Fiona, popping my head into her office as she tapped away at her keyboard.

She looked up, eyebrows raised.

'Also, you might want to send someone round. She's wrecked the place, but don't tell Chris that,' I continued.

Fiona leaned back in her chair, lips pressed into a tight line. 'I was worried this would happen. I warned Chris about employing her.' She bowed her head for a second. Perhaps Fiona had been talking about Amanda when I heard her use the word *unstable* the other day? I'd thought she was talking about me.

'Did you know that Mandy who used to work here was her sister?'

'I did.' Fiona was guarded, she clasped her hands together and I knew I'd have to push for information.

'Was she stalking Livvy?'

'Stalking is a strong accusation.'

I prepared myself for some diplomatic bullshit and interjected. 'Fiona, I'm leaving. Livvy is dead, Mandy is dead. Chris told me everything.' I was bending the truth but with only two days to uncover everything I was desperate.

'She was...' Fiona paused, looking for the right word, 'fixated, shall we say.'

'And Livvy complained?' My mouth was dry, tongue thick in my mouth.

'Yes.'

'Why did she never tell me?' I said, more to myself than to Fiona.

'It was before you joined. Mandy left soon after Livvy told me what was happening.'

'Did you know she killed herself?' I asked.

Fiona sighed, fiddling with the sleeve of her navy blouse and avoiding the question, clearly uncomfortable at where the conversation was heading. I'd heard enough anyway.

'Any word from Aaron?' I asked instead. 'He wasn't at the High Point photo shoot I organised.'

'Not yet, but I'll keep trying. He's probably in bed with a hangover or man flu,' she rolled her eyes before continuing. 'Cassie's not well either, perhaps there's a bug going around,' Fiona mused, but I knew she was trying to convince herself rather than me.

The silence stretched out between us until it became a little awkward.

'I'll see you tomorrow,' I said and Fiona nodded. Friday would be my last day. I'd run through everything one more time with Grace, with or without Aaron present, then I was gone.

I longed to be back in Lynn and Bill's kitchen, drinking tea and reminiscing about Livvy, but there was still the issue of getting my stuff from Jayden's house. Before I left, I found him alone in the meeting room using the big screen to run through a client presentation in preparation for a meeting.

'Hey,' he said as I pushed the door open. His wide-eyed expectance made my chest ache.

'Can you drop my stuff over to Livvy's later?'

'You're staying at Livvy's house?'

His incredulous expression irked me. 'What of it?'

'Nothing, just...' his words trailed off and I rolled my eyes. I couldn't bear his judgement.

'Can you bring my stuff or not?' I folded my arms, glaring at him. He owed me at least that. Otherwise I'd have to pay for an Uber and I didn't have any spare cash. Not until Cardinal Media paid me and that would be tomorrow at the earliest.

'Fine. Send me the address.' He turned his back, focusing on his presentation, tapping the screen to move to the next slide. We were done talking.

I sent over Lynn's address as I left, heading for the bus stop. Jayden didn't respond, but I didn't expect him to. He was still smarting at Amanda blurting out what they'd been up to. He wasn't who I thought he was, but it seemed everyone had another side to them but not one they revealed often. How many faces did he have? Amanda had many. What about Livvy? Could we ever really know anyone?

42

I got back to Lynn and Bill's to find dinner waiting for me. Another hearty meal, this time cottage pie, which she delighted in watching me eat. I made appreciative noises when really I wanted to retreat to the guest room and curl up with my thoughts. Guilt stabbed at me for their kindness, their hospitality, but I wasn't in the mood to socialise. I was on edge, waiting for the knock on the door and Jayden to arrive with my bags. I half hoped he'd dump them on the doorstep, knock and run. I couldn't face any more hostility. I was exhausted, my muscles ached and my head still throbbed.

'Do you have any paracetamol, Lynn? I've got one hell of a headache.' I pushed my half-eaten plate away. 'In fact, I think I'm going to go and lay down if that's all right.'

'Of course, I'll bring you some up,' she said as I stood, whisking the plate away as though she was a waitress at a restaurant.

I knew I should make more of an effort, repay their kindness with a little of my time, my attention, but I didn't have the energy. I was zapped after the hospital trip and the nightmare of the flat. All I wanted was to hide under the covers and sleep.

Within five minutes, there was a knock at the door and Lynn came in holding a sleeve of paracetamol and a glass of water.

'This arrived through the door for you today,' she said, passing me an envelope she had wedged beneath her arm.

'Thank you.' I took it from her, placing it on the bed.

She lingered, tucking her hair behind her ear and glancing around the room. I bit my lip to avoid initiating a conversation and encourage her to stay. I'd make it up to her tomorrow. We could spend all evening watching romantic comedies and eating ice cream. I knew she used to do that stuff with Livvy. It was the least I could do as it was my last night here and I had no idea when I would see them again.

'I'll bring you up some hot chocolate later,' she said as she left, as though I was seven years old. It made my heart break for her all over again. The need to love someone, to care for someone, doesn't die when they do.

I turned my attention to the envelope, plain white, with my name scrawled on the front, no address. I didn't recognise the handwriting, the ominous looping of the 'a' in my name made my temples thrum harder. I sensed whatever the envelope contained, wouldn't be good. Forcing my finger under the flap I ripped it open. Inside were folded pages torn from an A5 notebook. Like Livvy's journal, they were handwritten, erratic scrawls and I stared trying to make sense of them.

I went to the Kings Head, where they all hang out. I knew she was pleased to see me, the way she wrinkled her nose. It's cute and she only does it for me. It's like our secret sign. I sat in the corner, watching, waiting for her to invite me over to join them, but she didn't today. I know she will again, soon. I just need to prove myself.

And then on the next page.

Today wasn't a good day. She shouted at me. Told me to stop following her, but she doesn't understand how I feel. She's my best friend. We have a connection, but she won't admit it because I'm not as cool as the others. They laugh at me, at my glasses, how I dress.

I frowned. This wasn't Livvy's diary. Was it Mandy's?

No, no, no, no. There's a new girl. She likes her better than me, I can tell. They are always together. But she'll hurt her, I know she will. I can't let that happen. She needs me to protect her.

My toes curled as I squirmed. It was too intimate. Pages never meant to be read by anyone. The last sheet only had a few lines on it.

I tried to stop it. I tried to warn her, but I was too late. She told me she hated me, screamed in my face to leave her alone. Said I was driving her crazy. Now she's gone and I'm all alone. I want to be with her forever.

Those last words chilled me to the bone. Was it an admission of guilt? Did the person writing it spike Livvy's drink? Nausea rocked me and I sat up, concerned Lynn's cottage pie was going to make an appearance.

Just then the doorbell rang, footsteps on wood followed and I heard voices at the door. I froze, waiting for the sound of it shutting. Instead the bedroom door opened and Jayden stood bathed in the light from the hall. A bin bag in each hand.

'Here you go,' he said, putting them inside the room. 'There's another one downstairs.'

I opened my mouth to speak, but nothing came out. I clamped my lips, shut fearing I was going to be sick.

'Are you okay?'

I held the pages out to him and watched while he read them, before looking back at me.

'What are these?'

'Someone knows what happened to Livvy.' I was so confused. Chris was adamant Mandy wouldn't have given her anything. 'Did you spike her drink, Jayden?' I asked, clutching at straws.

'Oh for God's sake, Ria, are we doing this again?' Jayden flung the pages back at me.

'Did you?' I raised my voice.

'I don't do drugs, Ria, you know that!'

I raised my eyebrows unsure whether I could trust anything Jayden told me any more.

He scowled, flinging his hand out towards me. 'Anyway, we were all there that night, and no, I didn't spike anyone's drink. I was with you most of the time!'

'Not all the time,' I countered, although my argument was weak.

He glared at me, brows knitted together. 'You're mental, you know that? You need help.' He turned to leave as Bill came up the stairs.

'Everything okay, Ria?' His bulk filled the hallway, blocking Jayden's exit.

'It's fine, Bill, thanks.'

He shot Jayden a look, an unspoken warning, before retreating back down the stairs.

Jayden stared after him, before turning to give me a pitying shake of the head. 'Goodbye, Ria.'

I didn't know what to think any more. I was so sure Mandy had been the one to spike Livvy's drink, but looking at the pages again after Jayden had gone, the author wrote about trying to warn *her*. In reality, I couldn't say for certain Livvy was 'her', but I reckoned so. Which meant Mandy was presumably the author of these scribbles.

If I was right, Amanda must have delivered them. A shiver ran the length of my spine. She knew where I was and if I was the 'new girl' Livvy had ditched Mandy for, then maybe she was out for revenge.

Unsettled, I pulled the duvet up over me. I was safe with Lynn and Bill, wasn't I? She couldn't get to me here. Curling my knees up to my chest for comfort, I twirled Livvy's ring around my finger. Why hadn't she told me about Mandy? I was her best friend. I'd kept nothing from her, she knew about my messed-up relationship with my Mum. I told her everything, but it seemed Livvy had her own secrets. Ones she hadn't shared.

Eventually I drifted off to sleep, after I'd taken the painkillers Lynn had brought up, only to be woken a couple of hours later by my phone beeping incessantly.

I sat up, to find the glass of water gone, a lukewarm hot choco-late in its place. I rubbed my eyes, black mascara coming off on my fingers. What time was it? Half nine. I'd slept the evening away, but at least the headache had gone. I pulled myself up, leaning on the cushioned headboard to see who was messaging me.

I'd been added to a WhatsApp group with Cassie and Grace, who were texting back and forth.

Grace: Who's going to the fireworks tomorrow, ladies?
Cassie: Not me, I'm so rough, I haven't got out of bed all day.
Grace: Oh no ☹ I heard you were ill. What have you got?
Cassie: Stomach bug, feel like death. Haven't been able to keep anything down.
Grace: That sucks, Cass. Hope you feel better soon.

Grace: @Ria you up for it?

Cassie: How are you, Ria? I can't believe you're leaving!

Grace: You haven't seen Amanda or Aaron have you?

Cassie: Not since last night. Me and Amanda went for a cheeky Nando's. Probably where I got this bug. She was pissed about something but didn't want to talk about it. We weren't out for long. She said she had to be somewhere.

I chewed my thumbnail, watching the messages spring up before my eyes, twisting Livvy's ring again. It struck me Amanda might have poisoned Cassie somehow, like I was sure she did me with the lamb kebabs? What if she went too far this time? She was clearly angry with Aaron about something too. What if she had done something?

43

I considered not responding. Leaving the chat. But I was going to see Grace tomorrow at work, Cassie too if she was feeling better. I had to go in for my last day.

I began typing.

Ria: I'm okay, just had a nap. I haven't seen Amanda or Aaron either. They weren't at work. They've gone AWOL.
Cassie: Weird! How is Chris?
Ria: He's okay, I saw him today at the hospital. He's looking better.
Grace: That's great news. So, Ria, you up for the fireworks?
Ria: I don't think so, not feeling it this year. Plus I've got an early-morning flight to catch Saturday.

There was a pause, Grace was typing but stopped.

Cassie: So gutted you're leaving!
Grace: Yeah it sucks, Ria. Bummer, looks like it's just me, Rav and Jayden for the fireworks then.

The firework nights at the rugby club were usually fantastic, but I wasn't up for socialising. I didn't want to be around people I couldn't trust, especially with alcohol involved and I knew at least one of them was lying to me or knew more than they were letting on. Mandy had said she'd tried to warn Livvy. Had she seen someone put something in her drink? It had to be one of them, but who?

* * *

My alarm went off and I woke, groggy. It took ages to get to sleep last night. I made more of an effort at breakfast with Lynn. She was up and dressed by the time I wandered downstairs, ready to head off to work.

'I can give you a lift today if you like. I'm going that way,' she said as she handed me two slices of wholemeal toast. The table already decked out with butter, marmite and jam.

'That would be lovely. It's a good job I'm leaving tomorrow,' I said with a chuckle, 'if you keep feeding me like this, I'll be the size of a house.'

'Hardly. You need feeding up, girl,' Bill chipped in, a smidgen of marmite across his cheek.

'How about I bring home some ice cream tonight, we can watch a movie?' I suggested, watching Lynn's eyes light up.

'Oh yes, that new George Clooney one is out to rent on Sky Store and I haven't seen it yet.'

Bill rolled his eyes as Lynn bounced on the balls of her feet. 'You have everything you can possibly want with me, no need to be going all googly-eyed over Clooney,' he said, patting his small but perfectly rounded stomach.

I sniggered, almost choking on my mouthful of toast. Face glowing at the exchange, I couldn't deny it was lovely to be part of a family, to feel their warmth surround me. A stark contrast to what I'd experienced growing up.

We got in the car at quarter past eight. Lynn was a legal secretary and the firm she'd taken extended leave from after Livvy's death had welcomed her back with open arms. It was a job she enjoyed, and she told me as she drove they'd agreed to her return two days a week to ease herself back in gently. I could see she was glad of the distraction, citing life had to get back to some sort of normal.

Fiona was outside the front of the Cardinal Media office when Lynn dropped me off, shrunk back in an alcove to escape the elements, a cigarette dangling from her lips whilst she tapped at her phone.

'You okay, Fiona?'

'I don't know what's going on this week. Cassie is in hospital now, being treated for dehydration and kidney failure. Taken in this morning.' Fiona winced. 'Grace just told me. I'm sending her our best wishes.' She resumed tapping.

'Jesus, I was messaging her last night,' I said. First Chris, now Cassie. What on earth was going on? 'What about Aaron and Amanda?' I asked.

'I was about to ask you the same question. The others haven't heard a peep from either of them. Complete radio silence. I'm hoping they'll magically turn up this morning, grovelling for not being in contact.'

I doubted it. 'Maybe it's time we reported Aaron, and Amanda missing.'

'Chris tells me Amanda's parents are aware, but if Aaron hasn't arrived by ten then I'll contact his next of kin and check they've heard from him.' Fiona drew in smoke, pointing her face skywards to blow it out. She looked tired, but I wasn't surprised. Two employees in the hospital and another two disappeared.

'I heard about Cassie,' I said to Grace later in the toilets as we washed our hands side by side at the sinks.

'Crazy isn't it, to think we were both talking to her last night. Her flatmate Sara called for an ambulance this morning when Cassie could barely talk. Said it was terrifying.'

I shook my head. 'What do they think it is, a bug?'

'That or food poisoning I guess, who knows.' Grace shrugged, drying her hands on a paper towel.

I didn't voice my concern that maybe Amanda was behind it all. *One more day*, the mantra repeated in my mind. It was all I had to get through. I opened my mouth to warn Grace, tell her to be careful, but closed it again. Perhaps it was all a coincidence and I was putting two and two together and making five. No need to start a panic.

'Shall I come over at half past, we can do the final handover?'

'Sure, I've got a few more emails you need to have sight of, I'll forward those on, but we're kind of stuck until Aaron surfaces,' I said, grimly.

Grace rolled her eyes. She clearly didn't think anything was wrong, although I hadn't remembered Aaron ever not turning up for work. It was the place he felt most important, top of the food chain, the arrogant sod.

* * *

By lunchtime, Grace and I had gone through everything twice over. There wasn't any part of the proposals Aaron and I were working on she didn't know inside out. All this she'd have to take on while helping Rav with another project. I felt for her, it would get busier before the Christmas lull and Cardinal was working with half a team at the moment. Although it wasn't my problem, tomorrow Cardinal Media would be a distant memory.

I closed my eyes and imagined the sound of the waves, sand beneath my toes. Desperate to be back in the untroubled world.

'Well, Aaron's parents have said he's been in touch by text.' Fiona materialised at my desk like an apparition whilst I had my eyes shut.

'That's a relief,' I said, although something still niggled at me as far as Aaron was concerned.

44

Fiona left after causally mentioning she had my P45 and final payslip ready for me when it was time to leave. Funds would be in my account by close of business today – six months' pay, as Chris had agreed. I was grateful to be leaving with that. I pulled my phone out of my bag to see if I'd had any messages. Jayden had avoided me in the office, but that was no surprise after I'd accused him of spiking Livvy's drink yesterday.

A string of notifications were waiting on the screen. Mum had messaged to say she'd got my room ready and wanted to confirm what flight I was on as she would be there to pick me up from the airport. I sensed the general excitement in her words, which rubbed off on me. I swiftly sent her a screenshot of my ticket, with lots of excited emojis. This could be our chance to develop a real relationship and become a proper family, just the two of us.

Cassie and Grace had sent messages in the WhatsApp group. Cassie's were sent from her hospital bed, photographing her intravenous drip, then a selfie. She looked washed out, purple patches beneath her eyes. Thank God her flatmate had found her when she did.

I responded with well wishes, saying I'd keep in touch from Nice, although I knew I probably wouldn't. It was time to end this chapter of my life, I'd tried a break, a rest and recharge and it hadn't worked. It was easier to cut the cord.

There was one final message I hadn't got to yet and I let out an involuntary whimper when I saw who it was from. Livvy.

Tonight's the night

I rubbed at my throat, it constricting beneath my palm. Tonight was the night for what? I slammed the phone onto my desk before picking it up again.

'Fuck this shit,' I muttered, clicking on Livvy's contact and deleting it. I'd had enough. Tomorrow couldn't come soon enough.

When it got to four o'clock, I put my out of office on, directing all future queries to Grace and headed around to Fiona's office.

'I'm going to go, I've done the handover with Grace. Everything the guys will need is on Teams.'

'Brilliant, thank you,' she said, obviously distracted, then, remembering, she rose from her chair, reaching for an envelope in her tray. 'Here's your P45 and payslip. Obviously if you need a reference, then let us know.'

I smiled tightly, wondering what it would include.

'Do you have any plans?' she continued.

'No idea yet. I'm going to Nice tomorrow, so I'll see what happens, I guess.'

'Well, I wish you all the best. I know Chris does too.' She smiled but it didn't reach her eyes. I'd be one less headache for her to deal with.

'Thank you. Please say goodbye to Chris for me.'

'Shall I announce a trip to the Kings Head?' Fiona asked as I turned to leave.

'No, no, I'm just going to slip out quietly. No fuss.'

I looked over towards the huddle of desks where Karen sat, knowing I should go over and say goodbye, but I couldn't face it. I couldn't stand the pitying looks. Rumours as to why I was leaving were already doing the rounds. Another mental breakdown, not being able to hack the pace and the like.

I stepped out of the Cardinal Media office lighter on my feet. No more Amanda or Jayden, no more toxicity. I was cleansed as I headed into the supermarket to pick up a tub of Haagen-Dazs for me and Lynn to consume later, hoping it wouldn't melt as I waited for the bus.

* * *

Once back, with the ice cream safely in the freezer, I started to pack. Lynn let me have Livvy's old suitcase and with that, as well as my own carry-on one, I'd managed to get in enough stuff from the bin bags. The clothes I couldn't fit in I left for Bill to store in his garage.

'I'll be sad to see you go,' Lynn said, leaning on the doorframe, her eyes glassy. 'It's been lovely having you to stay.'

'Thank you so much for putting me up. I'll come back and visit, I promise.' I opened my arms for a hug, which Lynn stepped into. Hearing her sniff into my shoulder as she squeezed me tight. 'Right, let's go put the movie on,' I said as my phone beeped in my pocket.

I sat on the sofa, the ice cream and a huge bowl of popcorn on the coffee table. Bill had made his excuses and gone off to play darts, George Clooney having driven him from his own home, Lynn chortled.

I clicked play and checked my phone as the Universal Pictures logo came onto the flat-screen television. I'd been added to another WhatsApp group, this time by a number I didn't have a contact for.

Hey bitches, Fireworks party at mine tonight. 8pm sharp. Bring booze.
A x

A was Amanda obviously. She'd sent it to Grace, Rav, Cassie, Jayden, Aaron and me.

Grace had already replied.

Yes! Finally. I'll be there. X

Jesus. What was Amanda doing?

'Put your phone away,' Lynn chided, 'Clooney is on!'

I put the phone down on the table, my stomach tying in knots. What was Amanda planning? So now she was suddenly fine, back to normal and holding a party? Stranger still was the fact I'd been invited too.

Lynn handed me the ice cream, but the spoon lay still in my clammy hand. I couldn't face a single bite. Unable to concentrate on what was happening on screen, I froze as my phone beeped repeatedly.

'Perhaps you should answer, someone seems intent on getting hold of you,' Lynn said, taking back the untouched ice cream and helping herself to a mouthful.

I snatched the phone up, eager to find out what Amanda was up to. The screen full of notifications of responses to Amanda's invite. Rav and Jayden saying they were up for it. Aaron too. Cass said she was still at the hospital so wouldn't be making an appearance. Amanda replied that she'd roped in some of the neighbours, people I had barely acknowledged while I lived there, preferring to keep myself to myself. I shifted in my seat, crossing and uncrossing my legs. Rubbing my damp palms down the thighs of my jeans.

Outside, it was dark and the wind blew the tree in the front garden, its branches signalling at me furiously. Lynn laughed like a hyena at a particularly venomous exchange between Clooney and Julia Roberts. I chuckled weakly along with her, glancing at my phone again before getting up to draw the curtains. I didn't want to be reminded of the time, how the clock was edging ever closer to eight o'clock. The night pouring in.

'He's so handsome, isn't he,' Lynn said, drooling at the screen.

'A bit old for me,' I replied, forcing a smile.

'What's with all the messages?'

'There's a party going on.'

'Well, you should go, I won't mind,' Lynn said.

'No, it's fine. I want to be here.' I turned my head back to the screen as my phone beeped again. 'I'm going to put it on silent,' I said, giving Lynn an apologetic smile as I reached for it.

This time it was a WhatsApp from Amanda, sent separately to me. All the hairs on my arms stood to attention as I stared at the typed words.

If you come, you'll find out the truth...

45

LIVVY – BEFORE

Things have been so much better since she left. I don't know how, but Fiona came through for me and within a week work was no longer somewhere I felt constantly watched. I'm not sure whether she told Chris, I guess she had to, with him being the boss, but he hasn't spoken to me about it. It's taken a little time, but I've slowly started to relax, not seeing her skulking behind every corner, the tingling sensation of being watched. I was free again and then, Ria joined the fold.

We've clicked straight away, both having the same warped sense of humour and desire to elevate ourselves. She is a breath of fresh air after the past few months and it's easy to come out of my shell with her around. The others have welcomed her in, banter rolling off their tongues and she gives as good as she gets.

I saw the way Jayden looked at her almost the first second he saw her. I can't deny it didn't smart a bit, but if he was into me, he would have done something about it by now. Ria has the same whimsical look in her eye whenever he speaks so I know she feels it too. I'm not about to waste any more time hanging on his every word when he barely notices I exist. Weirdly, Aaron seems to be paying me more attention. Twice in so many weeks I've come in to find my favourite cinnamon whirl pastry and a coffee on my desk. It's sweet.

Ria has filled a massive hole in my life I hadn't realised was there. It wasn't long after she started before we began hanging out outside of work, just the two of us. Since Chris put her up in the company flat, we are there all the time. I've been distracted, unaware *she* is still around. Although no longer at Cardinal Media, her fixation on me remains. Not being as vigilant as I had been, I didn't notice at first.

It wasn't until Ria and I went to the cinema, that I saw her waiting outside, lurking in the shadows. She hasn't gone, not completely, not erased from my life like I'd hoped. Thankfully, Ria didn't notice, she was too busy chattering about the twist at the end of the film. I didn't want to admit my friendship came with baggage. That I've been infected by another's obsession with me.

It makes me feel dirty and incredibly angry. I'm not free at all. In fact, the only place I am safe is at work and from now on I'm sticking to Ria like glue. She is my anchor. She makes me want to live my life to the fullest, to enjoy every second, so I do the only thing I can. I block *her* out.

46

What truth would I find out? I stared at the message. The truth about Livvy?

I chewed the inside of my cheek, trying to ignore the urgency to get up and rush to the party. Finding out what had happened to Livvy had been eating away at me ever since she'd died. I didn't think anyone truly believed she had willingly taken drugs. Yet no one wanted me to pursue it, instead they got agitated whenever I made any noise on the subject.

Amanda was offering me the truth, whatever that was. Was she about to admit to doing it herself? If nothing else I'd find out why Amanda had been targeting me since I'd returned.

'Go on, go out,' Lynn chuckled, seeing I was absorbed in my phone but not registering the look of horror on my face.

I should leave it alone, block the number, ignore the message, but I knew I wouldn't. If it was my last night here, I had to make it count, for Livvy's sake.

'I'm sorry,' I squirmed under Lynn's gaze, grimacing.

'Don't be silly, go. At least I don't have to share the ice cream.' Lynn was so kind and Livvy was lucky to have had her as a mum.

'Thank you,' I said, jumping up to grab my keys and coat.

I didn't bother getting changed out of my jeans and sweatshirt, I wasn't dressing up for the occasion. It was freezing and I'd have to catch the bus there and back, but I was thankful it wasn't raining when I got outside. The fireworks wouldn't be a washout like they were last year. We'd all got soaked and came back slick with mud like we'd been to Glastonbury and not over the local rugby field. Perhaps if Amanda was throwing a party, she intended to watch the fireworks out of the windows of the living room. They were massive, practically floor to ceiling, with long drapes for privacy. I imagined she'd pull them back when the fireworks started. The flat was only a stone's throw from the club and the view was pretty good from inside. I remember Livvy saying, as we'd stripped off our muddy clothes, next time we should stay and watch them from the warmth. Neither of us knowing there wouldn't be a next time.

I waited ages for the bus, checking my phone every few minutes to see if there had been any more messages. The party had already started, eight o'clock had come and gone and still no bus. I stamped my feet impatiently. My toes had little feeling left despite the boots I'd worn and I had a horrible sensation in the pit of my stomach. Nothing good was going to come out of tonight and I half expected it was a trap, but I couldn't not know. The truth was my Achilles heel and Amanda knew it. All she had to do was dangle it in front of me like a carrot and out I went, a lamb to the slaughter.

Finally, after my fingers had started to go numb and sounds of distant fireworks echoed, the bus rumbled around the corner. I climbed on, sitting at the front and blowing hot breath into my hands. The knot in my stomach grew in size the closer we got to Crawley and I looked out of the window for the colourful streams of fireworks from back gardens that sprung up every now and again.

I practically dived off the bus, keys in my hand ready, racing towards the building as an explosion came from behind, making me start. The fireworks at the rugby club had begun, so the party would be in full swing. Music blared as soon as I entered the block. An old classic, 'Insomnia' by Faithless, was playing, slightly muffled by the door to the stairs. No wonder Amanda had invited the neighbours, they wouldn't be able to hear anything in their own flats anyway.

The lady from number 8, I knew as Linda Houghton from her buzzer, rolled her eyes as she passed me on the stairs and I smiled weakly at her. *It's not my party, I don't live here any more*, I wanted to say, but what was the point?

When I reached the flat, the door was on its catch so anyone could walk in. The bass thumped in my ears, and I was met with people throwing shapes in the living room. Amanda had bought a plug-in disco ball, which was projecting colour through the darkness and I put my keys down beside it.

I squinted at the bodies moving through the plumes of cigarette smoke, until I could make out Grace.

'Ria!' she screamed, seeing me at the same time and bounding over.

'You okay?' I said, trying to peel her arms from around my neck, she was unsteady on her feet. It was a little early to be drunk.

'Cool isn't it, love the ball thing. There's a bowl of punch on the side, but careful, it's bulletproof,' she giggled. Pointing back behind her, she said, 'Jayden and Rav are around somewhere. Amanda said Aaron is on his way, I'm just gutted Cass couldn't come.'

'Who are all these people?' I asked, but Grace shrugged.

'No idea, your neighbours, I think.' She jiggled, keen to get back dancing.

'Where's Amanda?' I shouted, trying to work out who the crowd were gathered by the window, watching the fireworks.

'I don't know, she was here a minute ago,' Grace replied and slipped back into the bunch of revellers.

The flat had about twenty people in it, all the remaining furniture had been pushed to the side. The broken TV removed, yet the wall still had paper ripped away, although it was barely noticeable in the disco lights. A bowl of punch was half empty, and snacks and shot glasses had been stacked in one corner of the kitchen, alongside bottles of vodka, gin and tequila. Gone were the broken glasses and plates which scattered the laminate the last time I was here.

I went back to scanning the crowd, but Amanda wasn't amongst them. I hung back, debating whether to explore the rooms, already nervous at what I'd find. Faithless gave way to Roger Sanchez and a cheer came from the impromptu dance floor as 'Another Chance' began to play, surprisingly loud from the small wireless speakers.

I made my way through the throng, the bathroom door was locked, someone was inside, so I waited. Two girls I didn't recognise came out, wiping their noses, not even trying to hide what they'd been up to inside.

Both mine and Amanda's bedrooms were empty.

I pressed my nails into my palms. I hadn't come all this way for nothing. Amanda had offered the truth and I was here to collect. Grabbing my phone, I typed a message quickly.

I'm here. Where are you?

I didn't have to wait long for a response.

We're having a party for two, on the roof

Party? It wasn't a party. It was a trap. But I had no choice, I had to know the truth.

47

The iron stairs to the roof were steep and I caught the skin of my palm on a jagged piece of the rusty handrail, wincing as I pulled it away, wiping the blood that followed. My legs seemed to become heavier the higher I climbed. Who was Amanda up there with? Unless she meant just me and her being the attendees of her party for two?

Whatever her plans were, I knew they weren't good. The roof wasn't somewhere I ever frequented. We'd been warned off by the owner of the building on more than one occasion. No one was allowed up there, it was off limits, the felt was cracked in places and it was technically unsafe. The exit was normally locked to stop any unwanted visitors.

Perhaps I was wrong and she'd gone up to get a better view of the fireworks? It was high enough to be the best in town. Maybe she wanted to make sure whatever she said to me was in private? She didn't want anyone overhearing the truth if that was what she was going to give me.

Mouth dry, I reached the metal door, which stood ajar, its broken padlock discarded on the step below. Fireworks whooshed, echoes of ear-splitting shrieks rattled around the stairwell and I could hear shouts over the explosions. Flashes of red and purple lights shot through the sky as I pushed the door open, its hinges creaking, almost tripping over some old pots.

My bladder loosened as I stepped out into the cold night, spying a figure illuminated by the falling sparks raining down on them.

'Over here, Ria,' Amanda called, her voice sharp as a pin.

As I shuffled closer, unsure of the stability of the rooftop, I saw someone slumped in a chair, head bowed, barely conscious, next to Amanda.

'What have you done?' I shouted to be heard over the fireworks blasting above us.

'I saved him for you,' she giggled, her eyes lit up, red lips peeling back from her glowing teeth.

As I approached, their faces sharpening in the gloom, her hand patted Aaron's shoulder. What was he doing up here?

'Is he okay?' I asked, anxiety swirling in my stomach at the state of him.

'Sure he is. Wakey, wakey, sleepyhead,' she said, her voice sing-song, as though she was addressing a toddler.

'Did you bring me here to tell me you killed Livvy?' I asked, the question burning inside me, I couldn't hold it in any longer. I waited for an answer, maintaining my distance. Aaron and Amanda were dangerously close to the edge with a low rail between them and a four-storey drop.

'It's beautiful up here, isn't it,' she said, ignoring my question. 'I love fireworks, Mandy loved them too, you know, we would always write our names with sparklers every year.' Amanda looked wistfully into the distance, tossing back her hair.

'Mandy is your sister?' I asked, stalling for time. Nobody knew I was up here and I had no idea what Amanda planned to do to Aaron. I hadn't thought to tell Grace where I was going. Unless Rav or Jayden came looking, but it was unlikely they'd feel the need to come and find me.

'Mandy *was* my sister. She lives on in me now.' Amanda pressed her hand to her chest and closed her eyes briefly. She looked almost ethereal, bathed in the glow of ice white shooting stars.

'You're Anna,' I said, unable to stop myself from correcting her.

'Anna's gone. I'm Amanda now, the perfect amalgamation of me and my sister. I'm doing this for her, you know.'

'Doing what?' I asked, my voice trembling. Blood sang in my ears and I shivered, fingertips quivering as I brushed my hair out of my face. The wind whipping it in all directions.

'You know they bullied her. She told me. She'd come home crying. "Dowdy Dowd" that's what they'd call her. Too straight, too boring, too plain. She tried so hard to get to know them and they ridiculed her.' Amanda snarled, baring her teeth, her face a mask of fury.

'Who?' I asked.

'Your bitch friend Livvy that's who!' she spat, her words stinging like she'd pelted me in the face.

I recoiled, tripping backwards over my feet, managing to right myself before I tumbled.

'But I can't get to Livvy now, can I,' she hissed, 'I can't make her pay for what she did. Tormenting Mandy until she hung herself.'

My mouth gaped. It couldn't be true. Livvy wouldn't have done that, not the Livvy I knew.

Amanda drank in my befuddled state, throwing her head back and cackling. She looked like Medusa, blonde strands fanning out like snakes.

'Mandy died after Livvy,' I said, knowing what Amanda was saying wasn't right.

'She was still the cause. Livvy wasn't whiter than white, trust me.'

I swallowed the lump in my throat, my extremities numb from cold and Amanda's revelations.

'You're wrong,' I said.

'Mandy was sent messages, invited out and then stood up. She was left on the side lines by all of them. They played with her, thought it was fun to trick her. My sister was sweet and kind, she didn't deserve their cruelty. Despite their games, she still wanted to be part of their group, she wanted to be Livvy's friend. You know, you've seen some of her diary.'

What I'd seen hadn't told me much, it sounded more like Mandy was delusional. Had she concocted her friendship with Livvy? Convinced herself there was one, when really it was a case of her trailing around after her?

I couldn't listen to Amanda slander Livvy any longer. Unable to control myself, I blurted, 'Your sister stalked Livvy and you know it.'

Amanda's eyes narrowed. 'If it helps you sleep at night,' she sneered.

'If what you're saying is true, why does no one remember Mandy? If they teased her relentlessly, bullied and ridiculed her?'

'They remember, they are just refusing to admit it... but it's okay, it'll be their turn next, but you – I wanted you to have Aaron.'

Amanda had lost it, she was making no sense.

I shook my head. Whatever she was offering, I didn't want it. All I wanted was to run back to safety, to the warmth and shelter inside, away from her madness.

Turning to Aaron, she shouted, 'I said, wake up!', smacking him hard around the face.

His arms twitched and he slowly raised his head, eyes wide as he came to.

'We've been hanging out for a couple of days, Aaron and me, we've certainly got *a lot* closer. He's really opened up, you know.'

Her eyes glistened and she ruffled his hair, his head wobbled like it was on a stick. 'Tell her, Aaron, tell her what you told me...'

Aaron mumbled something, a speck of drool escaping from his lips. He seemed to be having trouble getting his limbs to coordinate as he attempted to get up. His legs were like a newborn calf, unable to bear his own weight.

'Is he drunk or have you drugged him?' I said, taking a step closer.

Just like you drugged Livvy, the voice in my head piped up.

'A taste of his own medicine, wouldn't you say?' She nudged Aaron with her knee, but he barely responded. What had she given him and how much? And why?

Like a second timer clicking into place, her words suddenly made sense. I got it.

Amanda clocked the grief written all over my face as I held back tears. It couldn't be true. I shook my head as her lips curved upwards at my recognition. She paused, waiting for the revelation to hit before she spoke.

'Aaron is the one you've been looking for.'

48

The fireworks were still going strong, dizzying lights in front of my eyes as my head swam. The truth I'd been waiting so long to hear. Knowing it was one of us but not knowing who. My stomach recoiled like I'd been punched, the air knocked out of me.

Amanda stood behind Aaron, hands on his shoulders. He was becoming more lucid, looking around as Amanda spoke. She was like a hypnotist bringing him back again after clicking her fingers to send him to sleep. 'Aaron slipped ketamine into Livvy's drink the night of the awards ceremony.' She paused, watching her words hit me like bullets. 'I was convinced it was you. Mandy left a note when she hung herself, did you know that?'

I shook my head, the wind biting at my cheeks.

'Only had four words on it... Ria is to blame.'

I opened my mouth to speak, but nothing came out.

'At first, I thought she meant you'd drugged Livvy, but now I think you're the reason she hung herself. You came along and Mandy was dropped, you were the shiny new toy and she became the outcast.' Amanda's mouth pulled back in a snarl. 'You know, the irony is, Mandy saw what happened that night and she tried to help, she *tried* to get Livvy to listen, but she was told to fuck off. So... she did,' Amanda sneered, taking obvious delight in delivering the final blow.

Mandy had left Livvy, drugged up to the eyeballs, and she died in the toilet cubicle. She could have told someone, any one of us. We could have helped her.

'It was all recorded in her diary, but she left out the most important thing... scared there would be repercussions if she named the person responsible.' Amanda grabbed a handful of Aaron's hair, wrenching his head back, gritting her teeth, jaw flexing as the vein in her neck pulsed. 'Right up to her death, she was convinced *he* would come after her if she told anyone what she saw.' She let go of Aaron roughly and he slowly reached up to touch his head, arms uncoordinated.

Light-headed, I swayed in the gale. Senses overloaded by the screeching fireworks and beams of colourful lights reflecting back at me in Amanda's pupils. I watched as she slipped a phone out of her pocket, tucking it into Aaron's. His phone. Had she sent the texts from him, about coming to the party and the one to his parents confirming he was okay, whilst all the time grinding him down or drugging him to get him to confess?

Finally I was able to speak. 'No, no, no,' I wailed, crouching to my knees, palms flat on the ground. As though I'd been winded with her words, trying to fight the overwhelming urge to vomit on the flaking felt beneath my feet. It couldn't be Aaron, he liked Livvy, they were on the verge of getting together. It meant he'd been lying all this time, pretending he didn't know what had happened, covering his own arse. The coward! He must have been petrified at my return, worried I'd drag up the circumstances of Livvy's death again, start pointing fingers when he thought he'd got away with it.

'Afraid so... which is why I thought you might want to have Aaron all to yourself.' Amanda strode towards me and, still low on the ground, I flinched, waiting for her to put the boot in, but she passed without making contact.

I turned my head to follow her, what was happening?

'I'm leaving,' she said, glancing back and checking her watch. 'I've got a date with Grace, Rav and maybe Jayden too. They're next on my list, and we're about to do some shots.' She patted the bulbous pocket at the chest of her fur-lined denim jacket. 'It's not ketamine, just a little household bleach. I think I'll call these Liquid Panic,' she mused, swinging open the door and disappearing into the soft glow of the stairwell light.

My breath came out in rasps and I clutched at my chest, chin trembling as the horror of what was about to happen registered in my brain. Amanda was going to hurt my friends, but I was in the grip of an anxiety attack unable to command my limbs to move. I had to snap out of it. I had to stop her.

'Ria?' Aaron mumbled behind me. He blinked rapidly, lumbering upwards from the rickety garden chair Amanda had sat him on and immediately collapsing.

I stared at him, tempted to leave him where he'd fallen. He didn't deserve my help but Livvy wouldn't have wanted me to do that. It was that thought that forced me up onto my feet and over to him, trying to take his weight and steady the both of us. The chair fell on its side as he leant on it for balance.

'She got me up here to watch the fireworks, we've had a mad couple of days. I've been so out of it. We were going to do another hit...' he tried to explain, 'but she made me go first. Then she got all weird.' He still sounded under the influence, giggling to himself. Did he think this was a game? Had he not heard what she'd said?

'Aaron, what did you do to Livvy?' I shouted above the wind and the eruptions, already dreading the answer. Praying Amanda had got it wrong.

He was so heavy, I was struggling to bear his weight. I gripped him under the armpit, throwing his other arm around my shoulders, trying to use my body as leverage. He was moving too slowly and I had to get back downstairs. I had to save the others from Amanda, but I couldn't leave him here in such a state.

'Tell me, Aaron?' I cried, as we made a couple of wobbly steps. A gust whistled through my hair, fat droplets of rain had started to fall, splattering the floor. Despite this the fireworks were still going, ramping up to their finale. It was so loud, drowning out our voices, we had to shout to be heard.

'I... I was just trying to loosen her up, you know,' he stammered.

'You drugged her so she would have sex with you?' I screamed, tears mixing with the rainwater on my face. It was obvious he'd developed a thing for Livvy. We'd talked about it as we'd got ready, applying our make-up, excited for the evening ahead. She would have had no idea he intended to spike her drink and what was he going to do with her afterwards? Rape her? The idea of it repulsed me.

The heavens opened and both of us were soaked through in less than a minute. Aaron's teeth chattered, trainers skidding on the slippery surface. He stumbled to the left, dangerously close to the edge, pulling me with him. I forced my weight right, both of us trying to maintain our balance.

'No, I wanted to her to have a good time. We were celebrating the award, I didn't see any harm in it. She said she wanted to have fun,' he said.

My hair fell in front of my face, corkscrew curls dripping now, cheeks numb.

Fun? I recalled Livvy's lifeless body, her horrified expression, frozen forever. She'd had anything but fun.

'I never meant for it to happen. I was really into her. I didn't know she was so out of it. I went looking for her. One minute she was dancing and then...'

Another image hit me like a thunderbolt, Livvy's skin almost translucent, slumped over the toilet. Her blue lips and bulging eyes. Once beautiful but ugly in the face of death. The storm surged through me, my insides on fire.

'You killed my best friend,' I yelled.

'Ria, she fell. I didn't know,' he cried.

'She fell because she was off her face!'

As the crescendo of multiple blasts rang out, sparks of gold and green shooting into the night sky, I let go of Aaron. Ducking out from under him and shoving his arm off me, unable to bear his touch a moment longer. His proximity made my skin crawl. He'd tried to wheedle out from what he'd done. Taking no responsibility, sliding back under his rock, waiting for it all to blow over. I couldn't stomach the sight of him.

Without my support, Aaron stumbled sidewards, trainers squeaking as they tried to hold on to the watery felt. But there was no grip. He was too close to the edge, the barrier too low and he crashed into it. Arms flailing, Aaron was there one minute and the next he was gone. Over the edge of the rail and four storeys down.

My cries were drowned out by the final whizzing climax of screamers before the night was still once more. Frozen to the spot, dripping from the rain, I waited for signs Aaron had hit the pavement. Shouts or screams from below, sirens in the distance, but as though a conductor had swiped his baton, eerie silence washed over the rooftop.

I dropped once more to my knees. I wasn't responsible, it was an accident. *Just like Livvy's death was an accident?* my inner monologue tortured me.

What had I done?

49

'Ria,' a voice shouted, disappearing into the wind.

I shook my head. Was I imagining it?

The shout came again and, scrambling to my feet, I lurched towards the edge of the rooftop, holding on to the rail and leaning over.

Aaron was on his knees on what looked like a narrow maintenance balcony, only ten feet below the rooftop.

Relief flooded through me. He was alive. I didn't know how I would have been able to live with myself knowing I'd let him go, despite what I now knew he'd done.

Wind whipped his shirt, gluing it to him as he struggled to his feet, clinging onto the metal surround for support.

'Are you hurt?' I shouted.

'I think I've dislocated my shoulder.'

'I don't know how to get to you.' I looked around for inspiration, there had to be something on the rooftop that could help. A rope maybe?

'There's a door here, but it's locked.' I heard his fist hammering on metal, distant thuds.

'Okay, there's a ladder back up to the roof,' I shouted, leaning further over the edge, my fingertips grazing the top rung. 'It's not far. Can you climb?'

He looked up assessing whether he'd make it. One wrong move and it was a four-storey fall that would cause more damage than a dislocated shoulder.

With the crook of my arm around the railing, I leant as far as I could over, reaching my hand out, preparing to grab Aaron as soon as he was in touching distance. Awkwardly, Aaron tried to climb, using his good arm to pull his weight up the few rungs between us, balancing his feet on each one. Grunting with pain, he swore as his hand slipped and he had to catch himself with his other one, jolting his dislocated shoulder. He squeezed his eyes shut and blew out a long breath, body flat against the rungs, waiting for the pain to subside.

'Don't look down,' I called. 'One step at time. Keep going, I'm here.' I stretched my hand out, fingertips numb, watching his clumsy ascent.

The first part of him I could grab was the scruff of his T-shirt. With the inner sides of my boots buffeted against the low wall, I used my body weight to heave backwards, pulling him up towards me. His hand gripped the ledge and I leant over again, this time hooking my fingers into his belt and pulling the rest of him over the railing. We collapsed into a heap, legs entangled, panting and sodden from the rain.

'Fuck,' he said, sitting up, wincing and clutching his arm, but there wasn't time to waste.

'Aaron, we have to go, Amanda is going to hurt the others,' I said, already on my feet and pulling him up, my muscles screaming from all the exertion. The image of Amanda patting the pocket of her jacket was at the forefront of my mind. I had to stop her.

We hurried to the door, and I wrenched it open, fearing she

would have locked it behind her, banishing us up here. Hoping I'd exact my revenge on Aaron and be carted off in handcuffs, her score settled for Mandy and everything tied up in a neat little bow. I was glad to disappoint her.

Once we were over the threshold, I heard the screams, seemingly in stereo, coming from beneath me.

'Leave me here,' Aaron panted, slumping down onto the top stair, his eyes like pinpricks.

I didn't need telling twice.

When I reached the flat, chaos had descended. Jayden was on his knees, his hands clutching his throat as he coughed, eyes streaming. Rav was throwing up onto the carpet, a mixture of alcohol and blood. Grace was screaming, her hands clasped to her face amidst the horror. All of them were being comforted by people I didn't know.

Music still blared from the speakers and I rushed to turn it off, fumbling for my phone to get help, hands shaking so hard I could barely dial.

'I've called for an ambulance,' a girl with a high ponytail shouted towards me as she crouched down and forced Jayden to drink some water.

'Where's Amanda?' I shouted, frantically scanning faces for her, but she had gone. The small clear bottle which had contained the bleach was empty on the kitchen worktop along with upturned shot glasses. A bottle of Vodka and Baileys were on their sides on the floor in a puddle of liquid. The remnants of her crime.

'Fuck,' I screamed into the air, panic rising into my throat.

Rav had stopped throwing up, he was on his hands and knees, a puddle of vomit beneath him, still heaving. 'It burns,' he whimpered, voice scratchy.

'I know, here, drink this,' I said, rushing with water from the tap.

I had no idea if I was doing the right thing or not, but surely diluting the bleach would be a good thing?

I locked eyes with the ponytail girl, conveying our mutual panic as the flat emptied out. The party abruptly ending, everyone dispersing at speed knowing the emergency services were on their way. Unwilling to remain in case the police arrived and they were found with contraband on them.

Jayden was still coughing, lying on his side on the carpet.

'What's your name?' I said to the girl as we hurried to refill glasses of water at the sink, my heart racing in my chest.

'Natalie,' she whimpered, her glazed eyes meeting mine, she'd had to sober up fast and I was grateful I wasn't alone amongst the carnage.

'Ria,' I replied, before dashing back to Jayden, forcing him to drink.

As Natalie tried to comfort a hysterical Grace, who appeared not to have drunk one of Amanda's shots, a strange yet familiar smell assaulted my nostrils. My eyes were drawn from Jayden to see the kitchen was ablaze. A cigarette discarded on the laminate beside the puddle of vodka had ignited and flames climbed the cabinets like fast growing vines.

I leapt up from my crouched position, leaving Jayden vomiting up the water he'd just consumed and rushed towards it. Flapping at the flames with a tea towel only caused the fire to spread further and in seconds the worktop was alight,

'We've got to get out,' I screamed, turning back to Natalie and catching sight of Amanda frozen in the doorway to the flat. Smile twisted with intent, her eyes met mine and then she yanked the front door towards her, slamming it shut. I ran towards it, trying to pull it open, but it wouldn't budge. She'd locked it from the outside, imprisoning us. I looked around for my keys, but all I could see was the shattered disco ball, engulfed, its pieces melting.

'Amanda, no!' I screamed, hammering the door with my fists.

Natalie appeared behind me, eyes like a deer caught in the headlights. 'We're locked in?'

I nodded, continuing to bang on the door, hoping someone would hear me.

'Night, night, Ria,' Amanda's voice came from the other side before I heard footsteps then a scuffle. Aaron's muffled shouts and the sounds of a fight breaking out came from the corridor.

'Aaron,' I screamed as a loud thud shook the frame, a body thrown against it.

'Help us!' I yelled, hammering again, utterly helpless. Aaron was hurt but he had his size on his side, although Amanda would stop at nothing if she'd been cornered.

Blistering heat soared outwards from the kitchen, flames licking the carpet having already melted the laminate and searching for more to consume. Leaving the door, hoping Aaron would call for help, I raced back towards the screams of panic. The flat was filling with smoke fast, fire pushing us back further into the living room. The kitchen area now off limits. We couldn't even get to the sink for water.

'Help me!' I shouted to Natalie as she covered her face with her arm.

Instinct kicked in and I knew I had seconds to try and save all of our lives.

'We need to throw as much water as we can on the fire,' I instructed before racing to the bathroom to soak some towels in the shower. Natalie appeared beside me in the cramped space, filling up glasses from the bathroom tap. Not nearly enough to stop the spread. Grace's face was dirty with soot as clouds of black smoke swirled above our heads. Everyone was coughing now and she attempted to smash a window but the glass was reinforced.

'Open as many as you can, get Rav and Jayden into my room by the window, close the door and put a towel down, block the smoke,' I yelled over the incessant crackling.

It was already becoming hard to see inside the flat, my lungs were on fire. I carried on soaking as many towels as I could find, leaving the taps and shower running. Rushing to throw them over the worktop to put out the flames but they had already reached the walls, blocking the door to the tiny hallway. Even if we could get out of the flat, we wouldn't be able to unharmed. Flames crept ever closer to the sofa and the curtains, the fire now an unstoppable force. It was no use, in less than a minute the entire place would be engulfed.

'We need to get out of here,' Natalie's high-pitched scream of utter terror came from behind me as she looked desperately for a way to escape. But there was no escape. We were in a flat, with only one exit. Amanda had locked us in and left us to die. Even if Aaron had called for help, it wouldn't arrive before the whole place had gone up.

Near the fire its heat was indescribable, my skin felt like it was peeling back from my body, although I only had some minor burns to my arms and hands. I kept throwing water as fast as I could, exhausted by the relentless cycle but it wasn't fast enough to control the flames that licked the walls, spreading in seconds. Natalie was crouched down, struggling for breath. We couldn't fight the fire any longer, it was too strong. As if delayed the shrill fire alarm echoed, coming from the corridor, muffled by the crackle and hiss.

'We have to barricade ourselves,' I shouted, coughing, eyes stinging. Everything hurt, my throat and my lungs were searing. The oxygen was running out and it was getting harder to breathe but I wasn't about to give up. I wouldn't let us die here in this flat.

50

At that second I heard a smash of glass and cold water rained down upon us from the ceiling. A sprinkler in the centre of the room had kicked in, activated by the blistering heat. The feel of icy liquid hitting my skin brought hope as the flames sizzled beneath its assault.

I gestured towards my room where Grace was taking care of Rav and Jayden. We backed towards it, coughing, watching as the fire shrunk under the spray, losing its grip. A plume of black clouds rolled around the ceiling tarnishing everything it touched. Both of us already drenched, hair matted to our heads, and clothes dripping we gawped at the scene in front of us.

With the fire losing its battle we found Grace and the others gathered beneath the window, gulping air from a two-inch gap like it was precious nectar. Rav and Jayden were whimpering, their voices hoarse. Grace's bottom lip protruded as her tears fell in an endless stream.

'I think we'll be alright, the sprinkler is putting the fire out,' I said, wringing my sweatshirt. The others looked up, a tidal wave of relief washing over them despite the fact we were still trapped.

Head swimming, I replaced the towel at the bottom of the door, hoping it would give us a barrier from the smoke.

Praying we would be rescued soon I joined the group beneath the window. Natalie was sobbing, face blackened as though she'd painted herself with charcoal. Despite the sting from my burnt flesh I wrapped my arm around her and we huddled together, our salty tears mixing.

* * *

Detached and numb, all of us were quiet, apart from recurring coughing fits as we tried to rid ourselves of the ingested smoke and ash when the fireman pushed his way inside the room. I couldn't see his face, it was completely obscured by his mask and breathing equipment.

I was hauled to my feet and helped out of the flat, an oxygen mask placed over my nose and mouth and blissfully clean air pumped in. Every inch of me was coated in a layer of ash which had found its way inside my nose, mouth and ears, even clinging to my eyelashes.

Outside of flat twelve, the block looked untouched, although I doubted the flat below had survived intact. The fire door had done its job and contained the blaze which the sprinkler had put out, releasing gallons of water from one isolated unit.

I found Aaron with the paramedics outside, still clutching his arm. The street had been shut off with numerous emergency services vehicles, their blue lights flashing. His face was a mess of scratches and dried blood and he shivered uncontrollably, in shock from the events of the evening.

'What happened?' he asked.

'Amanda tried to poison Rav and Jayden,' I said before adding, 'and then the flat caught fire. She locked us in.'

'Where's Amanda?' I asked. Aaron turned and pointed towards a police car parked across the road. Amanda was sat in the back, nose pressed up against the glass, glaring at us. One of her eyes was swollen shut but she looked incandescent with rage.

'You got her,' I sighed, shoulders sinking, relief flooding my core.

'She put up one hell of a fight,' he said, pointing to his face. 'I had to sit on her in the end until the police came.'

'But I managed to smash the glass of the fire alarm panel.' Aaron's teeth chattered.

Exhaustion washed over me as the adrenaline left my system. All of my muscles ached but I breathed a sigh of relief that all of us had escaped the fire.

We travelled in ambulances to East Surrey hospital, where we were all triaged, then treated separately. I had oxygen administered initially then a chest X-ray to find out the damage from the smoke inhalation which thankfully was minimal. It seemed like I was there for hours and I kept asking about my friends but no one could tell me what was going on. The first-degree burns to my hands were bandaged and eventually I was given a prescription and discharged.

Grace was in the waiting area when I surfaced, her and Natalie had been treated with oxygen like me then discharged. Natalie had left the hospital already, desperate to go home and escape the nightmare we'd endured but Grace stayed, keen for news of us, clutching a bottle of mineral water from the vending machine. She had calmed down but her eyes were red and puffy from crying. Unable to believe what Amanda had done and how much carnage she'd caused.

Grace filled me in on what she'd witnessed. Rav and Jayden had downed shots with Amanda, unbeknownst to them, theirs a mix of household bleach and Baileys. Her shot containing only the latter. Grace had hesitated, lagging a few seconds behind, which was what saved her from burning her oesophagus like them. A vicious attempt to inflict suffering in the name of her sister. Someone who Grace barely remembered, let alone bullied as Amanda made out.

Aaron emerged next, at around midnight, his arm in a sling. They'd managed to pop his shoulder back into its socket and given him strong painkillers before discharging him. He sat with us in the sterile waiting room, amongst the weekend drunks and minor injuries while he waited for an Uber to take him home. There was so much I wanted to say, but I wasn't going to go into it with Grace present. Aaron kept glancing at me every few minutes as though I was a bomb about to go off, unsure how to handle me. I needed time to get my head around all I'd learned that night.

In a matter of hours, I was due to head to the airport, but I knew I couldn't get on that plane until I knew Rav and Jayden were okay. I sent Mum a text to say everything was fine, but I was going to miss my flight and I'd call her later. I sent one to Lynn too, in case she was waiting up for me to come home. With Grace yawning, I sent her off with Aaron when his Uber arrived and remained huddled in the plastic seat for news on Rav and Jayden.

PC Scoble arrived at the hospital shortly after Grace and Aaron left, asking me to come into a side room, where she could take a statement about the recent events. I'd still not been told anything about Rav or Jayden, although she assured me the doctors had told her they were fine but being kept in for observation.

I told her a version of the truth. I'd found Anna Dowd, known to us as Amanda, and an incoherent Aaron on the rooftop after being summoned there by text. Aaron was high on ketamine and as I'd tried to help him down, he'd slipped and fallen over the edge. Then I explained about the shots at the party and how she'd tricked Rav and Jayden into drinking bleach before a fire had started and Anna had locked us in to perish.

I decided to leave out what I knew about Aaron, the *truth* he'd admitted to me. His parents and friends didn't need to know what he'd done. The truth, after all the months I'd spent searching for it, didn't change a thing. Livvy was still dead and Aaron would be riddled with guilt for the rest of his life. Every time I closed my eyes, the image of his face as he realised he was falling flashed before me. Seared onto my brain the same as Livvy's before it. I was so glad the balcony had broken his fall. I already felt responsible for Livvy's death, I couldn't handle having another on my conscience.

PC Scoble drove me back to Lynn and Bill's house, watching from the patrol car until I was safely inside. The constable said she would be in touch if she needed any further information and would go back to the hospital to get statements from Rav and Jayden in the morning.

Inside, the house was dark, the clock in the hallway showing at just before two. I double-locked the door despite knowing Amanda had been apprehended. Surely the police wouldn't release her after what she'd done. Would her appetite for revenge be sated by all she'd put us through? She'd very nearly killed us all but at least I was safe now.

Bill's muffled snoring could be heard as I climbed the stairs to the bathroom, a comfort to know I wasn't alone. I finally had confirmation for him and Lynn that Livvy hadn't taken ketamine of her own accord. Deep down, they already knew. Livvy's memory wouldn't be affected by what Amanda had said up on that rooftop. Livvy hadn't bullied Mandy, she'd been trying to escape her.

Whatever reason Mandy hung herself, despite the words she'd written in her suicide note, I knew it wasn't mine or Livvy's fault. It was clear she had mental health issues, perhaps they both did. Chris had admitted Mandy been fixated on another student at college, she had history for it. He employed her at Cardinal despite knowing that and he should have kept an eye on her.

After cleaning myself up as best I could, desperate for a shower but not wanting to wake Lynn and Bill, I returned to the guest room. Stripping off my stinking, damp, clothes, I huddled under the duvet trying to process everything that happened, wanting to believe it was finally over. As my eyelids closed my phone beeped announcing a WhatsApp message had come through. It was from Aaron.

Thank you for rescuing me.

All of his bravado had gone. The Aaron I witnessed up on the rooftop was the real him. Stripped back and vulnerable, full of remorse for his actions. I was still angry. I'd always be angry, but as Lynn said, I couldn't change the past. I had no doubt he thought about Livvy and the part he'd had to play in her death every day. That had to be punishment enough.

I typed a quick reply.

I didn't say anything.

Aaron would know what I meant.

Sometimes the best thing you could do was nothing at all. Perhaps now I knew the truth, I'd find it easier to move on and leave the ghost of my best friend where she should be, in my happiest memories.

51

Mum called early, she'd been asleep when my text came through to say I was going to miss my flight. She panicked, thinking I'd changed my mind, or worse, that something had happened. I reassured her I was fine, but there had been an incident, going into as little detail as I could get away with. Promising I'd get another flight tomorrow and I'd see her soon.

Lynn and Bill were surprised when they got up to find me still in bed, my boots discarded by the front door, obviously not having left for the airport. Concern was etched on their faces as I relayed over breakfast how the party had ended in disaster. That Amanda had tried to hurt us. The whole sorry story came spilling out. How Chris's niece Mandy had latched onto Livvy when she'd arrived at Cardinal Media and Livvy's rejection and my subsequent arrival had pushed Mandy over the edge. After Mandy killed herself, her sister Anna, clearly with her own issues, reinvented herself as Amanda and began plotting her revenge for the treatment of her sister.

Lynn and Bill sat open-mouthed as I talked.

'We never knew Livvy was being harassed,' Lynn said, her chin quivering. Bill reached for her hand.

'Neither did I,' I said sadly.

'You have a room here as long as you need,' Bill said.

I knew he meant it too, but I was keen to escape the trauma of the past few days.

* * *

Fuzzy from only a few hours' sleep with sounds of fire crackling and Grace's screams still ringing in my ears, I was just out of the shower when Chris called, sounding distraught. Aaron had informed him of what Amanda had done the night before. Then it had all come out; how they were related, Amanda losing her sister Mandy to suicide and his subsequent concerns about his niece's mental health.

Chris's transparency had left Aaron shocked, he'd had no idea of the family connection or the intensity of Mandy's stalking, which had been kept under wraps by Chris and Fiona to protect Cardinal's reputation. He barely remembered the meek girl from finance who had only been there a couple of months.

I had no words of comfort to offer Chris. Most of the Cardinal team had been in the hospital over the past twenty-four hours, either directly or indirectly down to Amanda. I had a strong feeling Amanda was behind all of it, mine and Cassie's poisoning too although I didn't know how she'd done it. The team had no idea why they'd been targeted. I'd let Aaron fill them in on who she was in relation to Mandy and her quest for revenge.

Chris went on to say that Amanda was arrested for ABH and attempted manslaughter pending a charge. So far she had refused to say a word to anyone about what had happened. Even if she denied what they'd accused her of, they would have enough witness statements and evidence retrieved from the flat for it to be an open-and-shut case.

Chris ended the call as he was waiting for the doctor to discharge him, intending to go down to the ward to check on Rav, Jayden and Cassie before he left. He assured me he'd had confirmation from a nurse they were recovering well and I was relieved to know they weren't going to have any permanent damage, not physically anyway. I asked Chris to pass my love to them all.

When he said goodbye, wishing me well, I had the feeling it would be the last time we spoke. His voice carried the weight of what Amanda had done to the people he cared about, something I knew he'd find hard to bear.

* * *

The next day, I slipped away without any fuss, just a quick goodbye to Lynn and Bill, promising I'd be in touch. Once I boarded the flight, I counted the minutes until the plane touched down on the tarmac in France. Throwing my arms around Mum, who was waiting for me at arrivals.

It was strange going back to the house where Tarek had attacked me, sleeping in the same bed. Like I'd left one nightmare and re-entered another, but Tarek was long gone and not a trace of him remained in the house. Mum had made sure of that. She knew I wanted a clean slate and I needed to forget the horrors which had gone before once I told her everything that happened during my time in the UK. She was horrified I'd had to go through it alone.

Initially I spent my days inside, whilst Mum worked as a housekeeper for the other expats living in the surrounding chalets. I had no enthusiasm to do anything, too wrapped up in my own head. Occasionally Grace or Cassie would message me, checking in to see if I was okay. Word had got around about Amanda, and they felt

Chris had let them down, keeping information from them. I hadn't heard from Jayden or Aaron, although I hadn't expected to. No doubt they wanted to move on as I did.

News was Amanda had been sectioned after a psychiatric evaluation. She still wasn't talking. Her state of mind being called into question as her defence for her actions.

Mum said I needed counselling for my repressed emotions after Livvy's death and everything that followed. I wasn't so sure it would help. My solace was found on evenings walks along the beach, watching the waves and staring out into the horizon. Trying to empty my mind of everything, but despite knowing I was safe, I couldn't help looking over my shoulder.

EPILOGUE
MAY 2023

It was mid-morning on a sunny May day when I arrived at St Bartholomew's Church to find everyone already gathered by Livvy's grave. It was the one-year anniversary of her death and Mum had flown over with me for the occasion. Lynn and Bill had decided to hold a memorial, which continued back at their house, where we got to meet Bailey, the cocker spaniel, who was the newest addition to the family.

The day was different to Livvy's funeral, which I barely remembered because it was so raw. This time, we swapped stories and shared memories of Livvy. It was an emotional day, but there were more smiles than tears and it was lovely to see everyone again. Cassie and Grace had both left Cardinal Media to work for another advertising agency. Aaron had gone to a non-profit organisation which supported people with addictions. He looked happier than I'd ever seen him, despite his initial apprehension at our meeting again. I was cordial and we exchanged pleasantries although I'd never forgive him for what he did. At least I didn't have his face as a reminder every day.

Jayden was a little awkward, despite my assurances the past was in the past. He'd remained at Cardinal, although he told me Chris was in the process of selling the company and was planning to do some consulting instead. He'd been struggling to manage the business and support his brother, who'd split from his wife after Amanda's incarceration. He sent flowers but didn't attend Livvy's memorial.

I'd spent six months abroad but was still coming to terms with my involvement in Livvy's death. If I hadn't been so wrapped up in Jayden, I would have paid more attention to Livvy and potentially noticed something was wrong long before her fall in the toilet. Mum had been supportive, our relationship having turned a corner. She was trying to make up for lost time and I could finally rely on her. She eventually convinced me to have some sessions with a counsellor to work through my issues, which surprisingly was helping.

It was Beth, my counsellor, who thought it would be a good idea to visit Amanda, believing it might help me get some closure. I wasn't sure how, as even though I'd heard she'd started talking, she wasn't saying much that made sense. The doctors thought she'd had a complete breakdown caused by losing her sister and was living in an alternative reality. She was going for a not guilty verdict, by reason of diminished responsibility at her upcoming trial.

The day after Livvy's memorial, I visited Amanda at The Chichester Centre, unsure whether she'd agree to see me. Sat on the plastic chair, goosebumps peppered my skin as I waited. The room was cold and clinical, devoid of any personality, and with it a general feeling of morose hung in the air. A lump lodged in my throat as Amanda was brought into the room. They called her Anna as they sat her down but it was a name I couldn't correlate with the person opposite me.

She was a shadow of her former self. Hair cut short to her ears, dark greasy roots in stark contrast to the listless platinum blonde further down. Make-up-free, her full lips were dry and cracked and her cheeks hollowed from the weight she'd lost. The institution she'd ended up in was no country club.

'Did you really intend to kill us?' I asked, not bothering with any pleasantries. My clammy palms lay flat on the table as I took in her steely gaze. The slightest hint of a smile betrayed her stern expression.

'She blamed you,' she replied, avoiding the question, reminding me of the words Mandy had written in her suicide note.

'I never even met her.'

'Yet you broke her. You all did.'

I shook my head, it was a waste of time coming. Amanda would never take any responsibility for what she'd done, but she was speaking again.

'Mandy was never the same after our parents split up the first time. My mum left my dad, taking us with her. We changed our name and started again, but he came crawling back, promising he was going to get sober,' she scoffed. 'It hit Mandy hard, she was all over the place, desperate for some stability and she thought she found it at Cardinal Media. My beautiful sister thought she finally had a friend.' Amanda tilted her head to the side, choosing her words carefully. 'It was so easy to pretend to be Livvy. All I had to do was change her number in your phone to a burner I bought. I mean, who uses their birthday as a pin code anyway,' she sniggered, leaning forward in her chair interlocking her fingers, nails bitten to the quick. Angry inflamed skin surrounded her torn cuticles.

If only I'd scrolled through my messages, down to the ones I'd kept from Livvy, I would have seen the contact had been changed, but I'd been so caught up in it all, it hadn't occurred to me to check.

'Livvy had plenty of videos uploaded to social media. It wasn't hard to record her voice and play it back to you down the phone,' she gloated.

'Were you punishing me with the flowers, and the emails?' I asked.

'You're so stupid, Ria,' she sneered. 'I was sitting at Livvy's desk! Didn't you know they never cleared out her stuff. Her notebook with all her passwords was waiting for me to find it. It was easy to log on as her, and it was fun to watch you, like a rat in maze every time I did something. I wanted you unstable, off your game, I wanted you to trip up, to find out what you did.'

'I didn't *do* anything.' I repeated. We were going around in circles.

Amanda raised a solitary unplucked eyebrow.

'What if I hadn't come back from my sabbatical? Would you have hunted me down?' Just how far was Amanda willing to go in the name of her sister?

'Maybe,' she replied flatly.

'So all this was for revenge?' I asked.

'I lost everything when Mandy died. She was the most important person in my life. A void I'll never be able to fill. She could have been somebody, her spirit was so bright and they crushed it.' Amanda sucked in a breath as though willing herself to calm down. 'I think you'll all be a bit more mindful how you treat people in future, don't you?'

'You're crazy,' I spat.

'That's why I'm here, Ria,' she said, leaning forward like she was letting me into a secret, grinning manically. 'Although,' she continued, 'I never actually killed anyone, did I...'

I frowned, shoulders clenching.

'Neither did I,' I replied.

Amanda laughed, a tinny sound which went straight through me. I shuddered.

'No, you didn't have the minerals to give Aaron his just desserts, did you, but I wasn't talking about him.'

I stared at her, my eyes narrowed. What was she talking about?

'How do you think Mandy got in the club that night? I worked there, behind the bar, collecting glasses. I was there too.'

Something bubbled in my stomach, the urge to run from the room prevalent, but Amanda was on a roll.

'Livvy didn't want that final drink, did she. I didn't even know then Aaron had slipped the powder in. Mandy did, she'd seen it, but all I saw was you teasing Livvy for being a bore. "Drink up, Livvy, don't be a party pooper,"' Amanda put on a girly voice, imitating me, her eyes glistening now. 'I was collecting glasses at the next table. I knew who you all were, Mandy had told me. I heard Livvy say she was tired, she'd had enough and wanted to go home, but you... you weren't ready for the night to end.'

The memories I'd tried so hard to block out came flooding back. I'd squeezed myself in between Livvy and Aaron, she'd wrinkled her nose as I pushed the bottle towards her, encouraging her to drink up as I wanted to dance. I remembered her complaining her feet hurt and she was tired. I'd persuaded her to have one more drink. The drink that killed her. She'd chugged it and I'd left her to dance with Jayden.

My eyes welled with tears as Amanda laughed dryly.

'So now you have her death on your conscience,' she giggled.

I pushed my chair back, fighting the urge to be sick on the tiled floor. Guilt hitting me like a tidal wave. Livvy was my best friend. I'd loved her.

'I... I didn't know,' I stammered, my head in my hands. It wasn't my fault.

'Well, now you do. Consider it my parting gift.'

I opened my mouth to speak, tears streaming down my face.

'Times up, Anna,' announced the guard at the door. The stark reminder Amanda never really existed.

Slowly she got to her feet, her eyes trained on me. 'Night, night, Ria.'

ACKNOWLEDGMENTS

This so far has been my toughest book to write so firstly I want to thank my lovely editor Caroline Ridding for helping me wrangle *The Flatmate* into the book it has become. Same goes to my copy editor Jade Craddock for her attention to detail and fantastic advice.

I had so much fun using lots of friends and readers names in this one, so a big thank you to: Livvy Meadows, Chris Lightfoot, Fiona Hutchison, Michelle Forster, Mandy Dowd and Karen Brackstone for letting me!

Huge thanks to my lovely first readers, Mum and Denise Miller, who especially with this tricky one have been brilliant with their feedback and suggestions.

Lastly, thanks to my supportive husband Dean and two daughters, Bethany and Lucy, for letting me hide away for hours in front of my laptop without complaint.

MORE FROM GEMMA ROGERS

We hope you enjoyed reading *The Roommate*. If you did, please leave a review.

If you'd like to gift a copy, this book is also available as an ebook, hardback, large print, digital audio download and audiobook CD.

Sign up to the Gemma Rogers mailing list for news, competitions and updates on future books:

http://bit.ly/GemmaRogersNewsletter

Explore more gritty thrillers from Gemma Rogers.

ABOUT THE AUTHOR

Gemma Rogers was inspired to write gritty thrillers by a traumatic event in her own life nearly twenty years ago. Her debut novel *Stalker* was published in September 2019 and marked the beginning of a new writing career. Gemma lives in West Sussex with her husband and two daughters.

Visit Gemma's website: www.gemmarogersauthor.co.uk

Follow Gemma on social media:

facebook.com/GemmaRogersAuthor
twitter.com/GemmaRogers79
instagram.com/gemmarogersauthor
bookbub.com/authors/gemma-rogers

THE *Murder* LIST

**THE MURDER LIST IS A NEWSLETTER
DEDICATED TO SPINE-CHILLING FICTION
AND GRIPPING PAGE-TURNERS!**

**SIGN UP TO MAKE SURE YOU'RE ON OUR
HIT LIST FOR EXCLUSIVE DEALS, AUTHOR
CONTENT, AND COMPETITIONS.**

SIGN UP TO OUR
NEWSLETTER

BIT.LY/THEMURDERLISTNEWS

Boldwood

Boldwood Books is an award-winning fiction
publishing company seeking out the best
stories from around the world.

Find out more at www.boldwoodbooks.com

Join our reader community for brilliant books,
competitions and offers!

Follow us
@BoldwoodBooks
@BookandTonic

Sign up to our weekly
deals newsletter

https://bit.ly/BoldwoodBNewsletter